# NO STRINGS ATTACHED

LARA WARD COSIO

ROGUE PUBLICATIONS

Copyright © 2021 by Lara Ward Cosio

All rights reserved.

This is a work of fiction. Names, characters, businesses, places, events and incidents are either the products of the author's imagination or used in a fictitious manner.

Cover designer: Chloe Belle Arts
Cover Photo: Wander Aguiar Photography

**Also by Lara Ward Cosio**
Tangled Up In You (Rogue Series Book 1)
Playing At Love (Rogue Series Book 2)
Hitting That Sweet Spot (Rogue Series Book 3)
Finding Rhythm (Rogue Series Book 4)
Looking For Trouble (Rogue Series Book 5)
Felicity Found (Rogue Series Book 6)
Rogue Christmas Story (Rogue Series Book 7)
Problematic Love (Rogue Series Book 8)
Rock Star on the Verge (Rogue Series Book 9)

Full On Rogue: The Complete Books #1-4
Rogue Extra: The Complete Books #5-8

Hula Girl: A Standalone Romance

# 1

## KAYLA

**Author's Note:** The book you are about to read was expanded from a previously released short story called One More Try. It's the same characters but with a whole lot more story!

I don't normally stare at men's butts. It's just that the guy in front of me at my coffee place fills out his jeans *so well*.

With that view, I'm not exactly upset that the line isn't budging. I count six people ahead of me, including the woman at the counter insisting that her ridiculously complex order is repeated back to her. All I want is black coffee. The overpriced but freshly roasted brew is one of my few indulgences.

Sighing, I mentally review my to-do list. A lot of it is work related, but then there's the dry cleaning I need to pick up, the crafting supplies I've promised my daughter I'd get, and finally ... what was the other thing? I *just* dropped her off at her daycare center around the block, so why can't I remember?

I must have sighed again because the man in front of me turns around, his striking blue eyes bright and curious. With short but untamed brown hair and a scruffy beard, he's got a ruggedly handsome thing going.

He does a double-take and I seriously have to wonder if he spotted me looking at his butt.

I try to look disinterested, forcing an apologetic shrug.

The line starts to inch forward and he turns away. My eyes gravitate once more to his backside. This is clearly a man who does his squats at the gym.

What is wrong with me?

I avert my gaze, focusing instead on the crowd over at the order pick-up station. I'm definitely going to be late for my nine o'clock meeting.

Mercifully, the line moves again.

But that means Buns-of-Steel guy puts on a display I can't resist admiring once more.

This fixation isn't like me. It has to have something to do with the conversation I had with my best friend this morning. I'd confessed to having had the most intense sex dream.

"Fantastic," Nicole said, instantly warming to the subject. "Did it have a happy ending?"

I'd scoffed. "No, the ... desire disappeared when I woke up —alone. As usual."

"You know what this dream is telling you?"

"Not this again."

"Yes, this again. It's time for you to get out there and try to meet someone."

"Nic, you know better than anyone that with work and a

four-year-old who needs and deserves all my attention, I'm barely surviving most days."

"Honey, listen, you are beautiful, smart, and a wonderful mother. But you're a woman, too. And you deserve to have your needs met."

Nicole means well, but it's still hard for me to imagine expanding my world beyond work and Emerson, my daughter.

And, yet, here I am, salivating over a stranger. Maybe Nicole had a point.

Not that I'm going to do anything about it right now.

All I need today is my usual coffee.

Thankfully, another register opens and the line moves quickly. I avoid looking at Buns-of-Steel guy, even when I feel his eyes on me as we both approach the counter.

"You've been watching me."

*Please don't let it be him talking to me.*

Cringing, I turn to see he is definitely talking to me. There's amusement in his eyes that somehow makes him even hotter.

"What? Me? No, I don't think so," I say quickly. I order my no-frills black coffee, pay, and head for the pick-up area.

He joins me and we stand awkwardly together for a minute before he turns to me again.

"No, I'm sure it's you. You've been watching me."

My throat goes dry.

"Well, me and my crew," he clarifies.

"What?" Now I'm genuinely confused. He is definitely the only Buns-of-Steel guy I've been staring at just now. Definitely not a whole *crew* of men.

"I'm overseeing the construction crew up the street from

here. We've been getting the job ready for a few weeks and every morning, I see you in your window watching us."

Oh my god. I've just been ogling the construction guy from the site across from my apartment. Okay, I know I've been going without for too long, but this is just too ... clichéd.

And yet, it explains the buns of steel. A construction worker is bending and lifting and squatting all day, isn't he?

Ugh. I need to control myself. He's not the first gorgeous man I've run into. Why am I acting like a horny teenager?

"Yeah," he continues softly, "you're the one. Hard to miss with the way the sun shines on your hair in the morning."

Um, did he just give me a line? Like a pick-up line? I'm so out of practice I don't know how to take it. What I am capable of doing is reflexively smoothing my intensely red hair. It's naturally a paler red but I prefer a deeper shade to contrast with my soft gray eyes. That brief delay of me playing with my hair is enough time to wonder just what he's been seeing of me in the mornings.

"So, you're saying *you've* been watching *me*," I say in an obvious attempt to deflect.

His response is a knowing half-smile that's far too sexy for my own good. And then he leans in toward me and says conspiratorially, "Seems we've got some sort of mutual interest thing going here."

That was definitely a pick-up line. He's not wrong about our mutual interest. I'm fixed in his gaze, unable to move, the heat of attraction locking me in place for what seems like minutes.

"Kayla!"

My coffee is ready, offering me the perfect excuse to break

the spell I was just under. I rush forward, thank the barista, and take the cardboard cup from the counter.

"Wait," Buns-of-Steel guy says as I try to slip past him. "I didn't mean—"

"Sorry, I'm late. Have to go."

As soon as I'm outside, the cool air relieves the burn of my cheeks and I can breathe again.

What was that?

I laugh and shake my head. I haven't felt that kind of fierce attraction to someone since ... well, since my ex. That relationship ended up giving me my daughter, but nothing else good.

Makes me think Buns-of-Steel guy might just be too hot to handle.

## 2

TANNER

What was that? Actually, I know what that was. That was pure sexual attraction. Yeah, we had a moment there. But then she rushed away before we could get into anything more than that.

I'd guess she was unsettled by me telling her I've seen her watching our site. And that I've been watching her right back. Good thing I didn't confess to the fact that every time my alarm goes off at four forty-five in the morning, the idea of seeing her in her apartment window is the thing that gets me moving.

Still, I didn't set out to hook up with a stranger in a coffee shop. In fact, hookups are sadly few and far between. I just don't have the time, not with my job and other work aspirations. Then, I also spend every spare minute focused on being the most hands-on uncle I can be to my five-year-old twin nephews. My sister is basically a single mom with her Marine husband deployed in the Middle East. On top of that, she's pregnant. She needs all the support she can get, and I'm happy to help her. But it hasn't left me with much time for myself.

But all that self-sacrifice was lost just now because this gorgeous redhead sure got my attention.

My name is called out, forcing my thoughts back to reality.

With a nod to the harried barista, I take a sleeve of disposable cups under one arm while I grab a large catering-sized container of coffee in each hand.

Outside, the day is clear, the air still a little cool. But it's sure to heat up and get us sweating on the site, just as it's done for the last week.

"Take your time, boss. We're not thirsty or nothing," Ernesto says with a grin as I approach the site. "What, no donuts?"

He's one of my best friends and my most trusted worker, but he loves to bust my balls. Good thing, I like to give it to him right back. "You're lucky I did the coffee run at all. Don't know why I reward your shit-talking anyway."

Relieving me of the coffee, he sets it up on the folding table just outside the trailer that serves as my office.

"What took you so long, anyway?"

"Uh, it was busy there."

Something in my voice makes him look up from the coffee he's stirring sugar into. "And?"

I laugh. His attention to detail has saved my ass on more than one job. He's not just observant, he's fanatic about getting things right. I'm in debt to his OCD. Maybe that's why I go ahead and tell him the truth.

"There was a woman there who ... I don't know. She caught my attention, I guess."

Ernesto slaps me on the shoulder. "Good for you, man. About time you got into the game."

I smirk. "It didn't exactly go anywhere."

"Well, did you catch *her attention* back?"

"I think so. I mean, I think she was staring at my ass."

He laughs. "For real?"

"Maybe? Just caught her looking away."

"Geez, man, that's priceless. You'll be going back to the same place tomorrow, right? Try and get beyond the ass-starring part of your relationship?"

"I was thinking about it."

"You gotta. And bring donuts next time!"

I shake my head. "Stop hogging the coffee and call the guys over to get theirs."

"Yes, boss!"

He mock-salutes me before using his fingers to blast out a shrill whistle. In no time, my crew starts making their way over to us. Glancing at Ernesto, I see him craning his neck to look at something behind me.

"What is it?"

"Nothing. Just trying to see how fine your ass really is. Not my thing, as my hot-as-sin wife can tell you, but now I'm curious what your coffee lady was eyeballin'."

I regret saying anything to him. And, yet, I can't help but laugh again. "Get to work, man. Coffee break is over for you."

He raises his coffee as a toast before turning his trashtalking attention on the rest of the guys, leaving me to think about the redhead once again. Or Kayla, I should say. I caught that when her order was called out.

Looking up at the apartment building across the street, I

fix my gaze on the window where I've seen her watching our crew every morning.

This development has definitely made the job a whole lot more interesting.

# 3

## KAYLA

"Sorry, I was *almost* late," I tell my team with a smile and settle into my chair at the head of the conference room table.

We have a standing Monday morning meeting to start the week organized, and I've made it with just two minutes to spare. Being a marketing manager for a top-tier international real estate company based here in Denver wasn't my dream job, but it's the one I have, and I take it seriously.

"Problems with your daughter? Again?" Henry asks, a phony mask of concern on his face. He's been a pain in my side since I took over as manager for the group seven months ago, never missing an opportunity to point out what he sees as my deficiencies, namely that I am a single mother who has had to, on occasion, carve out some flexibility to my workday.

"Thanks for your concern, Henry," I say without looking at him, my attention on opening my planner. "I hope everyone had a great weekend. Looks like we're going to need to hit the ground running. I assume you all saw the email I sent through last night?"

My habit is to spend Sunday night putting together a detailed email with marching orders for the team. I've found that if I clearly set my expectations for all to see, then more gets done.

I hear the group of eight acknowledge the receipt of the email and I begin the meeting, going through the tasks item by item, clarifying any questions, and setting the tone for the week.

"Isn't there something that can be done to, you know, back Henry off?" Tracy, my biggest fan, has stayed after the meeting so she can curry favor with this question. She's the youngest member of the team and has told me point blank that she looks up to me as a role model. While I appreciate the vote of confidence, I'm still figuring out my place as a manager and don't feel ready to be a mentor. On the other hand, she's also ambitious, and so the stars in her eyes for me likely come with a goal of upward mobility.

"Oh, I don't give it too much thought," I say, though that's not true. He's been angling to find a way to knock me down a peg for far too long, and it frustrates me to no end.

"He's just so abrasive. I mean, you're the boss and he clearly can't handle taking orders from a woman. It's not okay."

She's right, and as much as I'd love to lead the fight in pushing back against his misogynistic inferiority complex, I can't afford to rock the boat. I may be in a position of power, but I'm also acutely aware of how fragile it is. Though I want to fight back for myself and other women, there are times when I have to force myself to stand down.

"Well, Tracy, I've found that the best thing to do is to simply deprive him of what he wants."

"Meaning?"

"Attention. That's what he's looking for. So, I'm just going to move on and not give it to him." I smile, trying to convince her as well as myself that I believe this is sufficient.

"Oh, um, okay."

She clearly isn't satisfied with my tepid rebuttal to that jerk Henry. But I have a full day of work to get to and can only do so much on this issue.

"We have a one-on-one at four, right?" I ask as a way to end this talk.

"Right. I'll have some preliminary designs ready by then for the internal communications branding refresh."

"Great. See you then."

The rest of my day is non-stop. I force myself to take a break out on the building's patio at two o'clock for some air and a quick bite to eat. I often take a late lunch because my day slides by so quickly, but I also prefer the solitude it offers. The area is usually packed during the lunch hour, but now I only see one other person and he's at the opposite end, leaning on the railing overlooking Syracuse Street while on his cell.

This is also the time that I take to check in with my daughter's daycare center. They have live cameras you can tap into, and their staff is incredibly communicative by text, which helps alleviate the guilt of being away for so many hours. I spot my Emerson at a crafts table working on her scissors skills while seemingly talking continuously to the two other children nearby. Smiling, I shake my head. That's my girl. She's crafty and chatty. And the very best thing in my life.

My conversation with Nicole comes to mind. She's my biggest supporter. If I hadn't had her help in the early days of pregnancy and just after Emerson was born, I don't know what I would have done. Now, she seems to have made it her mission to push me to get back into the dating world. I can't imagine even trying to meet someone, which I know disappoints her. She's sweet to tell me I need to do something for myself, but it's not that easy.

She will, however, get a kick out of the episode at Mean Beanz this morning. I laugh to myself, thinking of Buns-of-Steel guy. God, he was hot. I'll definitely look for him in the morning at the site across from my apartment, if only for the reminder of how, for a brief moment, I felt the heat of desire again.

"Kayla, Gregory wants to see you!"

Turning, I see Tracy waving me over from the doorway to the building. Gregory is my boss and is prone to calling me into his office rather than emailing or phoning. There goes my break.

# 4

## TANNER

"Was today the best day of kindergarten ever?" I ask my nephews as I double-check their car seat buckles.

"You always say that," Matt says with a grin.

"Yep, every time," Max confirms with a nod. He's the more analytical of the two. Matt is the goofball.

I help my sister Tatum out a couple times a week with whatever she needs. Could be minor repairs around the house, bringing over dinner, or picking up the kids from school and keeping them occupied when she needs time for a doctor's appointment like she has today.

"Only because every day should be your best day, right buds?" I say with a wink.

"Then it was your best day, too?" Max asks.

A flash of Kayla goes through my mind. And not for the first time since our little ... thing this morning. She may have looked buttoned-up corporate at first glance, with her black pinstriped skirt and starched white blouse, but I noticed the flower tattoo on her ankle and the extra piercings going unused on her left ear, both of which suggest a wilder side. Not to mention she was definitely checking me out. The more that I think about it, the more I'm sure of it.

"Yeah, it was a pretty good day," I say. Smiling to myself, I close the door and head around to the driver's seat.

We stop for Happy Meals on the way to my sister's place because I'm *that* uncle, the one who always gives the kids what they want. Once home, they eat at the kitchen island while I wash up the dishes left in the sink and we talk man stuff. You know, the usual: Legos, boogers, and Paw Patrol. Afterward, it's time for a little soccer in the backyard.

That's where Tatum finds us when she gets home.

"Hi, Mommy!" Matt and Max both say without stopping their chase of the ball.

"I hope you're wearing them out," she says with a smile.

She always says the boys have so much energy that she has to find ways to run it out of them so that they can get to bed at a decent hour.

"They're wearing me out!" I reply as I let Max steal the ball from me and make a goal in the mini net against the fence. "Oh, man. What is that? Zero to sixteen?"

"Zero to a million!" Matt says.

"You guys are too good for your old Uncle Tanner. Listen, I'm going to take a water break. You two keep at it, okay?"

"Okay!" they shout in unison.

"Love it when they do that," I tell Tatum as I follow her inside.

"Thanks for watching them, Tan." She looks at the tidy kitchen. "And for doing the dishes. You didn't have to do that."

"No problem. How was your appointment? Everything good?"

"I'm anemic. Doctor's not too worried, but it explains why I feel so much more tired this time around."

Nodding, I gesture for her to take a seat on the sofa and join her. "So, what's this mean? Steak dinners more often?"

"Yes, more beef and greens. Plus an iron supplement should do the trick."

I stand, ready to act. "Great. I can run to the market now, get you some of the stuff you need."

"Wait, I wanted to ask you about something."

"What is it?"

"Can we do that dinner I've been asking you to do forever? You know, invite my friend Cherylyn over? I really think you'll like her."

I've been putting off this attempt at a setup for a few weeks now. Not only are blind dates horribly uncomfortable, but I'm not interested in a relationship right now. My focus is on work and making sure my sister makes it safely through the last four months of her pregnancy.

"Right now's not a good time, Tate."

She shakes her head but with a small smile. "Come on, just give it a try. One dinner is all I'm asking. You might be surprised."

"I'm sure she's wonderful, but I'm just not feeling it right now."

Throwing her head back against the sofa cushion in frustration, she groans. After a moment, she takes a deep breath and looks at me. "I just want you to have someone in your life, you know?"

"I appreciate that, but—"

"I mean, aren't you even horny?"

That gets a laugh out of me. My sister and I are close, but

we don't usually go there. "That's nothing you need to worry about." And I'd definitely never share with her that I don't have trouble enjoying the occasional one-night stand.

"Why? Because you've got some chick on the side to take care of that?"

"Is this the anemia talking?" I ask with a smirk.

"You're just not making sense. I've showed you her picture. You've seen that she's really pretty. She has a nice body. And she's a great person. Why wouldn't you want to meet her? Or at least hook up?"

I don't want to tell her the real reason I'm not interested in getting involved—in any way—with a woman right now. She would hate that I'm putting my personal life on hold in order to help her out. As much as she appreciates my help, she's completely capable of handling her boys and her pregnancy on her own. It's just that I don't see any reason for her to *have* to. Another thing I can't tell her is that I promised Marcus, her husband, that I'd stand in as much as possible for him while he's away. It kills him that he can't be here, so knowing that I'm dedicated to helping out is a big relief for him. He has enough stress to deal with, so I'm more than happy to step in.

"Well?" Tatum asks. "Give me one valid reason. Just *one*."

"Uh, well," I say, scrambling. "I guess you could say I've got my eye on someone right now. So, I'm sort of preoccupied with her."

She eyes me skeptically. "Really? What's her name?"

"Kayla."

Wow. That slipped out fast. I mean, it's not exactly a lie. I'm all for seeing her again in the coffee shop. But the same goes with her as what I'd told my sister about her friend. It's simple. I'm not interested in dating.

None of that matters because Tatum is smiling at me, her eyes sparkling with excitement. "Well, then you can bring *her* to dinner. Thursday work for you and Kayla?"

"Oh, uh, I mean, I'll have to check with her."

"Great. You be sure to let me know as soon as you can. I can't wait to meet her!"

I can't tell if she's fucking with me or if she's really pleased with this turn of events. In either case, I have to figure out my next move.

Fast.

# 5
## KAYLA

I get to Emerson's daycare just before the cut-off point when they start charging a fee for every minute you're late and take her with me to the market.

"Baby cart?" she asks.

"Oh, yes, please!" I tell her. "You can be in charge, okay, Emmy?"

Her eyes go wide at the prospect and I smile. With dark hair and deep blue eyes, she takes after her father, but she's so beautiful in her own way that I've just about stopped connecting the resemblance.

Letting her push one of the mini shopping carts will stave off her fatigue after a long day. She and I both prefer when we can go straight home, but we've had one too many nights of eating whatever is on hand—most often vegetable soup and grilled cheese. Truth be told, she's so picky that it's our go-to comfort meal, but we need other essentials, one of those being wine. Mondays definitely require a glass of wine.

After shopping, we get home and have dinner, then it's bath time for Emerson, followed by reading books. Finally, I lay with her in her toddler bed, and we stare at the stars projected onto the ceiling from her nightlight as I sing songs until she falls asleep. There are quite a few nights where I fall asleep there, too.

But tonight, I manage to slip out of bed and blink my way awake enough to enjoy that glass of wine as I fire up my Mac. Just as I'm opening Photoshop to play with some graphic design, my cell rings.

It's almost nine o'clock. Not late by any means, but I'm still surprised.

Until I see the caller ID. It's my ex.

"Hi, Rad," I answer. Yes, he goes by Rad. Technically, his full name is Radisson, but being that he's both lead singer and lead guitarist in his own band, Rad definitely suits him better. "It must be late there, wherever you are."

"Stockholm, Kay Kay," he replies breezily.

Breezy is his constant state of existence. He goes with the flow, whichever way the wind blows. It was sexy when I first met him. He was committed to two things then: his band and letting life take him on a "journey." I was all for riding that journey with him back when I was a free and single twenty-two-year-old.

Back then, I was not long out of college, but with a jump start on a freelance career, making a reputation for myself in the graphic design business. I went out most nights, meeting a group of girlfriends for dinner followed by barhopping or clubbing.

It was in one of those clubs where I met Rad. He and his band were performing that night. Nicole and I had gone there, not even knowing there was going to be live music. The place was small but packed, creating its own humidity. Nicole

## No Strings Attached

volunteered to get us drinks and I drifted into the crowd watching the band.

Rad is one of those magnetic people, the kind people are drawn to—and that night, I was one of them.

We had one of those ridiculous things where we locked eyes, him on stage and me in the audience. With dark, longish hair and piercing blue eyes, he was the one all the girls were screaming for. But when he nodded his head, I knew he was gesturing at me. I made my way toward the stage, my heart beating wildly.

The band kept playing, but he stopped strumming the guitar and pulled away from the microphone, crouching down so he could look me in the eyes.

"I've forgotten how to play the fucking guitar because all I can focus on is you," he said. And then he ever so slowly *licked his lips*. At the time, I thought it was the sexiest thing I'd ever seen. Now, I realize it was his cheesy way of picking up girls. Still, I was hooked, especially when he continued, "Tell me you'll see me after the show so I can finish this thing."

Of course, I agreed. What girl wouldn't?

For four months, we were inseparable and insatiable together. I'd known from the start that he had plans to leave for a European tour. They were a no-name band at the time, so I figured he'd be back soon. But not only did he break up with me a few days before leaving, he never really came back, not even when I told him I was pregnant. The band is just popular enough in Europe to keep touring and eking out a living but has never caught on here at home, so he's permanently relocated except for random, short visits.

Speaking of random visits—I'm guessing this unexpected call is to let me know he'll be coming to town.

"Emerson is asleep, but you knew that, right?" I ask. "I'm sure you sorted out the time difference."

"Feeling feisty, babe?" he replies with a laugh.

I have to bite my tongue. It's not worth getting into things with him. He's incapable of taking responsibility. Or understanding all of my responsibilities. He's gotten off easy by being a barely present father while I raise our daughter. As much as I resent the lack of support from him, I don't want Emmy to grow up to resent him, so I try my best to be civil. I never even asked for child support because I didn't want to have to chase him all over the world to enforce it. It was better from the start to accept that I was on my own.

"What can I do for you?" I ask.

"Ooh, if you're offering, I'd love some help getting off before I crawl into bed," he says, amused with himself.

"Rad, stop it." He's continued through these past few years to act as if we can be fuck buddies when he's the exact opposite of what I want. Yes, we were insanely attracted to each other once upon a time, but I no longer think of that as a good thing. That kind of intensity, that heat, it only burns you in the end.

He laughs. "Anyway, I wanted to let you know there's a good chance I'll be in Denver soon."

My eyebrows shoot up. "Wow, that must be a record for giving me notice. You usually just show up. What could be bringing you here with such foresight?"

"I just wanna see my girl."

I don't believe that for a second, not when his daughter has never once been his priority. But I don't have the will to push back on him either.

"And I wanna see you, too, Kay Kay." He lowers his voice

to something husky and seductive. "It'd be good for us to get together. We should talk, you know?"

I take this as more of his odd insistence that we could hook up whenever he's in town and am thinking of a way to shut him down when he continues.

"Any chance I can stay there with you?"

"Nope. None. No chance at all."

"Geesh." He laughs. "Okay, well, I'll let you know when I'm there. Listen—" He cuts himself off and I can hear knocking and a girl's voice. Stockholm is where he lives, so I know it's not room service. It's much more likely that he's invited some random girl to his place after a late night of partying. Maybe some girl who fell for the same line I did once upon a time. "I, uh, I gotta go."

"Bye, Rad."

I end the call before I can hear him call me "Kay Kay" once more. It drives me crazy. It conjures up too many intimate memories. Times when I was going down on him and he'd moan that over and over. Times when he was making me come and saying it over and over. Times when he'd wake me in the middle of the night, whispering it as he slid his hand between my legs.

I need to stop thinking of him.

A better idea is to think of Buns-of-Steel guy. Yes, all I need is my vibrator and a hot fantasy. I down my wine, switch off the computer, and head to my bedroom.

## 6

### KAYLA

"Why do you sound so muffled?" Nicole asks early the next morning during our regular phone call. She moved to St. Louis two years ago, so these calls are our friendship lifeline.

"Because I'm hiding behind the curtains. I told you, I don't want him to see me."

"Oh, but think of how much fun you could have with this! You could put signs in your window. You could do a sexy dance for him. You could flash him!"

Laughing, I scan the construction site for him, but the crew is in full swing and all I see are a bunch of men in jeans and T-shirts, wearing tool belts and yellow hard hats.

"Seriously, I want you to promise me you'll jump on this opportunity," Nicole continues.

"What opportunity? It was a random encounter that lasted all of five minutes."

"Five intense minutes of sexual attraction is what you told me. Get yourself back to that coffee shop, at least, and maybe you'll see him again."

"And then what?"

"Then, flirt your ass off."

I groan. "I don't even know how to flirt anymore."

"It'll come back to you, Kay. You just have to give it a chance. I'm serious, honey. It's time to dust off the cobwebs and get you some."

Scoffing, I say, "I'm not some free single girl. I can't just 'get some.' I've got Emmy to consider, you know?" Glancing at the time, I see that I'll need to wake my daughter soon. I need to wrap up this call to get us both ready for the day.

"Your daughter will be better off if you're happy and your needs are taken care of, is all I'm saying. You've been super responsible and selfless since you got pregnant. You deserve a little fun for yourself, if nothing else. This guy could be a chance for the hot sex you've gone too long without."

"Okay, noted. I have to get going."

"Or, what if he has even more potential?" she says quickly before I can end the call. "What if, when you least expected it, you just met the love of your life?"

"You alternating between him being good for hot sex and the love of my life is truly dizzying."

"Well, why can't he be both?"

I think of my Rad. He was definitely good for hot sex. But that's all he turned out to be good for. I'll never regret that brief relationship because I got my daughter from it. At the same time, I don't want to mistake a superficial, intense attraction for anything more than it is ever again.

"Bye, Nicole. Talk to you tomorrow."

"Wait, pinky-promise me you'll get a photo of dat ass for me!"

Laughing, I'm instantly reminded of the little dares we

used to give each other, especially after a few cocktails during our nights out. Instead of saying, "I dare you to ..." we'd say, "pinky-promise me." We had a lot of fun, but that carefree girl feels like a thing of the past.

"Not gonna happen," I tell her with a laugh.

"No way. You know you can't refuse to pinky-promise me! Think of all the things I did when you asked!"

"That was years ago, Nic. We were wild then."

"Maybe you need to give your wild side a chance. Girl, you've been holding it together too long. You know you need a release."

"And taking a picture of a great ass to share with you will do it?"

She laughs. "I don't know, but it's a start!"

I think about that for a second, about how far I've overcorrected from the free girl I used to be to someone with no life outside of work and motherhood. Nicole's challenge seems like a relatively harmless kick.

"Okay, fine. I'll do it," I say.

"Knew you would!"

I shake my head and roll my eyes. There's a reason she's my best friend. She knows me inside and out and somehow manages to push me exactly when I need it. Now, I just have to rise to the challenge.

## 7

### KAYLA

The second I walk through the door at Mean Beanz, I recognize Buns-of-Steel-guy. He is, once again, hard to miss. I take a moment to enjoy the view because it's just so damn good. And then I get in line, one person between me and him. Retrieving my cell, I open the camera feature and as casually as I can, lower it to get the perfect shot of the "goods." I smile and shake my head, feeling pretty impressed with myself that I actually followed through on Nicole's pinky-promise challenge.

I manage to place my order, pay for it, and find a spot in the pickup area without drawing the attention of Buns-of-Steel guy. I realize with some disappointment that he must have gotten his order and left already. With no option for banter with the construction hottie, I instead prepare the text and photo for Nicole:

**Here it is in all its glory: dat ass**

Before I can hit send, I hear a man laughing behind me. I

turn so quickly that my hair whips Buns-of-Steel guy in the face. He had been leaning down and close enough to me to see exactly what I had done.

"Uh, that's not you. I mean," I stammer, "obviously. Not that you—"

"No, it couldn't be me," he says, fighting a smile. "I mean, what kind of woman would take a picture like that of a random stranger to share ... on social media?"

"Oh, god no. I was only going to text it to my friend." As soon as the words leave my mouth, I wince with the realization of what I've said.

"I see."

"Listen, I am so sorry. I'm honestly not usually this obnoxious, I swear. It's just, my friend, she made me pinky-promise her, and I just went with it—"

"Pinky-promise?"

I've overshared in my attempt to explain this all away. I need to regroup. Taking a deep breath, I open my mouth to start over but am interrupted by the barista shouting out, "Tanner!"

Buns-of-Steel guy holds up a finger to me. "Hang on a second, okay?"

I watch as he retrieves two catering containers of coffee and a large bag of pastries.

"Maybe I can buy you a coffee next time?" I ask. "To make up for—"

"'Dat ass'?" he asks with a raised eyebrow.

"I am so mortified, honestly."

"Kayla!"

"Oh, that's me."

"I know."

I stop in my tracks and look at him quizzically.

He shrugs. "Remember that mutual interest thing we discovered yesterday?"

"This is just so weird," I say with a helpless laugh and go grab my coffee.

"Do you have a couple minutes?" he asks when I turn back around.

"I, uh, not really. I need to go back to my place to get my car. I have to get to work."

"I'll walk with you," he says, and I hesitate. "You know, since we're going in the same direction? My site is across from your building, remember?"

"Oh, yeah. Right."

Another reminder of the fact that he's seen me watching him in the morning. Could this get any more awkward?

We walk together in silence at first. But then we both start to speak at once.

"You go ahead," he says.

"Oh, I was going to say again that I'd really like to make up for ... for that totally inappropriate picture I took."

He shakes his head. "No worries."

"No, I mean it. If a man had done that to me, I'd be—well, I don't think I'd appreciate it. So, I really do want to make it up to you to be sure you know I'm not a total creeper."

"Well, maybe you could do me a favor," he says slowly as if still thinking over an idea.

"A favor?"

"It's a little out there, I'll admit."

Oh god. What have I opened myself up to?

Before I can backtrack on my offer, he says, "You see, my sister is hell-bent on setting me up on a blind date with her friend. But I thought a way to get out of it was to say I'm already dating someone."

I wasn't expecting that. And I'm not even sure where he's going with it.

"Okay," I say and wait for more.

"You know what? Never mind. It's crazy. I don't know what I was thinking."

I laugh. "Well, now I'm curious."

He shakes his head. "It's ridiculous. I should just stand up to her."

"Your sister?"

"Yeah."

"She must be pretty tough if a guy your size is intimidated." He must be at least 6'3" and has muscles that strain against his short-sleeve shirt. On top of that, the smile he gives me is positively panty-melting. That crazy attraction I felt toward him yesterday is still there, despite my lingering embarrassment over being caught photographing his ass. I definitely need to steer clear of him. This feeling is all too familiar. It feels the same as it did with Rad. It's that thrilling sense of the unexpected and the reckless desire to chase that feeling just to see where it will go, all consequences be damned.

"Yeah, well, it's not so much that I'm intimidated by her as I want to make her happy."

"Uh-huh," I say, still preoccupied.

"Anyway, that's the favor I was going to ask you."

I feel like I've missed a vital piece of information. "Sorry, what was it?"

"If you'd come to dinner with me at my sister's house. This Thursday."

# No Strings Attached

Now I'm just confused. How did we make this jump?

"I know, that's why I said it was crazy," he tells me with a laugh. "It's just, there'd be no strings attached. To be honest, I'm not looking to date anyone, so you don't have to worry that this is some sort of convoluted come-on. I just want to give my sister the peace of mind she'd get if she thought I was seeing someone."

We're close to my apartment now, thankfully. I stop walking, and he does too. I gaze up at him, squinting against both the sunlight and his nonsensical suggestion.

"Tanner, right?"

He nods.

"The only reason I even know your name is because of the barista yelling it out just now. What on earth makes you think I'd go anywhere with you, let alone on some sort of fake date to your sister's house."

"I told you it was crazy. Yeah, I get it."

Now I'm the one to nod.

"Definitely been a hell of a morning," he continues. "What, with this beautiful stranger taking a picture of my—"

"Okay, we don't have to revisit that."

He laughs. "And then me coming up with an insane idea to ask this same beautiful stranger to do me a favor. You must think I'm some psycho."

"No."

"No?"

Again, with that sexy, charming smile of his that lures me in. "No, it's actually really sweet that you want to make your sister happy."

"So, you'll do it?"

I scoff. "No, I didn't say that." I smile at him, amused

despite myself, as I try to sort out what he's all about. "Anyway, I have to get going."

"Yeah, I have to get to work, too," he says, nodding to the site across the street.

"Ah, yes. I guess I'll see you around, then."

"Sure. See you, Kayla."

Before I turn away, I watch him take a long look at me, as if he's taking inventory. His eyes start low, fixing on the small tattoo on the inside of my ankle, then rising over my legs and lingering at the spot where my blouse buttons meet and expose the lightly freckled skin of my upper chest. After a split second of lingering there, his gaze travels again, finally meeting my eyes. The connection we make in that moment reveals the attraction I've been feeling is mutual. There's desire in his expression, and the way he leans slightly toward me feels like he wants to drop everything so he can throw me over his shoulder and ravage me. If I was the old me of just a few years ago, I might have invited him up to my apartment then and there to ravage him right back.

But with a sigh, I realize I'm not. I have to get to work and on with my day.

## 8

### TANNER

I follow the swish of Kayla's ass as she walks away, not even trying to hide how much I want her. Not that I have a chance of acting on that after what I suggested to her.

Rolling my eyes, I turn and head toward the site. What a fuck-up that was, suggesting she come to Tatum's house for dinner. What was I thinking? It was a half-baked, spur-of-the-moment fantasy that never should have left my lips.

So, why did I say any of that? There's no doubt that I'm attracted to her. But to jump from that to trying to get her to meet my sister?

Kayla was right when she said she didn't know me. And I don't know her. Why would I ever think to bring this stranger around my sister and her kids?

Simply because she's hot? Gotta admit it was a turn-on finding out I was right about her checking me out yesterday. Not only that, but she took it another step with that photo she wanted to send to her friend.

*Dat ass.*

I laugh to myself as I reach the folding table outside of my office. Setting down the coffee and pastries, I look out at the activity of my crew. They're a good bunch, mostly, with only a few guys I have to keep a check on. Everything has been going according to schedule so far, but it's a big job—a six-story, mixed-use building with retail space on the first floor and apartments above. It'll take fifteen months to complete. It's the biggest job I've been in charge of, in fact, and I knew it would keep me tied to one spot for a long time. There's potential for a generous bonus if I can get the job done in a year's time, and I've been using that as motivation to work long hours. But looking up at Kayla's window in the building across the street now, I'm beginning to think I've got an even more interesting motivation to get to work every day.

"All right! You got donuts this time," Ernesto says as he tears open the bag on the table. "Ah, what is this frou-frou shit?"

The scones, savory biscuits, and bran muffins aren't exactly what a construction crew craves.

"That's all they had," I say.

"Man, you need to go somewhere else. There's gotta be a Dunkin' somewhere, right?"

"Yeah, but I kind of like this place."

Ernesto looks up, mid-bite of a cheese and herb biscuit. "Oh, right. The place with your lady admirer. You see her again?"

"Turns out she saw me before I saw her," I reply, thinking of how she had obviously spotted me and taken that photograph before I ever knew she was in the coffee shop.

"What does that mean?"

"Nothing."

"No, not nothing. I see you trying to hide something. 'Fess up to your pal. Go on."

"I don't know what to tell you. Other than that, I think I fucked up whatever chance I had."

"Hang on, hang on. I gotta pour some coffee to go with this story," he says and makes a show of doing just that.

"We should get to work."

"No way I can work now, boss. I need to get the dirt first. What'd you do? Proposition her instead of pretend to be a gentleman?"

"Love that you're getting such a kick out of this."

"Ah, come on. I'm just here to listen. That is, if you can man-up and admit to however you fucked up?"

Ernesto always has a way of getting me to think things through, even if it is by goading me into it. And I realize that my fuck-up wasn't just suggesting to her that she fake date me for my sister's benefit, but that I also told her I had no interest in dating anyone. What a smooth operator I am.

"I guess I sort of gave her some weird mixed messages," I say, not wanting to get into it.

He watches me for a moment, then finishes off the biscuit and wipes his mouth with the back of his hand. "Well, tomorrow's always another day to get it right."

I laugh. "What's that mean? You're up for more frou-frou pastries?"

"For you, man, I'll sacrifice."

"Appreciate it. All right, let's get to work."

## 9

KAYLA

At the office, I have no choice but to put Tanner out of my mind and focus on the tasks at hand. We're going through a huge rebranding project, and my boss is keenly involved in the process, asking for full-scale mockups for multiple design options where the differences in color tone or font would be indiscernible to anyone not as meticulous as him. As tedious as it sounds, this is actually the part of my job I like the most. My promotion to manager means I rarely get involved in graphic design. Instead, I focus on guiding my team to produce cohesive products. At least with this project, I get to use some creativity.

It's not exactly the kind of creativity I got to explore when I was a freelancer during my last year of college and the one after I graduated. But it will have to do. I came to an understanding with myself when I got unexpectedly pregnant that I would from that moment on do whatever I needed to do to ensure security for my child. And so, I put aside my own desires for creative passion in favor of the predictability of a decent paycheck and guaranteed healthcare.

A text from Nicole comes through just as I'm ready to take my late, quick lunch break.

**Nicole: Well? Still waiting on dat ass!**
**Me: Can I call you?**
**Nicole: Yes**

I grab my turkey sandwich and bottle of water and head out to the patio, claiming a spot by myself at one of the picnic tables. Once I've had a couple bites, I call Nicole.

"Well?" she answers with a laugh.

"Oh my god," I tell her. "You won't even believe how busted I got."

"What?! Tell me!"

I laugh and that turns into more laughter. Nicole is begging me to tell her what happened but ends up joining me in laughter until I can get it together and tell her how Buns-of-Steel guy looked right over my shoulder to see the photo of his butt and my text.

"That is too good!" Nicole says.

"Easy for you to say. When—"

"Wait, before you go on, you *have* to send me that text. I need a visual, Kay."

"But the whole thing with him catching me made me realize how rude it was. I'm not some kid, I'm an adult, and I shouldn't have .... violated him that way."

"Girl, please. It's a *butt*. It's not that big of a deal. Now send it."

"Okay," I say reluctantly. "But don't go sharing it with anyone."

"Who am I going to share it with? My Mommy & Me circle? Come on."

"Hang on," I say, shaking my head and smiling. I send her the original text.

"Damn, that's a fine booty," she says. "On second thought, maybe it's a great idea to share this with those sleep-deprived mamas. Wake them right up."

"Nic, no. You said—"

"I am just kidding and you know it. Anyway, he's fine. You need to jump right on that."

"I don't think that's an option."

"Uh oh. What happened when he caught you?"

I give her the rundown on our awkward yet full of sexual tension encounter, finishing it off with his weird invitation to his sister's and how it was paired with his assurance that he had no interest in dating anyone.

"Huh," Nicole says. "That is a whole lot more than I thought you'd get out of the pinky-promise."

I laugh. "Me too. I guess it was fun, anyway. And nice to feel a little connection, even if it's going nowhere."

"I'm not giving up hope on this. I think this might just be one of those slow-burn things. You're going to see him again tomorrow and the day after that. And you'll have this 'thing' that will just keep building until you can't keep from tearing each other's clothes off."

"You've been watching Bridgerton again, haven't you?"

She laughs. "It's what gets me through the night when Lucas is up for feedings. I'm on my third viewing!"

"And you should enjoy it, but you should also know that Tanner and I are not some Regency romance."

"Oh, so you got his name, hmm? Well, I'm still gonna hold out hope."

"I have to get back to work, Nic. Thanks for listening."

"Always. And good job on that pinky promise. It's nice to see a bit of the old you, you know?"

Smiling, I tell her, "Yeah, I do."

# 10

KAYLA

I wake up early the next morning, unsettled by my dreams. Grabbing an extra pillow, I turn on my side and hug it to me.

In the dream, I'd been at the construction site across the street. But in place of a skeleton of steel beams, there was a stage and a massive audience. The person performing was Rad. But it wasn't Rad. The crowd was shouting "Tanner." I was in the audience, and when "rocker" Tanner beckoned me toward him, the crowd parted so that I could get to the stage. When he offered his hand to me, I took it, and he lifted me effortlessly into his arms, whereupon I somehow seemed to dissolve right into him.

I can't help but laugh. My dreams tend to be amusingly literal. Apparently, my subconscious is warning me away from Tanner with the worry that he'll be the same bad news as my ex.

The time Rad and I had together wasn't all bad, of course. That first night in the club where he interrupted his set to talk to me was incredible. After their show ended, he and I had a drink together at a back corner booth that quickly turned into the hottest make-out session I'd ever had. He had a way of holding my face, a way of teasing my mouth with his, that left me wanting more.

We left that club and went to my place. I thought it would be a one-night stand with a hot musician, but we ended up staying in bed together for two days straight, barely stopping to eat along the way. He was all-consuming and made me feel like I was the absolute center of his world.

He talked about his journey and how it was now entwined with my journey, that together we were going to explore new territory. It was exciting and I was so swept up in him that I didn't think twice about just going along for the ride. Whenever we had to part, my body vibrated with anticipation until I could see him again. And when we reunited, it was as if we hadn't seen each other in months. The passion was explosive and incredibly satisfying. And addictive. I got lost in him, ignoring Nicole and my other friends except when I convinced them to meet me at one of Rad's gigs. But even then, I only had eyes for him. As soon as he was off stage, I was back in his arms, with barely a wave to my friends.

Thankfully, Nicole has forgiven me for my friendship sins. She's had her own time of overwhelming desire, too, chasing after that rush of pheromones. Only, she ended up marrying her hottie, moving to St. Louis, and having a baby.

By the time Rad was getting ready to head to Europe, our fanatic need for each other had leveled off. He was spending a lot more time with his band, and I was back to hustling for freelance work. But I still thought we were planning on being together when he came back from tour. His casual breakup line of "Listen, Kay Kay, it's time for me to go on my journey and you to go on yours" didn't register at first. It was just the way Rad talked about everything. He's a fervent believer in the idea that you go where life takes you. You don't overrule that concept by trying to *plan* or make yourself beholden to what society deems appropriate.

But I soon realized that his lack of commitment—not just to me, but to anything in life other than his band—meant he and I were done.

When I tracked him down to tell him I was pregnant, his response was "that's really great for you Kay Kay" and it told me everything I needed to know. I was on my own. And once I had some time to think about it, I realized that him not taking any responsibility was the best thing in the end. If he had suddenly rushed back to me and committed to making us a family, I'd have to be on my guard for when he'd suddenly decide it wasn't his "journey" after all and took off. This way, I could create a life for the two of us that was based on the stability and security that Emerson deserved. I'd had my fun, my days of wild passion. And it was time to put that away and be a grown-up.

It hasn't always been easy, that's for sure. There have been so many times that I wished I had a partner, not just for help in raising Emerson but to have someone to simply share the amazing moments of parenthood with. When Emerson does something especially cute, I have to tuck it away to tell my Florida-based parents when we have our weekly video call.

This isn't to say that I feel sorry for myself. Not at all. I think I've made a very nice life for Emerson and me. In fact, I'm protective over it to the point where I haven't dated anyone since Rad, not wanting to disturb the balance we've created.

But the lack of intimacy must be wearing on me, whether I realize it consciously or not, because I keep thinking about Tanner—even dreaming about him. Though, I would have preferred something sexier than what I got.

Maybe seeing him today at Mean Beanz will trigger a better dream next time, I think with a laugh.

EMERSON and I get through our morning routine easily enough, and so after she's dropped off at daycare, I feel a rush of anticipation when I open the door to the coffee shop. It's busy, as usual, and I scan the crowd for Tanner, but there's no sign of him.

Glancing at my watch, I see that I'm here at about the same time as I always am. So, it's not likely that I've thrown things off by being especially early or late.

With no other choice, I get in line and order my regular. Once I have it in hand, I hesitate, looking around for him. All I see are other pre-work caffeine hounds or those setting up their laptops to make a day out of it. No tall, handsome, incredibly fit men ready to engage in casual conversation and heated subtext like Tanner.

Before I can feel completely pathetic for lingering, I take my coffee and head back to get my car. As I walk, I realize Tanner not showing up was a good thing. The chemistry we had was only bound to turn combustible. It's not a good idea to even entertain the idea of him being an option. I learned my lesson with Rad, after all. A sexual attraction like that can only lead to costing you what you both want and need out of life.

So, it seems he did me a favor by bowing out of our little back and forth. Maybe he even felt the same sense that we had the potential for something too risky.

Nodding to myself, I'm determined to shake off the whole incident and move on.

## 11

KAYLA

Emerson has gone to bed and I'm in the zone, working on what is now a hobby: graphic design. Since I don't have the time for freelance jobs, I entertain myself by selecting an existing logo to redesign for my own amusement. Lately, I've been toying with something new for Mean Beanz. Their current logo never made sense to me. It's a frothy cup of coffee with coffee beans spilling over the side. Nothing about that says "Mean Beanz" to me. So, I've designed a logo that is a to-go cup with a grumpy expression on a cartoonish face on one side, and as you turn it, a trail of coffee morphs into a contented cartoon face slurping up the coffee. It's cute, but I feel like it needs fine-tuning, and I'm working on shadows of the "grumpy" face when there's a knock on my door.

The interruption startles me into throwing my hand across my chest and holding back a yelp. Looking at the clock on my computer, I see that it's just after eleven o'clock. On a Wednesday night. Who on earth ...?

"Kay Kay, open up."

*Rad.* Is he kidding me right now? I'm wondering if I can just keep quiet and hope he'll go away when he knocks again, this time louder. If he doesn't wake my normally deep-sleeping Emerson, he'll wake all my neighbors, including Mrs. Trujillo down the hall, who is always looking for a reason to engage.

I rush to the door and swing it open to find Rad leaning against the frame, a duffel bag and a guitar case at his feet.

"What are you doing here at this hour?" I hiss.

"Is it late? I don't even know what time zone I'm in, to tell the truth." He grabs his bags and lets himself in, inspecting the living room.

It's not a big place, but the living room is cozy with a dusty-red brick accent wall, a gas fireplace, and pale wood floors. A glass coffee table sits in between two burgundy loveseats, all of which are centered on top of an oatmeal rug with hints of rust threads.

None of this has changed since the last time Rad dropped by unannounced about eight months ago, so what could he be looking for?

"You alone, babe?" he asks.

Oh. That's what he's looking for. A man. Not that he has any right to ask such a thing.

"Emerson is asleep in her room."

He nods and eyes me up and down. My leggings and an old, oversized John Mayer concert T-shirt are bound to disappoint him—both because it is a decidedly unsexy outfit and because he believes he's been miscast in the US as a poor man's John Mayer. They do have a similar blues-pop-rock vibe, along with a husky singing voice; I can't deny that. He's also tall with dark hair, but I personally always found him more classically handsome than John Mayer. And though he does have natural talent, the comparisons to the other artist have always made audiences and critics dismiss him as an unintentional tribute band. That unrelenting mischaracterization is behind his devotion to Europe where the audiences are more open-minded.

"Lovely," he says, trying unsuccessfully to hold back the bitterness in his voice as he continues to eye my shirt.

"Oh, come on, I didn't even know you were coming. Nicole forced me to a show a few years ago and bought me the shirt."

"Hmm." His gaze falls to my neckline, where it dips low enough that I'd guess he's getting a glimpse of my lavender bra.

I check him out right back, taking in the European cut to his leather jacket, black button-up shirt, and slim-fit dark wash jeans. He's wearing the same Doc Martens boots he's had forever, the ones that used to be oxblood but are now more scuffs than a deep red color. They're also the ones he had carved my name into on the toes. Or, I should say, he carved "Kay" on each toe to form that nickname I've grown to hate. Despite that, he's in good shape, has a decent haircut, and definitely exudes *rock star*.

The intense physical attraction we used to have is gone, though. At least it is for me.

Gone are the days when I lived to just breathe in his scent. Gone are the days when I convinced myself that his grand romantic musings of our "entwined journeys" meant he wanted a future with me.

That all dissolved when he walked away without a shred of hesitation or regret, and I was left to process what our time together had actually meant. I was devastated to admit the truth to myself but, in the end, there was no denying it: I had been nothing more than a good time, someone to be enjoyed in the moment but not savored for anything more. It was a rude awakening once I realized I'd basically been the only one in that "relationship." Like a lovesick dope, I took his sweet talk for what I wanted it to be rather than see it for what it was—simply a very good way of getting girls into bed. I questioned everything about my own judgment after that.

I will never go down that road of obsession again. There is nothing to be gained from it. I'll always put Emerson's needs above my own and what she needs is a mother focused on her well-being.

"So, what brings you to town, Rad?" I ask, folding my arms across my chest in a defensive pose.

He smiles the smile that had hooked me that first night when I was at his show. It's just the quirk of one side of his mouth, but it's enough to showcase the dimple in his cheek. I used to melt when I saw that dimple. Now, all it does is make me think of Emerson because she inherited the same dimple from him.

Instead of answering me right away, he walks a slow circle around the loveseats and over to where my desk is tucked into a corner at the far side of the living room. He nods at my logo.

"That's ... cute."

He's always dismissed my art as something like a pastime, whereas his music is something serious and takes priority over everything.

I shake my head. "It's just me messing around. I don't do freelancing anymore."

"That's right. You're on a corporate world journey, aren't you?"

Scoffing, I say, "I'm on the having-a-stable-job-to-provide-for-my-daughter journey."

"*Our* daughter."

Whenever he corrects me this way, a shiver of fear runs down my spine. I've taken it for granted that our arrangement —informal, though it may be—will continue indefinitely. But every now and then, he makes some stray comment hinting that he might want something more. It is his right as her father, and I don't begrudge him that. Not at all. What I do worry about is his inability to commit. I worry that he'll become invested in Emerson for a time but that it won't last, and she'll end up heartbroken by his disappearance. After all, he's only ever seen her a half-dozen times in her life. Luckily, she's been too young for it to affect her for very long. That's how it seems on the surface, anyway. I fear, though, that she's absorbing the instability of his presence and that it might cause problems in her own relationships when she's older.

"Yes, our daughter," I say to placate him.

"Can I go look in on her?"

Wincing, I shake my head. "I don't want her to wake up." If he knew his daughter, he'd realize my excuse doesn't hold water. Emerson is such a heavy sleeper that once she's out, nothing disturbs her until she's fully rested. But he doesn't know that or any number of things about her, and that's part of my hesitation to give him this small parental pleasure.

"Kay Kay, I'm fully capable of doing it quietly. I just want to see her."

"And then you'll go?"

He raises his eyebrows. "We can talk about that after."

That's not an answer I like. Still, I shrug, and he heads down the short hallway, though it's clear he doesn't remember which bedroom is Emerson's because he hesitates at the closed bathroom door.

"End of the hall, on the right," I tell him.

Collapsing onto the sofa, I stare at the unlit fireplace and will myself not to follow after him. Not even after I hear him saying Emerson's name several times without getting a response.

Rad soon rejoins me, sitting on the same loveseat next to me. I get up and sit opposite him.

"What's the plan, Rad? How long are you in town this time?"

"That is entirely up to you."

"What does that mean?"

"I think I've gotten to the part of my journey where I need to spend some time with you and Emerson. I think we need to give this family a shot."

I honestly try to hold it back, but in the end, there's no stopping the laugh that comes out of my mouth.

"What's so funny, babe?"

"Is Europe done with your band?"

"What?"

"I mean, there's really no other explanation for what you just said. You've *never* wanted 'a shot' with us before. Why now?"

"Don't question it so hard, babe. It's just what I'm feeling right now. It's the path I'm on."

I stand. "You're about four years too late. You need to go to your hotel or wherever you're planning on staying."

"Oh, about that ... I was hoping to stay here." He sees the

rejection of that notion on my face and rushes to continue, "At least for tonight. I really want to be here when Emerson wakes up. I want to surprise her, Kay Kay. Come on, I just got off the longest flight, and I'll crash so hard you won't even know I'm here."

"You can crash at a hotel. Or anywhere else, really. Doesn't your cousin Cary live here?"

"It's Cody. And no, he's in Telluride now. Anyway, can't you give me this? I haven't seen my daughter in so long. Can't I get a little leeway here? I just want to see her beautiful smiling face in the morning. And you can't tell me she won't be happy to see her dad, right?"

I have my doubts about that, but exhaustion and the hope that my daughter might actually have a good experience with her father overwhelms that.

"Fine. Just one night. Figure out how to sleep on that loveseat, if you can."

"Thanks, babe," he says.

I head down the hall to my bedroom, locking the door behind me, lest Rad gets any ideas.

## 12

### KAYLA

I wake earlier than normal again, but this time it's to be on guard for Rad. He's still sprawled and asleep on a loveseat, his legs dangling over one end when I come out to the living room.

"Time to get up," I say, shaking his shoulder.

"Hmm?" He half-opens his eyes and yawns. "Oh, what time is it?" When I tell him, he asks, "Do you have any coffee?" He groans as he sits up, his body likely full of kinks from being in that awkward position all night.

"No, I don't make coffee here. I get it from my coffee place after dropping Emerson off at daycare."

"No coffee?" He rubs the back of his neck. "That's inhumane."

"Yeah, well, it's how I do it. Listen, wake yourself up and I'll get Emerson. You wanted to surprise her, right?"

He looks confused for a moment, and I want to snap my fingers in front of his face to get his attention but I restrain myself.

"Yeah. Oh, yeah. Give me a minute. Bathroom is ..."

"First door on the right."

Giving me an annoyingly self-satisfied smile, he heads off down the hall. I go to the kitchen to get Emerson's breakfast ready. Her favorite thing right now is strawberry yogurt with a side of plain Cheerios. It's easily prepared, and so once I'm done, I look out my window at the construction site. It's just past seven o'clock, but they're already in full swing, which must mean that Tanner has been leaving his crew each morning to pick up coffee for them. The gesture of the boss doing that for his team is a nice one. Makes me think I should try that with mine during our next Monday meeting.

"Hi, Mama."

I turn to find a bedheaded Emerson in front of me, her favorite purple teddy bear held against her chest.

"You're awake, huh, sleepyhead?" I scoop her up and cover her face with kisses.

She laughs and buries her face into my neck.

"There's my girl!" Rad says, joining us in the kitchen with outstretched arms.

Emerson jumps at the unexpected appearance of someone else in our home and wraps her arms around me as tight as she can.

"It's okay, sweet pea," I say soothingly while shooting daggers at Rad. "It was a surprise, I know. But your daddy wanted to see you."

"Not daddy," she says with a shake of her head.

"Sure, I am," he says and reaches for her. "Come on and give me a hug. I've missed you so much."

"No!" She shakes her head violently and then looks at me with wide eyes.

"Shh," I tell her. Rocking her, I press my lips to her forehead. "Emmy, I know you haven't really seen your daddy in a while, but he's here now. He took a long plane ride all the way from Europe to come see you."

"Don't break my heart and tell me you don't remember me," Rad says with a furrowed brow.

I try to keep my voice neutral as I tell him, "Let's just give her some space. She was still half-asleep, okay?"

He hesitates, and I can see that he wants to just rip the Band-aid off and force Emerson into acknowledging him, but, in the end, he thinks better of it and takes a few steps backward.

"Sweet pea," I say, "sometimes surprises are good, right?" She looks at me but doesn't say anything. "Like that time I picked you up early from daycare and we got ice cream?"

A smile slowly creeps over her face. "With sprinkles."

"Yes, with sprinkles!" I stroke her cheek. "But sometimes surprises are unexpected and we need to sort out how we feel about them. Like when your class got a pet turtle but you thought you were going to get a fluffy bunny. Remember?"

"Turty," she says. "He's slow and cute."

I laugh. "See, you know exactly what I mean. You didn't expect Turty, but now you love him." I take a deep breath. "So, this is a little like that. You didn't expect Daddy to show up this morning, but he's here. And he's so excited to see you. So, what do you think? Do you want to go say hi?"

She thinks about this for a moment and then nods. I bend down to release her to her feet and then watch as she takes a few tentative steps toward Rad where he's standing in the living room. This time, he holds back and lets his daughter take the lead, offering only a gentle smile.

"Daddy," she says softly as if to confirm it for herself.

He nods. "I like your teddy bear."

She looks at the stuffed animal and then holds it out toward him, not to give it to him but to offer him a better view.

"I bet you have a lot of stuffed animals."

She nods. "I have all the animals. Mama says it's my very own zoo."

He laughs. "How about I take you to the real zoo?"

Her eyes widen? "I love the zoo!"

"Perfect. You can show me all of your favorite animals there."

"Want to see the zoo in my room?" she asks, beaming.

"I'd love to, Emerson."

My heart swells as I watch her offer her hand to show him the way to her room. Rad turns back and mouths "thank you" to me. I nod but am filled with mixed emotions. I'm delighted that Emerson will get some time with her father but worry that it will end abruptly, just when she's latching onto the very idea of him. That's all it's ever been with him so far.

## 13

### TANNER

I'm eager to break away from the site this morning since I couldn't leave yesterday and missed out on seeing Kayla. We had a mini-crisis when part of the crew realized they were using the wrong materials for a section of the build and I couldn't get away. But today, things are under control, and I step out of the trailer ready to get to Mean Beanz earlier than I have before just to be sure I don't miss Kayla.

Not that I have a grand plan for what to say to her after how I screwed things up with my admittedly weird invitation to have dinner with me at Tatum's.

Still, as Ernesto optimistically suggested, today is another day to get it right. Exactly what "right" means, I can't exactly say. All I want is another chance to see her, to talk with her, and maybe even make sure she understands that *I'm* not the one who is a creeper. Thinking of her use of that word in relation to how badly she felt over taking the picture of my ass makes me laugh. It was a little surprising, I'll admit. But also, somehow endearing. Especially when she made it sound like it was part of some sort of harmless prank with her friend.

Anyway, the thing is to just connect with her at least one more time today and see if we can be on good terms.

I haven't even left the site yet when my cell buzzes. It's Tatum and I don't hesitate to answer.

"How are you feeling, Tate?" I ask.

She sighs. "Do you have any idea how many times I get asked that?"

I can hear noise in the background. She's probably getting the boys' lunches ready, and it sounds like they're chasing after each other and shouting taunts along the way.

"No, how many times?"

"Too many," she deadpans. "Yes, I'm pregnant. And yes, my belly is *huge*. That's apparently what happens when you get pregnant again after twins. It's all stretched out and ready to grow a gang. But that doesn't automatically make me so feeble that I'm a walking cause for concern."

"Calm down," I tell her mildly. "It was a simple question about the well-being of my *anemic* pregnant single-mother sister."

"Well, that's even more flattering," she says, and I laugh. "I'm fine. Getting the boys ready for school and after that, I'm going grocery shopping. But what I need to know from you, dear brother, is whether your Kayla will be joining us. You never did get back to me, which was pretty rude, if you ask me."

"I couldn't get back to you because I don't have an answer yet," I lie. "But at this point, it's unlikely she can join us, so go ahead and plan for it to be just me. Sorry to disappoint you."

"I am disappointed. But only because I was looking forward to meeting the person who has captured your interest. The last woman you were with was that awful Chloe, wasn't it?"

My sister doesn't beat around the bush. She either likes you, or she doesn't and there isn't much that can change her mind one way or the other.

Chloe was something else. We met at a sports bar. I was there with Ernesto and some friends, blowing off steam on a Friday night after a long week. She was there with a few friends, too, but we gravitated toward each other and left together without saying goodbye. I thought it might be a one-night stand, but she was fun and up for anything, so we kept it going. We were totally casual, seeing each other once or twice a week at most. Nothing serious.

Until that all changed one night when we were out to dinner together and we ran into Tatum. She had escaped for a girls' night and so was all done up and tipsy. She greeted me familiarly, of course, with a hug, and Chloe about lost her mind with jealousy. I mean, it went from zero to sixty and was not pretty. She actually told Tatum to meet her outside so she could show her who I really *belonged* to. Needless to say, that relationship ended right there.

"Yeah," I say as I near Mean Beanz, "that one is long over."

"Thank God. Okay, so I'll see just you tonight?"

"Yeah. Looking forward to it. Let me know if I can pick up anything on the way over, okay?"

She sighs again. "I probably will. Mom-brain is real, you know? Add to that pregnancy-brain, and I'm bound to forget half the things I need for tonight."

I laugh. "You're doing great, Tate. Hang in there and I'll see you later."

We disconnect just as I reach for the door, already scanning the place for a gorgeous redhead.

# 14

## KAYLA

Emerson's renewed connection with her father lasts all morning as he follows us through our routine of walking to daycare where he makes a big show of being impressed by her crafts projects on display. She hugs him goodbye when it's time for us to go, and I have a flicker of hope that all will be well.

It's only when we're outside and headed toward Mean Beanz that the old, true Rad emerges.

"Kay Kay," he says, "it's so good to see Emerson. Jesus, she's growing up fast."

"She is," I agree.

"You don't want her to grow up without her father, do you?"

"What does that mean?"

"You and I ... we had a wild connection back in the day. We can get back that spark again, don't you think?"

"Not interested," I say shortly.

He tries to take my hand in his, but I pull away. "Listen, maybe I got it wrong when we parted ways. Maybe I didn't understand my journey was supposed to be with you and Emerson."

Furrowing my brow, I don't hide my skepticism. "What is suddenly making you think this?"

"I ... isn't it enough to say that I miss you, babe? I miss that intensity we had. Jesus, we needed nothing when we were together, right? It was a rare kind of bliss, that's what I've realized."

I'm still not buying this line. I know for a fact that he's with a different woman just about every night, and that's the way he likes it. I was an anomaly. I lasted months rather than a single night with him. In the end, though, he still moved on.

"Rad, why would I ever give you another chance? I mean, you've never even apologized for walking out, for never being there when you should have been."

"How can I apologize for following my journey?" he replies.

He's so self-serving and obtuse I want to shake him. But it would do no good.

"Do you know how ridiculous you sound?" I ask instead.

He covers his heart dramatically as if I've wounded him. "Okay, what about trying us again for Emerson's sake, if nothing else. We could be a family, the three of us, couldn't we?"

I laugh bitterly and stop walking, turning to him. "A family? A family has to be together. At the most basic level, a family has to be there for each other."

"Well, that's why I'm thinking you two should move to Stockholm." When I roll my eyes, he continues quickly. "The band is on fire there, babe. We're really on a roll. So, yeah, you'd need to come to me."

"Except for the fact that you and I are not together, Rad."

"But we could be," he murmurs, pulling me to him with his arm around my waist.

I push against his chest until he lets me go. "There are a lot of reasons why you and I are not an option. You need to accept that."

"I don't. I don't accept it. Not when I know how much that little girl needs me in her life. Not when I know I could make you happy. It could work. This could be my jour—"

"Don't you dare say that word. I am so sick of hearing about *your* selfish needs. My world is not about you."

He watches me for a beat, trying to decipher this cool rejection. Despite never quite achieving the fame he's always wanted as a musician, being rejected by a woman is a rarity.

"Come on," he says. "What do you even have worth sticking around here for? A soul-crushing corporate job and this boring-ass town?" He gestures to the block we're on, but I'm stuck for a moment on how he's characterized my job. I don't think I've ever talked with him about what I do and how much it has stifled my creativity. But he somehow knows. Or has made a good guess, anyway.

As for this neighborhood, Highlands Square, I actually really like it. It's just west of downtown with a great variety of distinctive architecture, along with boutiques, salons, coffee shops, and restaurants. I have easy access to everything I need, including Emerson's daycare. It's got a community feeling, too, as we've made a tradition of going to the Sunday Farmer's Market, the summer Highland Street Fair, and the holiday event in December.

But that would all apparently be too quaint for Rad because he says, "Where's my up-for-anything girl? Don't you want to get out of this bland town and live an adventurous, sophisticated life with me in Europe? I promise you we could be so good together again."

I'd almost forgotten how persistent he could be. He's like a dog with a bone when he decides he really wants something. That's how we ended up basically having a four-month hookup. It's how I neglected my freelance clients because he'd always have an argument for why staying in bed with him, or going to his show, or simply being his audience of one as he played guitar and came up with new song lyrics was a better use of my time. I don't want to be sucked back into falling for all that again. I won't.

Looking just past Rad's shoulder, I see Mean Beanz. But more importantly, I see a tall man just inside the door, looking around expectantly.

"I need coffee," I say and forge ahead.

I'm only vaguely aware of Rad behind me as I walk straight up to Tanner and throw my arms around his neck.

"Hi, sweetheart!" I say and kiss him quickly on the lips. "Please go along with this," I whisper to him before pulling away.

His eyes lock on mine, and for a moment I think I see fear there. Of course, he thinks I'm a psycho. But as soon as I saw him, I thought this could be the way to put an end to Rad's efforts at a reunion. Yes, I should have just shut him down myself. But the more guilt he lays on me about creating a family for Emerson, the more I'm susceptible to doing something I don't really think will make any of us happy in the long run. I've spent the last four years making a good life for us, but Rad has a way of making it seem like it's lacking. I just need to shut him up for a little while. And if I get to fall into

Tanner's strong arms and kiss his sexy lips while I do so, then that's a hell of a bonus.

Thankfully, his hesitation is brief.

"Hi, honey. I've been looking for you," he says far more smoothly than I could have even hoped for.

"Uh, Kay Kay?" Rad says.

"Oh, I forgot you were here for a second," I reply. I suddenly realize Tanner and I have been holding hands and I start to pull away, but he holds me in his grip. His hand is large, rough, and protective. It feels perfect. "Tanner, this is Emerson's father, Rad. I've told you all about him." I take a breath and continue quickly. "Rad, this is Tanner."

"And you've told me nothing about him," Rad says, eyeing me skeptically.

"Well, we didn't have a lot of time to talk, what with you showing up so unexpectedly last night."

"We could have pulled an all-nighter. Like we used to."

I force a smile onto my face. "Anyway, I need to get my coffee and get to work."

"You two work together?" Rad asks, looking Tanner up and down.

Tanner is wearing the same jeans that flatter his ass so well, a navy T-shirt, and work boots. Before he can come up with a lie to try to indulge my outlandish roleplay, I jump in.

"Does he look like he's in marketing?" I ask with a smile. "I mean, he could be the *star* of some marketing materials for the company I work for, but he's not the one handling the graphics."

"Cute," Rad replies with a thin smile. "Maybe we can talk more about what I was saying earlier at dinner tonight?"

I stare at Rad for a moment, trying to think of an out.

"Honey, we've got dinner at my sister's tonight. You didn't forget, did you?" Tanner asks.

"Oh, right!" I shake my head as if I'm just a silly dummy. "See, I really need that coffee."

"So, you're busy, then?" Rad says. "Great, I'll babysit Emerson. That'll be awesome."

Tanner must sense that me reflexively squeezing his hand is a sign that I don't like what Rad's suggested because he says, "Thing is, my nephews were so looking forward to seeing Emerson. You know how much they adore her, Kayla."

God, he's good. Now I stare at him for a second too long, lost in his reassuring gaze.

"Tomorrow, then," Rad tries.

"Um, yes. Tomorrow after work, sure."

"Good. Let's get some coffee." He goes and joins the line.

Pulling my hand from Tanner's, I smile up at him. "Thank you so much. I promise I'll explain it all to you one day."

"You can explain tonight when I pick you up."

"Oh, you don't really have to—"

"Quick, tell me your cell number."

"You'll remember?"

He nods. "I'm good with numbers."

I rattle it off and he leans down to kiss my cheek. "See you tonight at six-thirty."

"Um," I say and turn to see that Rad is watching us. "Yes, see you then."

"Don't worry," Tanner says. "There really are no strings attached."

I nod but can't help wondering what I've gotten myself into.

## 15

TANNER

I've spent the last couple of hours after leaving the site for the day running errands. When I let Tatum know that Kayla would be joining us after all, she asked me to pick up another bottle of wine and find a dessert that would be both kid-and adult-friendly. Once I checked that off my list, I washed and thoroughly vacuumed my truck to take care of the stray snack crumbs in and among Max's and Matt's car seats. Finally, I swung by my house just long enough to shower and change before driving back to pick up Kayla.

I don't know what's appropriate in this situation. Should I go inside her building and to her door or should I just text her to say I'm here. If this were a real date, I'd definitely go inside. If this were a real date, I might have even brought her flowers.

But it's not a date. It's a ... what the hell is this, anyway? I laugh to myself as I set the truck in park. Kayla has been a surprise every step of the way, but certainly not a bad one. Even if she did use me as some sort of wedge against her ex. The expression on her face as she implored me to go along with her was familiar. I've seen that same sort of trapped look on my sister's face before when a boy in school or a man in a bar was giving her unwanted and aggressive treatment. That's why I didn't hesitate to step up and help her out.

I could have left it at that. I could have let her out of going to dinner tonight. Maybe I should have. But maybe one good deed deserves another. This way, Tatum will get the impression that I'm dating someone and get off my back. It'll be a harmless little bit of pretend, just like with Kayla and her ex.

The fact that I'll get to spend some time with her outside of a coffee shop is an extra perk that I won't deny I'm looking forward to.

Dialing her number on my cell, I wonder if she'll screen the call or pick up. After a couple of rings, she answers with a wary "hello?"

"Hi, Kayla. It's Tanner. I'm downstairs. But I could come in to get you if you want?"

"No, that's fine. Um, I'm going to bring a car seat for my daughter."

"How old is she?"

Kayla hesitates, and I continue, "Just asking because I actually have car seats for my nephews. They're five, so if you think they could work—"

"Oh, that's perfect. She's four, so I bet it'll be fine. Okay, we'll see you in a few minutes."

As I wait, I get out of the truck and lean against the front passenger door. The sun won't set for another hour or so and the early June day is just starting to cool off. I've changed out of my work clothes and into clean jeans and a gray Henley with the sleeves pushed up. I opted not to shave, wanting to keep this whole thing as casual as it can be.

Kayla has chosen to dress up a little more, I see, as she and a cute little girl who clearly favors her father emerge from the apartment building. The dress Kayla is wearing is a sleeveless, V-neck cream thing with bands of mustard and rust colors where it falls to mid-thigh. It's loose, and with her red hair falling around her shoulders, she looks free and relaxed in a very welcome contrast to the more buttoned-up work outfits I've seen her wear.

I can't stop the broad smile that spreads across my face.

"Hi," I tell her, and she returns my smile. Bending down, I address her daughter. "You must be Emerson. I'm Tanner. It's very nice to meet you." I offer her my hand but she just looks away shyly.

"It's okay, Emmy. You can take Tanner's hand," Kayla coaxes.

I shake my head. "Tell you what, when you're ready, you let me know. No need to push it, okay, kiddo?"

Emerson nods solemnly and Kayla thanks me.

I shrug that off and open the extended cab door for Emerson, letting Kayla help her up and into Max's car seat. She adjusts the straps expertly and we're ready to go.

"Tatum—that's my sister—her place is about fifteen minutes from here," I say.

"Okay," Kayla replies. After a moment, she muses with a playful smile, "Tanner and Tatum? Any other 'T' named siblings?"

I laugh. "No. But my nephews are Matt and Max, so apparently, the alliteration naming thing carried through with my sister." I pause. "Don't worry, I have no intention of doing that with my own kids."

"Glad to hear it."

Glancing at her, I see she's fighting a smile, causing me to do the same.

We drive for a couple of minutes in silence, the oddness of our situation overwhelming conversation.

In an effort to normalize things, I ask, "How was your day?"

She turns to me and opens her mouth to answer, but then stops. After a second, she laughs. She continues to laugh, and it's a beautiful sound: genuine and relaxed.

"What's funny?" Emerson asks.

Kayla holds up a hand as she tries to get herself together. "Nothing, baby. I'm just being silly."

"Mama's being silly," Emerson agrees with a smile.

"I need to apologize again," Kayla says. "I seem to have the bad habit of being totally inappropriate with you."

I smile and raise my eyebrows. She's not wrong. Still, I won't let her feel too bad about it. "Can you tell me what was going on this morning? I mean, is your ex some sort of threat?"

She glances back to check on Emerson and I realize I need to be careful about how I speak. I see in the rearview mirror that Emerson has picked up a Pete the Cat book that the boys had left in the truck and doesn't seem concerned about us.

"No," she says. "He's not a threat. He's just a pest, to be honest. Um, he actually lives in Europe, but he showed up last night. And this morning he was pushing me ... to a place I didn't want to go."

Clearly, she doesn't want to let me in on the whole story, and that's okay. She's confirmed what I thought, that she needed help getting him to back off.

"Well, glad I could help," I say.

"You were incredible, really. Very smooth, in fact."

"Yeah, I guess it came easy."

"So, your sister thinks we're dating?"

I shrug. "Something like that. I sort of told her I had my eye on someone and that's why I couldn't let her set me up with her friend. I had just met you that day at Mean Beanz and your name kind of fell out of my mouth."

Her eyes widen at that, but at the same time, the corner of her mouth tugs upward.

"What can I say? You made an impression on me. What with taking a photo of my a—" I stop myself with a quick look in the rearview mirror at Emerson. She's still enjoying the book, thankfully. "With that whole photo thing, I mean."

"I see," she says.

"Anyway, this will just be a good way for Tatum to see that she doesn't have to worry about me. She's got enough to deal with right now."

"What do you mean by that?"

"Her boys are twins. Five-year-old twins. They're awesome. I love them to death, but they're a handful. She's also about five months pregnant. And her husband is in the Marines, deployed in the Middle East. So, I help out as much as I can." I laugh. "Even though Tatum would hate to think she ever needs help."

Kayla nods. "Sounds like you're a really good brother."

"Well, as long as she doesn't know that this whole thing is a put-on."

"I can put on a good show."

I glance at her just as she's crossing her legs and realize I don't think I'll have to fake much about my attraction to her.

## 16

KAYLA

Tanner stops the truck in front of a small Craftsman-style house. It's painted gray-blue with a deep red door, and the slightly overgrown lawn is littered with a couple of scooters, a soccer ball, two jumbo nerf guns, and a sprinkling of nerf darts. It all adds up to create the impression of boys who have recently enjoyed themselves there and makes me smile.

"So, this is it," Tanner says. "I, uh, well, we didn't really come up with a game plan for how to play this."

Turning to him, I see doubt coloring his face and have to think mine looks the same. This is the weirdest situation I can remember being in. When he insisted we really follow through with what I thought was a bluff for Rad's sake and come to dinner, I wasn't sure it was the right thing to do. But I spent the day convincing myself that he had done something really nice in Mean Beanz, and so this was the least I could do.

I second-guessed all that when Emerson and I came down from my apartment, and I was ready to just tell him in person that we couldn't go anywhere with him. But then he greeted us so warmly. And the sweet, respectful way he treated Emerson was enough to sway me right back into wanting to help him with his sister.

So, I'm up for playing along. It's just a few hours of pretending we're dating. Of pretending we know each other and are attracted to each other.

Only, I've already established my attraction to him from the moment he caught me with that photo of his ass. And he … he's given me more than one indication of his feelings on the matter, including the other day when he devoured me with that long look. He replicated that same hungry look just a bit ago when he let his eyes travel over my legs.

Okay, so maybe we won't have to fake the attraction part. Just the rest of it is fake. He made it clear—twice now—about his "no strings attached" policy. This is going nowhere beyond tonight.

Time to go ahead and get it over with.

"We can just sort of fall back on the idea that we're newly seeing each other, right?" I ask. "I mean, that would account for me not actually knowing a lot about you and vice versa."

"Yeah, you're right. That's good."

I turn to Emerson. "Are you ready, Emmy?"

She looks up from the book she's been studying and smiles. My sweet girl got pulled into this thing, and I can only hope she isn't negatively affected by it somehow.

Tanner opens my door before I realized he's gotten out of his side. He offers his hand and I take it, once again noticing the callouses and warm strength in his grip.

After hauling out my oversized purse, I pull Emerson from the car seat and walk with her hand in hand toward the house. Tanner leads us by half a step, seamlessly opening the gate for us and plucking a frisbee from the branches of a quaking aspen tree. When he uses the toe of his running shoe to pop the soccer ball up and into his free hand, Emerson squeals.

Tanner grins down at her. "I've gotta show you later how I can bounce it on my head. My record is forty-three times!"

"Wow," I say with a laugh.

He leans down and whispers in my ear, "Not my only talent, just so you know."

I catch a whiff of his cologne as he pulls away. It's a subtle mix of cedar and citrus that makes me want more.

"I'm intrigued," I admit, and he raises his eyebrows with a suggestive smile.

And, boy, am I in trouble. He's far too tempting to just play some silly game with.

There's no choice but to jump right into the charade, though, because the front door opens and a pregnant woman is nearly toppled by two boys rushing past her and to Tanner.

"Hey, boys!" Tanner says, giving them a hug.

"You must be Kayla," the woman at the door says with a welcoming smile. "And Emerson?"

I nod. "Yes, thank you for having us. I'm sorry it's so last minute."

"No problem. I'm Tatum, by the way. Those wild things are my boys, Max and Matt." She pauses to look at Tanner and her adorable boys who have fallen into horseplay. "Tan, did you bring the things I asked you to get?"

"Yeah, they're in the truck. Matt, Max, help me with this stuff," he says, and they dutifully follow him back down the walkway.

"Come on in, ladies," Tatum says, opening the door wide.

I hesitate for a split second, not wanting to start this night off alone with Tanner's sister when I have no idea what she'll ask or how I should answer without him there to give me clues or nudges. But with no other choice, I quickly recover and follow her inside.

"I just love your name, Emerson," Tatum says as she leads us toward the combined kitchen and living room.

Emerson is too fascinated looking at the complex Lego tower on the carpet in front of the sofas.

"She's shy at first, but then she's the biggest chatterbox, I swear," I say, smoothing Emerson's dark curls away from her forehead.

Tatum has a dreamy look on her face as she watches Emerson for a moment. "I'm having a girl," she says with a rub of her belly. "I'm thrilled. And not just because of the girly things we'll get to do but for the way that it will stabilize the testosterone around here!"

I laugh with her but can hear the exhaustion behind her words and feel for her. "Tanner says your husband is out of the country. That must be hard."

She sighs. "Yes, Marcus is doing his duty, god love him. But I will be so happy to have him back. Counting down the days, actually."

"Oh, will he be back soon?"

"One hundred and eighty-four days," she says, forcing a cheerful smile. "Or, a couple of months after I give birth."

"Is there no way he can get leave?"

She waves away the concern. "It's part of the plan. This is his last tour and then he's retiring. But Tanner probably told you that he and Marcus are planning to start their own contractor company, right?"

I'm saved from having to come up with a reply to that by

the sound of Legos crashing. Tatum and I both turn to see that Emerson has knocked over the tower and has tears welling in her eyes.

"Oh no, sweetie," Tatum says soothingly. "Don't you worry about that. The boys can build that up in no time, believe me. Now, would you like lemonade or apple juice?"

Emerson, whose chin was quivering a second ago, is now smiling. "Lemonade, please!"

"So polite," Tatum says. "I adore you already, Emerson. Kayla, if my brother ever comes in, maybe you'd like a glass of the wine he was supposed to bring?"

"I'd love one," I tell her. I'm enjoying Tatum already. She's easy and genuine, not trying to put on a show, and it has the effect of making me feel welcome.

"I'm here," Tanner says. He's got a bottle of red wine in one hand and a *French for Sugar* bag in the other hand that the boys are trying to peek into.

"Finally," she replies with a smirk. "Hurry up and pour Kayla a glass. And then you can tell me all about how you two met."

I bite my lip and look at Tanner. He flashes me a rakish grin.

"Should we tell her the truth?" he asks. "Or the PG version?"

My cheeks are probably as red as my hair as I'm left speechless.

"This has some serious potential," Tatum says with a laugh. "Let me get the kids set up to play together so we can talk."

She gets the boys' attention and introduces them to us before gathering all the kids to play in the living room where they are within view but not earshot.

I take this brief moment to go to Tanner on the other side of the kitchen island. He's working the cork out of a bottle of Bordeaux.

"What was that about?" I whisper.

"Just having a little fun," he says. "I won't really tell her about how you took a pic—"

"What do I have to do to get you to never mention that to anyone, including me, again?"

His smile tells me he enjoys that I saw him as a sex object. And then his eyes drop to my mouth and I get that tingling sensation again. When he leans toward me, it feels like he's going to kiss me. And I'm not opposed to it. But, just as he did outside, he whispers in my ear instead.

"Give me time. I'll come up with something we can both agree would be an ... enjoyable arrangement."

When he pulls away, I look up at him, my mouth slightly open in a silent "oh" response just as he pulls the cork free from the bottle.

"God, I wish I could have some of that wine, too," Tatum says as she joins us in the kitchen.

It takes me a second to blink back the heat of desire that had washed over me just now, thinking of what kind of *arrangement* Tanner and I could agree on. Having him close to me like that and offering the promise of something very likely intimate has reawakened parts of me that I've buried for years now.

The only question is, can I play with fire again without getting burned like I did with Rad?

## 17

### TANNER

I can't lie. I enjoy the hell out of teasing Kayla. It's just so much fun to see her react with a mixture of shock and desire. And now she's dangled this idea of what she can do to get me to stop bringing up the photo she took. I couldn't *not* take the bait on that one.

Though, it'll have to wait because Tatum is making good on wanting to hear how we met. I jump in to answer before Kayla.

"Funny story, actually," I say. When Kayla looks at me with wide, imploring eyes, I laugh. "It is, though. Remember when we were in line together at the coffee shop and I told you that I recognized you?"

"Well, that's not exactly how you put it," she replies.

"Yeah, that's true. I think I said, 'you've been watching me.'"

"I'm not following," Tatum says as she eases herself onto one of the stools on the other side of the kitchen island.

Kayla laughs. "You basically *accused* me of watching you."

"I didn't mean it that way. I was just surprised to see you. To recognize you."

"So, where did you recognize her from?" Tatum asks.

"It was her hair I recognized, actually," I continue. "Her gorgeous red hair. I recognized it from seeing her watch my construction site from her apartment window across the street."

"You mean," Tatum says, "you were watching her in her apartment while she was watching you at the site?" Her eyes dart between us in amusement.

I nod, remembering the first morning I saw her, picturing that sighting as if it were happening all over again right in front of me.

"The sun rises at around five-thirty and it's at a perfect pitch by the time she's standing at her window about a half an hour later. The light this time of year is this rich warm yellow and it lights up the face of her building. But what got my attention was the way the sun seemed to light her hair on fire. It just mesmerized me, honestly. I stood outside of my office for almost ten minutes because I couldn't take my eyes off of her."

Kayla's been watching me during this description, her expression slowly relaxing and turning into something almost dreamy.

"Wow," Tatum says. "Obsessed much?"

We all laugh. But what I don't say is that once she turned away from the window and moved out of sight, I felt like I'd just stumbled into darkness. It was disorienting and left me wanting, like something essential was just out of reach.

It was an oddly intense reaction, I know. But it's also what made me look for her the next day, to see if I'd have the same sensation. I did. And it continued for the next couple of days, motivating me to get out of my warm bed and to the site. So, when I heard a woman in line behind me at Mean Beanz sigh and turned to find that same redhead, I was thrilled.

"Yeah, seeing her in the mornings made an impression," I continue. "And so, when I saw her in the coffee shop, I had to say something."

"Well, lucky for you, Tan," Tatum says, "that Kayla didn't get weirded out by the whole thing!"

I laugh and exchange a look with Kayla. "Yes, lucky for me."

Of course, there's a whole lot we're holding back, including the fact that this isn't real and that, after tonight, I don't know if I'll see Kayla again. But for now, I just want to soak up the *idea* that it's real. Because I don't want to step away from the light she radiates.

DINNER IS rowdy as the kids dominate with their non-stop chatter. The boys fight to tell Kayla a story about their day at school where they teamed up to score a soccer goal. All the while, Emerson has come out of her shell and has a running commentary about everything she's eating (beef stroganoff), seeing (the photos covering the refrigerator, among many, many other things), and smelling (the garlic bread). The kids even engage in a little conversation with each other as Matt and Max take turns using all-knowing "big boy" voices to explain various things to her.

I watch Tatum taking this in, knowing it pleases her to see her kids acting so well with a younger child. I can imagine she is seeing a slice of her future once the baby is born. That's four months away and when I think she'll *really* need me. Our parents have passed and Marcus' are in New Hampshire, and while Tatum has friends who can help out, no one is as invested as family. So, I'm committed to being there for her. On top of that, I've got the job I'm working on *and* the plans for starting the contractor business. It's a full plate that only enforces my no-time-for-romance rule.

Which brings me back to Kayla. I enjoy how she watches over Emerson. She's attentive and curious with her, purposefully guiding her into expressing herself. She's a good mom. That doesn't stop me from also seeing her as a beautiful, sexy woman. I'm reminded of the arrangement I'd said we could come to so that there would be no more talk of the infamous "ass photo." I can think of a few things, all of which involve very few clothes.

"What do you do for work, Kayla?" Tatum asks, pulling my attention back to the present.

I realize in the moment when I've let my mind wander to what I'd like to do to Kayla, the kids have left the table and are off playing.

"Marketing," I reply, wanting to seem like I was paying attention and not imagining Kayla naked and positioned on all fours with me behind her, plunging deep as my squeezes and light slaps leave marks on her ass as red as her hair.

Kayla looks at me with an arched brow, obviously sensing something is off with me.

"Yes, I'm a marketing manager for an international real estate company. Corporate communications, branding, some design, that sort of thing," she tells Tatum.

"You enjoy it?"

"It's fine." She shrugs and takes a sip of wine.

"Not your dream job?" I ask. I'm aware this reveals that I don't know her very well, but I'm curious—and hope Tatum won't notice.

"No, not exactly."

"Why do you do it then?"

"We all have compromises we have to make, right?" Kayla says shortly.

I follow her gaze to where Emerson and the boys are playing in the corner of the living room. It hits me that even though I spend a lot of time helping my sister with her kids, my efforts and responsibilities are limited. After all, I get to go home and have my own life with only myself to consider. Kayla looks like a young mom. She must have given up a lot to dedicate herself to her daughter.

"What if you didn't have to compromise? What would you do?"

She smiles. "Well, in an ideal world, I'd go back to freelancing graphic design. In my last year of college, I managed to get a few jobs and that carried me through so I could set up my own business. It was great. I got to really develop a vision for my clients but with my own stamp on it."

Nodding, I say, "There's nothing like creating something out of nothing with your own hands, right? That's what I got a kick out of when I started doing construction straight out of high school."

"My god, you should have seen my friends," Tatum says with an eye roll. "Tan was already the school heartthrob but then put him in a tool belt on a construction site and all the girls went absolutely crazy."

"Come on, Tate," I say as Kayla laughs.

"Seriously. They used to drag me with them to cruise the

site!" Tatum shakes her head mournfully. "It was so embarrassing."

"Yes, it really was," I agree.

"Well, I can agree that you do look good on a construction site," Kayla says with a wink.

I enjoy the flirt, even though it may be the product of the wine loosening her up. Her body is relaxed and she's leaning toward me slightly. If these were any other circumstances, I'd lean in to meet her, slide my hand into the hair at the nape of her neck, and take her mouth with mine.

But that's not an option. Instead, I try to focus on the conversation we'd been having before Tatum pushed it into embarrassing territory.

"Anyway," I say, "I loved the whole process of building something that had a practical use, of imagining how people would make it their own eventually. It was so satisfying to see all that hard work come to something, you know?"

"All that is in past tense," Kayla says. "You don't do the work anymore?"

I shake my head. "Thing about construction is that there are opportunities to rise in the ranks if you're a hard worker who actually shows up. And, I suppose, I had some project and people skills because the company I work for groomed me to move up quick. I still like to jump in and help where I can, but it's not nearly often enough."

"Good thing I have endless projects for you," Tatum says.

"True. This house may look sturdy, but I've slowly been rebuilding it."

Kayla looks deep in thought for a moment before murmuring, "It's funny that we have this in common. I mean, we both take orders for someone else's vision instead of getting to build something out of nothing like we want to."

Meeting her eyes, something unspoken passes between us. It's a kind of understanding of the connection we've just discovered about who we are and what we want.

"Can we have dessert now?" Max asks, having corralled Matt and Emerson to join him in the request.

The kids' appearance breaks the spell between Kayla and me and I get up and bring out a platter of cupcakes for the kids to choose from. I made sure to get a blueberry cupcake for Tatum, since it's her favorite. Kayla chooses a frosted animal cracker cupcake to share with Emerson, who sits on her lap.

The sugar soon has the boys running around the house tagging each other but it seems to have the opposite effect on Emerson who has curled up against Kayla's chest and fallen asleep, her lips tainted pink by frosting.

I skip the sweets and instead start to tackle the dishes, ignoring my sister's weak call for me to leave it to her. With one ear, I listen as she and Kayla talk.

"Emerson really is just the most precious thing," Tatum says.

"Thank you. She is my everything," Kayla replies.

"Is her father... around?"

"Funny you should ask. He actually just came back into town last night. Totally ambushed me at my place and guilted me into letting him stay the night."

The "Oh?" my sister utters is dripping with her brand of full-on protection mode. It seems she doesn't like the idea of Kayla's ex sleeping at her place any more than I do. Not that I have one single reason to make such a jealous claim. Still, I drop some cutlery into the dishwashing machine caddy a little more forcefully than necessary.

"He spent the night curled up on the living room loveseat by himself," Kayla says with a laugh. "I should have sent him away, though. I just fell for his grand plan to surprise Emmy in the morning. She doesn't get to see him very often."

"So, there's no shared custody agreement?"

"No, nothing official. Rad—that's my ex—he's never been committed to the idea of fatherhood, I guess you could say. He spends most of his time in Europe and just sort of floats in and out of her life."

I hear Tatum sigh. I can only imagine the eye roll that goes with it.

"And I suppose he's not the child-support-paying kind of guy, either?"

"No, not exactly."

"Well, I don't have the pressure of supporting the family financially, but I understand how hard it can be to raise kids on your own," Tatum says.

"I'm fine. Completely used to it being just me and Emmy. But I can't imagine having two energetic boys and another on the way. You're incredible."

Tatum laughs. "Sure doesn't feel that way. Thank goodness Tan is such a help, though. I mean, I could handle all of the household stuff and the running around to get the boys to school and soccer practice and all that. But having him here as a solid male role model while Marcus is away is just invaluable."

I shut off the water and turn to face my sister and Kayla, wiping my hands on a dish towel. "Ah, it's nothing. The boys are a blast."

"I know you love them, but I worry that all the time you spend with us means you miss out on other parts of your life," Tatum says. Then she eyes Kayla. "But looks like you've got that covered?"

There's an awkward silence before I decide to not even try to answer that. "Anyway," I say. "Fantastic dinner. Thanks, Tate. Looks like we need to be heading out, though." I nod to Emerson who is still fast asleep.

"Yes, thank you so much," Kayla says, and I'm relieved that she's in sync with me on this.

**18**

KAYLA

I get Emerson buckled into the car seat without waking her and then turn to find that Tanner has opened the passenger door for me.

The night air has cooled and in the dim light of the evening, he's partially in shadows. But I can see that he's watching me with an expectant smile.

"Thank you for tonight," he says. "You were really great."

I shrug. "No problem. I actually had a nice time. Your sister and her boys are sweet."

Though he nods, he doesn't make a move to the driver's side. Instead, he lingers, his eyes doing that thing again of leaving mine to focus on my mouth and back again. I lick my lips in anticipation of him leaning down to do what we've both wanted to do all night. We're standing close enough to each other that I can feel his body heat, and when he reaches out to touch my bare arm, I shiver. I want to feel the pressure of his lips on mine, be pulled even closer to him, to melt into his strong chest.

"Mama?"

But Emerson has other plans. Since her door is already closed, I jump into my seat and turn to her, holding out my hand. She holds me weakly in return and I don't think she was even really awake. Still, I tell her, "I'm here, sweet pea. Everything's okay. We're heading home."

Tanner's apparently got the message that we need to go because he's slid into the driver's seat and started the engine. We drive for a few minutes without saying a word. When Emerson's hand has slipped from my grasp and she's sleeping deeply, I shift to face forward.

"You're a good mom," he says.

"Thanks."

"Must be rough, though? Being on your own?"

"It was at first. I was only twenty-three when I had her. But I was lucky to have my friend Nicole. I guess she was sort of like you are for your sister. She picked up the slack a lot."

"That's great." He pauses. "She was the one you were going to text that photo to, wasn't she?"

I cringe. "Yeah, she's the one who pinky-promised me."

"Which means what, by the way?"

"It's a little game we used to play when we were in college together. We'd 'pinky-promise' each other with harmless pranks—usually after we'd had a few cocktails."

"What kind of pranks?"

I hesitate.

"Come on, you said they were harmless, right?"

"They were … but also just ridiculous, mostly. And the success depended on other people sort of going along with it."

"Now I gotta know."

Shaking my head, I tell him, "Once we had these guys in a

bar convinced that we were French, couldn't really speak English, and didn't know how to order drinks."

He smirks. "Okay, I've probably been suckered into buying a pretty girl or two a drink. No big deal."

"Then, one time, we tried to convince some other guys that we were twins."

"I'm guessing you don't look anything alike?"

"Nicole's parents are from Ethiopia, so no, we don't look alike at all," I say with a laugh. Guys used to love seeing us together because of how my fair skin would contrast with hers. We got more than our fair share of offers for threesomes. Not that we ever indulged them.

Now he laughs. "And did this most recent pinky-promise come about the same way? You two were out drinking and came up with it?"

I laugh. "Nope. We were sober as can be."

"Okay. But you didn't actually send her the photo, did you?"

When I hesitate too long, he looks over at me. I raise my eyebrows and give him an impish smile.

"Oh, no way," he says with a laugh. "Well, what did she think?"

He seems to be taking this really well, so I say, "Do you want the truth?"

"Sure, why not?"

"She said you have a nice ass."

That raises an even louder laugh from him.

"Shush, Tanner," I say with a nod to Emerson even though I'm smiling with him.

He quiets and then goes completely silent.

"Wait a second, we're talking about the photo. What happened to you being all weirded out by it?"

"Must be the wine," I say with a shrug.

"Damn."

"What?"

"I was really looking forward to coming up with something that could buy my silence."

"What did you have in mind?"

He glances at me with a suggestive smile, and I feel a rush of heat in my cheeks. The fact that he makes me *blush* is just so not me. It has to be because I'm so out of practice with this. God, I can't believe I haven't had sex in five years. Not since Rad. I've been so focused on being a mom and creating our life that I've put everything else on the backburner. Including my libido. I would have thought it had shriveled up and died by this point, except for the fact that whenever Tanner looks at me, he ignites a fire in my core.

But it's an all too familiar, too dangerous, attraction. I'm not the same girl I was just a few years ago when I spent days in bed with someone because I couldn't stand to not have his bare skin against mine. I have more than myself to consider now. Which means that I need to steer clear of the impulse to get lost in another man.

"Tatum said you're going to start a business with her husband," I say in an obvious effort to ignore the moment of undeniable sexual tension we just had.

"Uh, yeah." It takes him a second to shift gears. But then he continues, saying, "It's a big commitment. Marcus wants to come back when his time is up in the Marines and hit the ground running, so I'm crazy busy trying to get a lot of the framework for it ready."

"Exciting, though, right? Being your own boss will be amazing."

"I hope so."

"You don't sound convinced," I say with a laugh.

"I think I'm just too busy to be excited, honestly. I've basically got two full-time jobs. And then I'm trying to help Tatum out as much as I can, too."

I nod. "Yeah, I'm all too aware of that feeling of having no time for yourself." Looking back at Emerson, her peaceful face makes me smile. "But it's all worth it in the end."

"What about your ex? You're having some kind of trouble with him?"

"Rad? No, I can't imagine he'll be anything more than a passing nuisance."

"That's good." He's quiet for a moment. "What kind of name is Rad, anyway?"

I laugh. "It's short for Radisson. His parents were romantics when it came to choosing a name, I guess, and wanted to honor the hotel where he was conceived."

He shakes his head. "That's ... something."

Letting my head fall back against the headrest, I turn to him with a smile. "It is. But it suits him. He's a guitarist in a band called The Rad Band. Yeah, I know it's cringe, but he's married to it. You've probably never heard of them, but they're pretty established in Europe."

"Ah, that's why he's never around?"

"Yep. And it's fine, really. Emerson and I are good on our own."

He pulls up in front of my building and puts the truck in park. "I'll help you get her up to your place," he says with a nod to Emerson who hasn't stirred.

"It's okay. I've done this a million times."

"No, really, I insist."

He's out of the truck and carefully unbuckling Emerson before I can protest. Instead of making a big deal out of it, I watch as he pulls her into his arms and against his chest. She flings her arms around his neck reflexively and rests her cheek against his shoulder while releasing a contented sigh. He holds her confidently, effortlessly. They look like such a natural fit that I'm struck for a moment by the sight of them.

"You're on the fourth floor, right?"

I'm startled that he somehow knows my floor for a second. But then I remember that he's made a study of me in the mornings as I looked out of my window at the site. His description of the impact seeing me that first morning had on him overwhelmed me. It was so unexpectedly romantic that I wanted to sigh with the pleasure of it. The whole thing made me realize how starved I am for that kind of attention, for someone to take their own pleasure in me. I had to tell myself that it was a fleeting moment for him that he's already predetermined to go nowhere.

"Yes. This way," I say and lead him into the building and to the waiting elevator. The ride up is short and soon I'm unlocking my door and showing him down the hall to Emerson's room, where he lays her down gently without disturbing her sleep.

After stepping out and returning to the living room, I offer him a drink. "More wine? Or a whiskey? I'm sorry, I don't usually have beer."

"Thanks, but I'm good."

"Okay. Well—"

"Is that the window? The one I've seen you in?"

Following his gaze to the living room window, I say, "Um, actually, it's the other one. The kitchen window."

"You mind?" He nods toward the window. "Just curious what your view is exactly."

"Be my guest."

He goes to the window and I trail behind him. The kitchen is dark and neither of us make a move to turn on a light. The nearly full moon casts enough of a glow over the room to keep us from bumping into the small dining table. I watch him surveying the site, his eyes sweeping over the barebones structure, the stacks of materials, the idle equipment, the trailer. The construction is still in its infancy, and I can't even imagine what it'll look like completed. I tell him as much.

When he turns to me, I expect him to give me a description of the plans, to paint a picture of the building he will have a major part of making a reality. But he doesn't say anything for a long moment. He just looks at me, surveying me much the way he did the site just now, though his eyes fall over me less critically and more with a kind of hungry wonder.

"What?" I ask softly.

Tilting his head, he says, "You're just as stunning in the moonlight as you are in the sunshine."

"Oh," I reply on a caught breath.

When he then pulls me to him with his hand on my lower back and leans down to kiss me, I forget all the reasons why I shouldn't give in to this intense attraction. His lips against mine are tentative at first, the pressure a mere suggestion, a tease. I'm breathing quickly, my chest expanding and pressing against his with each inhale, lost in the way our bodies are drawing even closer together.

Taking complete control, he slides his hand into the hair at the nape of my neck and seals his mouth over mine. It's the kind of connection that leaves me instantly needy for more. My hands rest on his chest, the ridges and definition there promising incredibly toned muscles. I want to explore every part of his body, and yet I haven't even tasted his tongue. He seems to have the restraint I don't. Then again, I'd guess he hasn't gone five years without having sex like I have.

When he pulls on my bottom lip with his teeth before sucking on it, I whimper. This is sensation overload, and yet, he's barely touched me. This reaction isn't because I'm so turned on. It's because I'm scared to go down this path with another man, scared to lose myself to an insatiable need that blinds me to the things that should take precedence.

I pull away and press my forehead to his chest, trying to catch my breath and get my thoughts together.

"You okay?" he asks before pressing a kiss to the top of my head.

"Um, yeah." I look up at him. "Is this—I mean, could this be something real?"

He looks confused. "What do you mean?"

"Just that you said you're not interested in dating anyone."

"Oh." He pulls away from me just enough so that the heat of his body is replaced by cool air.

"It's just that I have to be realistic. I have spent the last four years completely focused on my daughter. I don't date. I don't hook up. I put what's best for Emerson first, including who might or might not be in her life. So, if you're not open to dating, that's completely fine. I just need to know that's where you are."

His eyes leave mine and I know his answer.

Before he can open his mouth to reply, I create some physical distance between us, moving over to the living room.

"It's okay," I say. "I know a single mom probably isn't the kind of thing you're into. You've seen how hard it is with your sister, after all." I attempt a self-deprecating laugh, but it comes out flat.

"It's not that, Kayla," he says. But he doesn't make a move to come closer to me. He's still in the darkness of the kitchen. "I'm just at a bad place to be dating right now. I've got so much going on and—"

"It's fine. Really." I wave my hand as if to dismiss the whole topic. I'd rather not hear him tell me he has no room in his life for me. Not that I was ready to marry the guy, but it still doesn't feel good to be shut down like that.

"I think you're an amazing woman. I really do. I just have to be honest with where I am right now. It wouldn't be fair—"

"Got it." I go to the front door and put my hand on the knob. "Well, thanks for helping with Rad. And I hope you got what you wanted with me being your pretend date for your sister's sake." I open the door because he still hasn't moved from the kitchen.

"Yeah, thanks again for that."

"Yep, sure." I avoid his eyes as he finally starts toward me.

"See you around, then?"

I swallow and nod. Because I'm not looking at him, I'm surprised when he leans in to give me a kiss on the cheek. I pull away and smack my head on the door.

"Are you okay?"

Now I look him right in the eyes. "Absolutely. Have a good night."

He hesitates for a moment before nodding and stepping out.

As soon as I've locked the door behind him, I fall onto the sofa and tip my face into my hands. I'm not crying. I'm not sad.

I'm just... disoriented.

I thought he and I had a real connection. And not just a sexual one. It felt like there was something deeper between us, like we had some kind of understanding of what we need at the core of who we are. At least as far as creativity and ownership in work. Apparently not so much in common when it comes to what our attraction amounts to. Turns out he really meant that whole "no strings attached" thing. And I... I don't even know what I want from him, to be honest. But he just made it clear that he's not an option for dating.

There's nothing to do now but laugh about it. The whole episode has been ridiculous from start to finish, what with him knowing I was ogling him to the weird way we both pretended to be a couple for our own reasons to me banging my stupid head on the door as he left.

"Well, that's that," I say aloud.

The problem is that it doesn't feel so easy to dismiss how I was beginning to feel about him.

# 19

## KAYLA

"Okay, wait a minute. I'm not getting this," Nicole says.

I'd called her, as per usual, in the morning, but this time, I'm not chatting idly with her while staring out the window. After a fitful night's sleep, I've gotten up and curled into a corner of one of the loveseats with a blanket wrapped around me. I brought her up to speed on how the fake date with Tanner went, confessing to how his sexy little whispers in my ear had me revved up so that when we kissed in my kitchen, my knees practically went weak. But then I told her how I'd sent him on his way when he admitted he wasn't interested in dating.

"What's not to get?" I asked. "It's not like I'm going to just hook up with the hot construction guy from across the street."

"But that's exactly what you should do, Kay!"

Shaking my head, I close my eyes. "I know you really want to see me getting back out there, but this isn't what I need."

"Why not, though?" When I scoff, she quickly continues. "I know you think you can just deny your needs because you're a mom now. But, honestly, what is wrong with allowing yourself a little no-strings attached fun?"

Opening my eyes, I stare at the empty fireplace. "What if I'm not capable of doing a 'no strings attached' thing?"

Nicole sighs. "Girl, you have built your thing with Rad up to far more than it ever was. Yes, you had some mind-blowing sex for a couple of months, but he's not the only one who can get your rocks off."

I laugh. She's probably right. I may very well have convinced myself that Rad had cast some kind of spell over me rather than take responsibility for the fact that I chose to lose myself in him. He's just a man, after all. And I've come a long way since then. I've not only raised my daughter on my own, but I've fought my way into a management position to create a solid career. I need to give myself more credit.

"Okay, you have a point. So, you really think I should use him for sex?"

"Yes. And here's how you need to look at this: as the empowering move that it is. Be Angelina Jolie—after Billy Bob but before Brad Pitt. You know, when she'd meet up with men in a hotel room to satisfy her needs?"

"Um, no, I don't think I was aware of the details of Angelina's sex life," I say wryly.

"That's what I'm here for, Kay," she replies without irony. "Anyway, just think about it like our girl Angie did. It's a basic human need. You need to be touched. You need to be satisfied. You need to be worshipped. And you happen to know a guy who is totally down for it. Go. Get. Him."

That takes me aback. "Go get him? Like—"

"Yes, like *now*. Go make it clear to him that you're up for a one-and-done. And *enjoy* the hell out of it! Play hooky from work and get yourself some of that hot construction booty. Now, go!"

Instead of giving her reasons why I can't do something like that, I envision being that bold. And that leads to flashes of stripping down in the bedroom with him, of taking from him what I need, and letting him take from me right back. And it doesn't make me worry about being out of control or losing myself. It makes me feel just the opposite, like I can take charge of this part of my life, just like I've done in every other part in the last few years. Only, this would be something just for me. After over four years of being pretty damn selfless, I'm suddenly ready to indulge in what *I* want.

And I *want* Tanner.

BEFORE I CAN TALK myself out of it, I dress in a black lace bra and matching panties, a low-cut wrap dress, and heels. As soon as Emerson is safely deposited at the crafts table at daycare, I stop in at the drug store across the street and grab a box of condoms. There's no way I'll go into this escapade completely spontaneously.

With that taken care of, I head to my destination, strutting into the coffee shop and spotting Tanner sitting at one of the bistro tables near the pick-up counter.

How appropriate, I think with a smirk, and go straight to him.

He sees me coming and stands quickly. "Hey, good morning. How—"

"Do you have time this morning to be away from work?"

"What?"

"If I, say, offered you a daytime view of the site from my

apartment, would you have time? And interest?" Not the smoothest line, I know. My flirting skills are truly long gone. When he hesitates, I add, "No strings attached."

This seems to get the reaction I hoped for. His eyes leave mine to do a scan over my body.

"Absolutely," he says, his voice low but insistent.

"We'll skip coffee, then?"

"*Yes.*"

"Great." Turning and heading toward the door, I feel a rush of nervous excitement. I'm really doing this. I'm going to take this man to bed.

That thrill drifts away as we walk side by side to my apartment two blocks away, replaced instead with awkwardness.

"About last night," he starts, but I stop him cold.

"Let's not talk about that, okay? I really don't want to talk at all."

He looks surprised but not put off. Thankfully he takes my lead, going quiet and following me into my building, and then into my apartment.

But that's where his submission ends. As soon as the door is closed behind us, he grabs me by the hand and pulls me to him, spinning me so that my back is pressed against it. I let my purse fall off my shoulder and onto the floor as he leans down and takes my mouth with his. There's nothing tentative about this kiss, no searching to find the right connection or rhythm. It's pure domination, and I melt into him, savoring the pressure of his lips against mine, the warm heat and insistence of his tongue toying with mine, and the way his large, rough hand holds my jaw and neck possessively.

I wrap my arms around his neck to get closer to him. One of his hands falls to my ass, squeezing so that I moan softly.

# No Strings Attached

It's been so long since a man has touched me like this and I'm hyperaware of every sensation.

When his mouth leaves mine so he can trail kisses down the side of my neck, I take in a shaky breath. I'm practically desperate with need for him. I want his lips on mine, but I also want him to keep planting those slow kisses and gentle bites on the sensitive skin along my collarbone, too. His mouth reaches the lowest point of the V-neck of my dress, and he grazes his teeth over one hardened nipple while he rolls his thumb over the other one, making my legs tremble.

The tie of my dress loosens and then comes undone before I realize he's discovered this easy access. He straightens so he can push the fabric off my shoulder, then gazes lustily at what he's revealed.

The black lace lingerie isn't especially provocative, but paired with the black heels I'm still wearing, it's enough to bring a wolfish grin to his face. He runs his hand along my side and sucks in a breath.

"You're fucking beautiful, Kayla."

I know I'm not anything more than pretty on a good day. I have stretch marks and would love to be more toned. But right now, under the heat of his gaze, I believe him. I feel beautiful. And desired.

"You're wearing too many clothes," I reply.

He nods and starts to unbutton his shirt. I stop him, replacing his hands with mine to undo his flannel while kissing him hungrily. He's got a white T-shirt underneath and pulls away to yank it off over his head. His chest is muscular with defined pecs and abs and a drool-worthy 'V' leading into his jeans.

I run my hands slowly over his smooth, deliciously hard

chest slowly, reveling in the feel of his solid body before turning my attention to his arms. His biceps are thick, his forearms tight.

But then he takes my hands in his, stopping my touch.

"I am hoping more than you can know that you have a condom?" he asks urgently.

I nod and lean down to pick up my purse. "Follow me."

I must be high on endorphins because I strut my thong-bared ass down the short hallway toward my bedroom without hesitation, even knowing he'll be watching. I'm leaning into this experience as my one chance to just *feel* and *enjoy*.

At the door of my bedroom, I pull him to me and kiss him hard. He responds by wrapping his arms around my waist, lifting me up and carrying me to the bed, where he drops me down so he can loosen his belt. I lean back on my hands and watch him. He kicks off his work boots, drops his jeans, and steps out of them in one swift move.

In just boxer briefs now, he's sporting an impressive bulge at the crotch. But I'm just as interested in his backside and motion with a twirl of my finger for him to turn around.

"I'm beginning to think you're obsessed," he says with a laugh.

I bite my bottom lip. "Busted."

With a little shake of his head, he does as I ask, slowly giving me a view of that incredible butt. I know no shame, reaching out to tug on the waistband of his boxer briefs. He helps me slide them down to reveal a smooth, firm ass that is just as exceptional as the rest of his body.

"Come here," I say softly, moving onto my back against the pillows.

When he turns back to me, he's got his cock in his fist. Then he lets it go to climb onto the bed and it springs to attention up against his abdomen. And, *check*. It's just as impressive as his ass. Crawling between my legs and kissing me once more, his heat and hardness has me writhing under him.

The fact that we are basically strangers is completely irrelevant. At this moment, we are one in our desire for each other, in our need to please and be pleased. There's no first-time hesitation, just a natural instinct to explore this connection, to draw out each other's satisfaction.

He's slipped his hand inside my panties and I have mine wrapped around his cock. We work each other, alternating between kissing and pulling back to meet eyes, a hint of a smile on both of our faces.

"I'm going to make you come. And while you catch your breath, I'll grab that condom you said you have. So be ready, honey, because then I'm going to fuck you until you come again."

"Promise?" I ask with a naughty grin and stroke him faster.

He moans but isn't put off from rubbing my clit just so. I feel my core tighten and warmth radiate as I break, crying out uncontrollably.

"I could watch you come all day," he whispers in my ear.

Closing my eyes, I fling my forearm over my face. I can't stop smiling. I haven't felt this free, this insanely good, in such a long time.

I hear what he's doing, how quickly he's found a condom in my purse, managed to open the packet and roll it on, but I don't watch. Soon enough, I feel him touching me once more. He runs his hands from my shoulders over the peaks of my breasts, along my abdomen, until he gets to my panties, where he hooks the side straps with his fingers and pulls them off. Next goes my bra, and he takes first one, then the other nipple into his warm mouth, teasing me with sucking and bites, bringing me close to the edge all over again.

"Tanner," I say, "I want to feel you inside me."

"Yes," he agrees and positions himself at my opening. But there's more teasing as he rubs his tip over my swollen clit.

I half-moan, half-laugh at the delicious torture and then grab his flexed biceps to urge him on. When he sinks into me, I lose my breath. The sensation of him filling me is somehow both exactly what I expected and more. It's a revelation of the kind of pleasure I've gone too long without. It's a reawakening of the sexual woman I used to be. The woman I am right now, with him. He may not be Mr. Forever, but he is everything I need right now.

Bringing my knees up, I rock my hips against his. I grab his fine ass, enjoying my first real taste of it as he flexes and relaxes with his thrusts. In return, he cups my ass with one hand while bracing himself with his other arm over me, and I take pleasure in watching his face change with each movement. He's getting into a groove, his eyes closed.

"Wait," I say and raise myself up on my hands to kiss him.

In one quick motion, he grabs me around the waist and pulls me up and with him as he leans back so he's sitting on his heels. Now, with me on top, he doesn't need to do anything but let me move my hips in just the right motion to draw another orgasm.

Just as I'm wilting, coming down from the high, he grabs me again and pushes me gently off of him, turning me so I'm facedown against the pillows. He uses both hands to squeeze my ass hard before pushing into me once more. The depth he gets this way as he lifts my hips just right is enough to make me cry out in a hurts-so-good way.

"Jesus, I can't get enough of you," he moans with his final thrusts before letting go.

He doesn't drop his dead weight onto me like most guys do. Instead, he braces himself on his elbows and leans over to kiss my shoulder and neck and cheek again and again until he's ready to slip free and deal with the well-used condom.

Turning onto my back, I wait to feel some sense of regret over this. But it doesn't happen. Instead, I simply feel relaxed and satisfied. I did something for myself, an experience of pure pleasure, and it was incredible.

Tanner joins me in bed again, leaning over me as he strokes my cheek. "You are something else."

"Enjoyed the view of the site, then?" I ask with a laugh.

"Best come-on line I've ever heard." He smiles before giving me a long, slow kiss.

"Just so you know, I've never done this before."

"I find that hard to believe. I mean, you have a daughter, after all."

I roll my eyes at his lame joke. "I meant, I've never brought someone back to my place for sex like this."

"Lucky me."

My smile for him lingers for a moment. "It's too bad we're not the right fit."

He arches a brow. "I think we fit exceptionally well together."

"It *was* good," I concede. "But you know what I mean. That this is all it is."

"Well, not quite yet."

Before I have a chance to question what he means by that, he's dragging his fingers between my breasts and downward until he finds my legs closed. With a swift motion, he pushes them apart and claims me with a possessive hand over my still sensitive pussy. Taking in a sharp breath, I arch against him, eager for him to use those fingers on me all over again.

## 20

### TANNER

Jesus, that was good. I'm still catching my breath, even after Kayla has slipped out of bed and gone to shower. She needs to get to work, but I'm in no hurry. While we've been devouring each other in bed, the sky has darkened and rain has started coming down in sheets. It's a summer storm, perfect for lingering in bed.

My crew will have taken off, but I still have work to do in the office. Finding the motivation to get up and leave is proving to be a problem at the moment, however. All I can think about is what a fantastic connection we just had. It was more than just hot sex. We were in sync, and as satisfying as my two orgasms (and her four) were, I still want more.

But that's not part of the plan. In fact, I set the boundaries between us to say that I didn't want anything more than this. That this, sex alone, was all I had time for in my life. So, why am I wishing she would come out of that shower and sink back into bed with me so we could spend the day alternating between dozing off, making love, and talking about everything and nothing? That's not what this is supposed to be.

This was *no strings attached* sex. No obligations outside of fucking.

Maybe it's because the fucking was *so* good. We've got incredible chemistry, that's for sure. It's the kind that makes you want to come back for another taste. Another hit. Like an addiction.

Which, if I'm thinking of it like that, means I need to quit this thing now. I really don't have time to get involved with someone, not even someone as promising as Kayla. The pressure on me with work and organizing everything to start my own business with Marcus is intense. Throw in the time I put in with Tatum and the boys, and I'm tapped out.

With a sigh, I sit up on the edge of the bed, resting my hands on the mattress. Just then, Kayla emerges from the bathroom in a baby blue silk robe. Her hair is wet, her skin pink from the heat of the shower.

"It's raining," she says with surprise.

I follow her gaze to the window. "Started a while ago," I tell her with a small smile. "Guess you were too distracted to notice."

Her eyes meet mine before falling over my bare chest and down to where the sheet covers my lower half.

"Must have been." She does the cutest thing of raising an eyebrow and looking away. As if she wasn't just riding my dick a few minutes ago and begging me to make it last.

"Come here."

She hesitates before doing as I say. I pull her close to me so she's standing between my legs and wrap my arms around her slim waist. Pressing my face to her abdomen, I take a deep breath in and let it go as I feel her hand fall through my hair. I enjoy the heat of her, the comforting softness of her body, the fresh, lemony smell of her skin.

"Tanner," she says after I've held her this way for a long moment. I look up at her. "I, um, I know you know I had a good time."

I laugh, thinking of the sexy way she moans when she comes. "It was fantastic, for sure."

She smiles at me and plays with my hair for a second. And then she blinks and pulls away abruptly, as if she just remembered that kind of intimate touch isn't part of our arrangement.

"So, I need to get ready for work."

The suggestion that I get dressed and get out is clear enough. Not rude, but clear. "Yeah, I've got to get going, too."

She nods, and when I stand, the sheet slips from me. I hear her let out a breath and find that she's enjoying the view once again, this time a full frontal.

"You have to get to work, like, soon?" I ask. I don't reach for my clothes, not when she's drinking me in like I did to her a couple of mornings ago. She'd lingered when I did that, knowing I was surveying every inch of her, making the moment all that much hotter. Now, she takes me in, slowly, deliberately. And it gets me halfway hard before she shuts me down.

"I really do," she says reluctantly. "I have meetings I can't miss."

Now I grab my boxer briefs. "That's too bad. But, yeah, I'll get out of your hair. Can I just take a minute in your bathroom?"

"Of course." She steps out of the way so that I can pass by.

I glance back and see that she's been watching my ass as I

go. "Obsessed," I say with a smirk.

"You are too cute for your own good," she calls out to me with a laugh just before I shut the door.

Smiling, I shake my head at my reflection. This woman, she's just too *everything* for my own good. Doesn't mean I want this to end, though. Just that I need to tread cautiously.

KNOWING that she doesn't have time to linger, I clean up as quickly as I can and get dressed. I'm not sure what kind of goodbye we should have in this situation. I mean, I've had one-night stands before, but this doesn't feel like that. Even though it's supposed to be exactly that in its own way. Do I kiss her? Does a hug seem to fit the occasion better?

In the end, she walks me to the door and gives me a quick kiss on the cheek.

"I'll see you around?" she says.

It's become something of a vague non-goodbye between us, somewhat hopeful and definitely not final.

"Yeah, definitely. Have a good day, Kayla."

"Oh, I think my day's already been made."

Again, with the shy arched eyebrow and looking away. It makes me want to throw her over my shoulder and take her straight back to the bedroom.

Instead, I just smile and say, "Mine, too."

Once she closes the door behind me, I hurry out of the building with a sudden plan, going right into the rain that is still coming down with force. I start jogging, not because I want to avoid getting wet. There's no escaping that, not when my destination is a couple blocks away. But the rain doesn't bother me at all. It certainly can't stop the smile on my face.

## 21

KAYLA

When I swing open my front door, ready to rush out and off to work, I have to stop short. There is a to-go cup of coffee and a pastry bag on my welcome mat. It's from Mean Beanz, which means it's from Tanner. For the first time since I moved into this building, I'm glad there's no main lobby security door since it means he was able to go back to leave me this surprise.

I bite my lip to keep from smiling too big. To keep from reading too much into this gesture. Still, my heart does a little flip as I pick up the still-warm coffee and peek into the bag. He chose well. It's an almond croissant drizzled with dark chocolate.

There's also a note written on a napkin: *Couldn't have you miss out on your morning coffee — Tanner*

That does it. I can't keep from smiling at that. Why does he have to be so sweet and sexy and charming?

Why does he have to be so unavailable is the bigger question.

"He was cute, that man."

Startled, I look up to find my neighbor, Mrs. Trujillo, watching me from two doors down. Though she looks every bit her eighty-two years with a tight perm to her silver hair and a deeply wrinkled face, she's also sharp and spry. She does two long power walks a day, one at five thirty in the morning and one at four thirty in the afternoon. In between those activities, she somehow finds a reason to be out in the hallway or in the lobby of the building and is always eager for conversation, usually starting with some observation about a subtle thing she's noticed about me or Emerson. At first, I found it a little intrusive, but I soon realized that she's lonely and is looking for ways to connect. Since then, I make a point of chatting with her when I can or picking up something extra at the store for her. She's even sat with Emerson on the odd occasion when I've needed the help, though she's strictly a "light duty" kind of babysitter who needs everything to be in place before she comes on board.

"That man," she says again, "he was cute."

I feel my cheeks heat at what she must be thinking in seeing a man leave coffee for me like that. "Oh, yes. That's Tanner. A friend."

She eyes me for a moment, a knowing sparkle in her eye. "Sweetie, we all need a friend like that once in a while."

A laugh sputters out of me as I shake my head.

"I think you're right, Mrs. Trujillo. I have to get going. I'm sure I'll see you soon."

"Bye now," she replies, smiling.

I take the coffee and pastries with me on my drive into work. Just as I'm exiting the elevator to my floor where my office is, I get a text from Nicole:

**Nicole: Status update, please.**

I don't have time to go into details since I've already burned half of my day in bed with Tanner, but I know I can't leave her hanging either, so I text back:

**Me: Just call me Angie.**
**Nicole: OMG! Tell me EVERYTHING!**
**Me: No time. I'll call you as soon as I can.**

Even as I slip my cell into my purse, I hear it buzzing with her back-to-back texts. The ego boost of knowing she's impressed by my morning activities puts an extra pep in my step.

Until I see Henry in front of my office door. He's alternating between looking at his cell and looking up at me as I get nearer, clearly indicating he's been waiting for me. I wouldn't put it past him to have had the receptionist in the main lobby alert him when I came in.

"Hi, Henry," I say. "Did you need something?"

"Everything okay with your daughter?" he asks.

"My daughter?"

"Oh, I just assumed that's why you were late coming in today," he says with a smug smile. "In fact, that's what I told Gregory when he came by looking for you, that you must have had a babysitting emergency or something. Again."

I force a smile. "As it turns out, my daughter is fine. Thanks so much for your concern. It's really so sweet that you think of her well-being ... so often."

He bristles at that, knowing full well that I see exactly what he's doing.

"Since you're here," I say, "why don't we bump up our one-on-one from two o'clock to now."

Clearing his throat, he says, "Now?"

I moved past him and into my office, setting down my purse and leather laptop satchel. "Is that a problem? I assume you're ready to go with the color pallet schematics I've asked for?"

"Of course, I am. It's just that I have them in my office. I can—"

"Surely you have them saved to the team's shared drive?"

He visibly stiffens and we stand there staring at each other for a long moment. Finally, he says, "I'd like a little extra time to go over everything before presenting it to you."

I nod and sit at my desk. "Probably time better spent than lingering outside my office, right?"

"I, uh, well, I'll see you at two o'clock."

In a move to make sure it's clear to him that I'm the boss, I don't bother to look up from the planner I'm examining when I tell him, "See you then."

THERE WAS no time for lunch today, late or otherwise, so by the time I've picked up Emerson and we're walking down the hallway to our apartment, I'm starving.

"How about we order pizza?" I suggest, too tired to even throw together our usual grilled cheese and soup.

"With pep-roni!" Emerson says.

I smile down at her. "Yes, with pepperoni."

"How about sausage on that, too?"

I look up at the man's voice to see Rad waiting by our door

and my smile fades. What is it with men waiting by my door today?

"What are you—"

"Daddy!" Emerson's hand slips from mine as she runs to Rad.

He picks her up and swings her around. "There's my girl! How was your day?"

"We made crafts with pop-sticks and buttons and yarn," she replies.

I unlock the door as she keeps up a running list of all that she did that day. Rad kicks the door shut behind him and then sits down on a loveseat with her on his lap, listening attentively. It gives me the chance to put down my things and head to my bedroom. It's just as I left it this morning, the bedding askew and empty condom wrappers on the nightstand. A flash of being with Tanner comes to mind. The sex was phenomenal. I so wanted more, especially when he was standing butt-naked in front of me and growing hard as I eyed him. I'd wanted to drop to my knees to take him deep into my mouth, to give us both that pleasure. But I had to force myself to end our time together to go to work instead. And I have to assume that I won't get the chance to be with him again.

Thinking of him reminds me that I should at least text him to say thank you for the coffee. I was too rushed earlier, but it's only polite to do so now ... right? Or am I just making up an excuse to reach out to him?

I debate the pros and cons for a minute before reaching for my cell.

**Me: That coffee was exactly what I needed. Thank you.**

With that, I quickly straighten my room and change into

leggings and a soft sweater perfect for the still gloomy weather. Then I make a quick call to order delivery of pizza and a Greek salad. In the living room, I find that Rad and Emerson are no longer chatting. She's on the floor, drawing a rainbow on scrap paper and he's looking at his cell. Guess their father-daughter Hallmark moment is over.

"I take it you're staying for dinner?" I say as I pass through and into the kitchen.

"Well, yeah, Kay Kay. We had plans. You remember, don't you?"

As I'm pulling a bottle of sauvignon blanc out of the refrigerator, I remember I'd agreed to meet with him tonight. To continue talking about "us" becoming a family.

"Do you have any beer?" he asks.

"Nope. Just wine."

"What, your 'boyfriend' doesn't expect beer when he's here?"

I sense that he's not convinced by the act Tanner and I put on. But I'm still game to go along with that charade if it'll help back Rad off.

"No, we're usually too busy with other things to worry about beer," I say with a mischievous smile.

"Really?" His tone is dubious. "Who is this guy, anyway? Why don't I know who you have in my daughter's life?"

"Our daughter," I correct him.

"Just answer the question."

"It's still new with Tanner."

He contemplates that, nods, and then lets out a breath. "Good. That means my suggestion for us getting back together is still good, right? If you're not about to marry this guy or something, then we still have a chance."

"Honestly, Rad, what makes you think you can just come back into my life–into *our* life–and expect me to uproot everything I've worked for to run off with you?"

"Oh, I don't know." He pointedly looks over at Emerson who is still happily coloring. "Maybe you should tell me why you *wouldn't* want to give her a real family? She needs me in her life just as much as she needs you, don't you think?"

I have to fight to keep my voice even. "Don't you dare make me out to be the selfish one here. You didn't even walk away from us. You were *never* there. But now I'm supposed to just fall for your guilt trips?"

"Kay Kay, it's not–"

My cell ringing has stopped him and I realize that I'm shaking with anger. I force a deep breath before looking at the caller ID. It's Tanner. A wave of relief washes over me. I don't know if it's because of the welcome interruption or just because I'm happy that he's reaching out.

In either case, I hold up a hand to Rad and take the call.

"Hi, Tanner," I say and turn to the kitchen window. The rain has slowed to a drizzle but I can see large puddles dotting his construction site. "You got my text?"

"Hey, hi. Yeah, I did. But I'm actually calling to check in on you," he says.

"Um, thanks. But–"

"I remembered your ex planning to see you tonight."

"Um, yep, that's happening."

"As I recall, you weren't too thrilled at the prospect?"

"Exactly."

"So, if there's anything I can do to maybe help you out again, I'd be up for it."

The kindness of him not only recalling Rad inviting himself over and also offering to be a buffer makes me smile.

"That's so sweet," I say. "But I don't know."

"Is he right there?"

Glancing back, I see Rad has pulled down two wine glasses and is giving them both a big pour. "Uh, yeah, that's true."

"Feel free to use me," Tanner says, and I laugh in surprise. "I mean, if you want to back him off, just tell him you and I are a real thing. I can swing by and back that up if you want."

"Do you have time for that?"

"I'm still across the street. Been working late since I got interrupted this morning—in the best way possible."

Smiling, I focus on the trailer at the far end of the site. There's a light on there that I hadn't noticed before. "Okay, yeah. I just ordered pizza, if you're hungry."

"Didn't stop for lunch, so yeah, I'm hungry. Speaking of which, mind if I get a little hands-on with you when I get there?"

I laugh again. "What do you mean?"

"You know, just to give *Rad* the impression that he's got some competition."

Another flash goes through my mind from this morning. This time it's of the way that Tanner had caressed my whole body with his hands, lips, and tongue in one way or the other. I'd dismissed Nicole's suggestion that I needed to be "worshipped," but Tanner had made me feel exactly that.

"You there?" Tanner asks.

"Yeah. And yes. See you soon."

"See you."

Disconnecting the call, I take a moment to collect myself before turning to Rad.

## No Strings Attached

"Did you just invite him to join us?" he asks, incredulous.

"I, um, I did."

"Thanks a lot, Kayla. Really, I can't believe you're not even having a discussion with me about our future."

"I will. I promise. Tanner's just going to come by for a minute. Maybe have a slice of pizza."

He watches me as he raises his wine glass. In three large swallows, he's emptied it. And I'm suddenly not so sure I've made the right decision in having Tanner come over.

## 22

### KAYLA

My anticipation builds as Tanner takes longer than I thought he might, given that he's just coming from across the street. Thankfully, Rad hasn't tried to get back to our conversation and is instead busy on his cell, responding to the band's social media messages.

The pizza guy shows up before Tanner, and I start to think he's changed his mind about doing this pretend thing once more. But within minutes of setting the food on the kitchen table, he finally arrives.

As soon as I open the door, he leans in and kisses me full on the mouth. It's such a deep, committed kiss that it takes me a second to recover. When I open my eyes again, he's smiling at me like we're sharing a secret. And I suppose we are.

"Sorry, it took me longer than I thought," he says. "But I wanted to pick up a few things."

I step aside so he can enter the apartment.

"You didn't have to do that," I say.

"It's just that wine you like. And I brought some beer since you never seem to have any."

He turns so only I can see his expression of hopeful, raised eyes. It was well remembered on his part since I mentioned the other night that I don't usually have beer on hand.

"Right, I always forget to pick it up for you," I say, and he looks relieved.

"I also brought this for a certain someone." He pulls a package of Circus Animal cookies out of a plastic bag and looks at Emerson.

She must have a sixth sense that sugar is being offered because she drops her crayons and gets up.

"Hey, you," Tanner tells her, leaning down.

Eyeing him for a moment, her serious expression soon breaks and she gifts him with a smile. And then she offers him her hand for a handshake. It seems they've both remembered something about each other: for her, it's the way he had tried to shake her hand yesterday; for him, it's how much she liked the Animal Circus cookie flavored cupcake at his sister's house.

I watch this interaction happily, without even remembering Rad is there. Until he forces himself into my line of sight by moving between me and Tanner.

"I could use a beer, thanks," he says, relieving Tanner of the bag.

"Hey, how's it going?" Tanner asks.

"Fantastic. Couldn't be better," Rad mutters as he goes to the kitchen.

I give Tanner an apologetic smile. He leans down and whispers in my ear, "I'll follow your lead with this." I start to nod in anticipation of him pulling away, but he doesn't.

Instead, he slips his hand into the hair at the nape of my neck and brushes his lips against the shell of my ear. "You smell good enough to eat."

"Oh," I whisper. When I pull away, I raise a brow and look away.

He strokes my cheek with his fingers. "I love when you get shy like that."

Before I can reply, Rad says loudly from the kitchen, "Food's ready!"

Meeting Tanner's eyes, I force a smile and say, "This is going to be awkward."

He laughs. "Yeah, it is."

THE FOUR OF us squeeze around the small kitchen table and conversation is mercifully stalled while we dig into the food.

"Hey, Emerson," Tanner says, and she looks up at him mid-bite of a slice of pizza. "I'm going to ask you a question I ask Matt and Max all the time. Are you ready?"

She puts her slice down and wipes her mouth. "Ready."

I hold back a laugh at how absurdly cute and solemn she is.

"Did you have the best day ever today?"

Her eyes go wide as if she's shocked that he could read her mind. "I did!" She launches into an animated description of her day in only the way that she can, where no detail is too small to spare.

And despite how awkward it is for the three of us being there together, we all laugh with her and encourage her to go on until she's had her fill.

Finally, she takes a deep breath, and asks Tanner, "Did you have the best day ever?"

The question is simple, innocent. But the air somehow suddenly feels charged. As soon as I meet Tanner's eyes, a rush of heat finds my cheeks. It's the way he's holding me in his gaze. It's openly sexual, as if he's reliving everything we did to each other this morning. It's a look that says he's ready to ravage me all over again.

When he breaks our connection to give Emerson his attention, I have to force a deep breath and blink hard to clear away inappropriate thoughts of how he had touched me like he owned me just a few hours ago.

"Yes, Emerson," he says, "I had the *best* day ever. Something unexpected happened, actually."

"Like a good surprise?" Emerson asks.

He laughs and winks at me. "Yes, a *very* good surprise."

As if sensing the subtext of Tanner's answer and wanting to change the course of things, Rad says, "I was thinking you and Emmy should come to Stockholm. You know, for a trial visit? To see about moving there."

I'm silent as I digest this request. Rad has never once asked for us to visit him, let alone suggested a "trial" for actually moving there to be with him.

"Stock home?" Emerson asks, her face scrunched up in cute confusion.

"Where daddy lives," he tells her. "Wouldn't it be great for us all to live together?"

"Yeah!" She turns to me. "Can we, Mama?"

And that's when it hits me. He's made this suggestion in front of our daughter so that he can use her as leverage in the guilt trip he's been crafting to get me to uproot my life at his whim.

I'm so furious at this manipulation that I'm paralyzed by it.

## No Strings Attached

I wish I could conjure up a cool, cutting response like I can at work. But when my heart is involved, it's not nearly as easy.

Tanner must sense my unease because he steps in, saying, "Well, that would actually be a problem for us. Wouldn't it, honey?" He takes my hand and rubs his thumb over the inside of my wrist.

"What *us*?" Rad asks. "I thought you guys were new, not even serious?"

"It may be new, but that doesn't mean it's casual," Tanner says, smiling at me with such warmth that I almost believe his doting boyfriend act.

Rad clears his throat to remind us he's still here. "Yeah, well, anyway," he says, "this isn't up to you. Right, Kay Kay?"

"Well, yes, but—"

"Hey, another thing I was thinking about you moving is that it could be a chance for you to go back to doing the graphic design. You know with us together, you'd have more freedom. No more silly coffee cup graphics. You could get back to the stuff you used to do. Fuck the corporate gig. Feed your soul instead."

"Rad," I hiss and gesture to Emerson.

He shrugs, unconcerned by his four-year-old daughter hearing profanity. "I remember how fired up you'd get when you were inspired. Man, that was a turn-on. Yeah, you'd get this gleam in your eye and I could see your mind working on overdrive. We had that creative thing in common. You remember that, don't you?"

I do. I remember the very brief time we connected on that level. I thought it meant we were destined for each other. He thought it meant we were destined for great sex.

"I gotta say," Tanner steps in, "you're so out of line right now. I mean, Jesus, maybe wait until I'm not here to try this line of bull?"

Rad levels his eyes on him, his mouth twitching up at the corner. "That mean you're leaving?"

"No," Tanner says firmly.

To my surprise, Rad says, "Well, turns out I am. I'm going to Telluride tomorrow to see Cody for a few days and—"

"Wait, what? You just got here. And you promised to take Emmy to the zoo."

"I'll be back, Kay Kay. And it seems like maybe it'll be a good thing to give you time to think about what's best for our family's jour—" He stops himself when he sees my eyebrows shoot up. "What's best for our family."

"Yes, having some time would be a very good thing."

Rad looks disappointed, and I'm reminded again by how much he lives in his own reality. He really thought simply suggesting Emerson and I move to Europe was something I'd readily agree to and is truly surprised that there has to be thought given to it. I'd rather him think that I might consider his asinine idea than shut him down because doing so in front of our daughter would only confuse her.

When I don't say anything more, he sits back in his chair and stares at me for a long moment. And then his eyes fall to where Tanner is still holding and stroking my hand. The familiar gesture is just intimate enough to make him uncomfortable, and I almost feel bad about this whole ruse.

Before I can make a move, Rad enlists Emerson into his plot all over again and my sympathy for him disappears.

"Emmy, I'm going to go on a little trip, but while I'm gone," he says, "you make sure Mommy knows how much you want us all to live together, okay?"

"Okay!" she dutifully replies as I bite my tongue.

There's an uncomfortable silence while I'm still trying to sort out how to respond.

"How about some dessert?" Tanner asks Emerson.

"Cookies?"

"You got it!"

"I'll skip out on that," Rad says, standing.

"Somehow not surprised that you're ... skipping out," I say under my breath.

"Easy, feisty girl," he says with a laugh. He pulls Emerson up so she's standing on top of her chair and gives her a big hug, promising he'll be back soon.

I stand, ready to show him to the door but Tanner intervenes. "I got this."

Rad looks amused and shakes his head before following Tanner to the door. Luckily the apartment is small enough for me to hear what my pseudo-boyfriend has to say to my ex.

"Listen, man, Emerson's your daughter and I'd never step between you and her, but this game you're playing isn't fair to Kayla."

"Hey, *man*, I'm not playing any games. This is about my family. *My* family. Whether you like it or not, that includes Kayla."

"You might want to take note of the fact that Kayla has been doing this family thing on her own just fine while you've been doing your own thing. You can't just snap your fingers and change all of that."

Rad glances past Tanner and sees me watching them, my hand frozen inside of the cookie bag. "You want to get your boyfriend out of our business before this gets ugly?"

I quickly give Emerson enough cookies to make her squeal

in delight and then go to the door. Wrapping my hands around Tanner's surprisingly tense bicep, I lean into him. "He's just being protective," I say. "Let me know when you'll be back in town, okay, Rad?"

There's a moment where the air crackles with tension. Rad's never been a fighter, but I suddenly feel the anger radiating off of him. I can see in the way he surveys Tanner that he's calculating his odds if he were to throw a punch. Tanner stands his ground, straightening his spine so that he's even more formidable. With a dismissive shake of his head, Rad relents.

"Yeah, I'll let you know."

As soon as the door is closed behind him, I turn to Tanner, my mouth agape at how he challenged Rad.

He winces. "Too much?"

"I mean," I say with wonder, "if you were really my boyfriend, I'd love for you to have done that. But, I don't know. This seems like game-playing right back, doesn't it?"

"Don't let his guilt trips get to you. That's what set me off, seeing you caught up by that."

I think about the way it all must have looked to him. My moments of silence after Rad used Emerson to pressure me. The way I just let him plant these ideas into her head because if I refused him, I'd be the bad guy. I must have seemed like I had no defense against it all. In truth, I'd been torn over how to respond because it's a shock to have Rad suddenly want us in his life. I need to process all the implications of that, of what's best for my daughter. Even if my instinct is to be furious with how he's going about it.

"Um, I appreciate that," I say. "And I really appreciate you going out of your way to come over. It's above and beyond, that's for sure."

He nods but his gaze soon turns wary. "Are you actually considering moving to Europe to be with that guy?"

"What? No." I shake my head. When he doesn't look convinced, I laugh. "I think I'm just overwhelmed by all of this right now. I've got so much on my mind."

"Yeah, it must be a lot."

The warmth is back in his eyes. It's that same expression as before where it feels so real that he cares for me. It's such a good feeling that I want to believe it. I want to sink into it, into him.

"Do you want to have another beer?" I ask. "Stay while I get Emmy bathed and to bed?"

And just like when I'd asked him if he and I could be something real, his face changes. The warmth slips away and is replaced by something like regret. Regret, I assume, that he's allowed me to hope for something more between us. I can see he's going to reject me again, so I correct myself before he can say a word.

"Never mind. I totally get that's not what we're about, and it's all good." I clear my throat and blink. "Emmy, want to say goodnight to Tanner?"

She perks up and comes galloping over in that silly new way she has. "Thank you for the cookies," she says.

He leans down and taps her on the nose. "You're welcome, kid. Enjoy them."

"When do you come back?"

"Let's get you ready for a bath," I say brightly and scoop her up into my arms. "Bye bye, Tanner."

"Bye bye!" Emerson parrots.

This time, when he leans in to kiss me on the cheek, I brace myself and let it happen instead of throwing my head back against the door like an idiot.

"Hope to see you around, Kayla," he says softly in my ear before pulling away.

I nod, but that's all. No use in replying with the same sentiment or offering another booty call. Our odd little connection is officially over now.

## 23

### TANNER

If I could kick myself, I would. Instead, I take out my frustration by slamming my fist on the steering wheel on the way home, knowing that my so-called effort to "help" Kayla with her ex is bullshit. What the hell am I doing? I didn't need to volunteer to be a buffer. Hell, I didn't need to even see her again after this morning. We both got what we wanted—a fantastic time in bed, no strings attached. So, why did I not only offer to keep up this fake boyfriend thing, but then go even farther by confronting her ex?

Shaking my head does nothing to dismiss the fact that when I remembered she'd be seeing Rad tonight, I was jealous. I didn't want her to be with him. I didn't want the helpless feeling of knowing she'd be alone with him without me being able to do a damn thing about it. And so, I forced my way into her evening, even going so far as to confront the jerk over the way he was manipulating his own child into helping him guilt Kayla into a move to another country.

Granted, I don't know the whole story. Maybe Kayla is open to the idea. She never actually told him no. Maybe that was because she didn't want to get into it in front of Emerson. Or maybe it was because she's actually considering it, despite her denial when I asked. None of which is any of my business.

On top of all that, my mixed messages with her are doing nothing but hurting her. The look on her face when I hesitated after she asked me to stay ... I feel like such an asshole. I was actually trying to convince myself it would be okay to stay, to prolong our time together, even as I knew it wasn't a good idea. I know all too well that you can't go in halfway with a single mom. I either need to commit to giving this a real chance or step off. And so, for the second time in our short history together, I had to disappoint her by letting her know I wasn't interested in something real.

The problem is that I am undeniably drawn to her. She's smart and sexy, charming and complex, and worthy of getting to know better. But since I've already decided that I can't invest the time that dating her would take, I have to back off. Even if I'm already wondering if she keeps up her coffee routine on the weekends.

My cell ringing is a welcome distraction and I answer with the hands-free option.

"Hey, boss!"

It's Ernesto. I can hear the sounds of a bar in the background and the alcohol in his voice.

"Where'd you go today, man?" he asks.

I didn't cross paths with him because the rain had cleared the crew out before I got back to my office on the site.

"Hey, I, uh, had to run some errands for Tatum," I say.

He hesitates for a moment and I worry that his ability to

read me has somehow come through this call, even with the distractions of an obviously good time going on in the bar.

"Come on down and meet us at Pancho's. It's just me and Jenny."

It sounds like a lot more people than just him and his wife, but I welcome the offer of a distraction. A drink or two might be just the trick to get a certain redhead off my mind. I agree and disconnect.

I have to turn around and head back toward the job site because the place where I'm meeting Ernesto and his wife is the crew's designated after-work drinks spot. I don't usually indulge with the guys since it's better as the boss to keep a bit of a buffer. But I'm not worried about that if it's just Ernesto. We have a friendship, not just a work relationship.

Pancho's is a little Mexican restaurant with over the-top-decorations and an even smaller terrace bar area. The food is greasy, the prices cheap, and the margaritas go down easy. The place is, as usual, packed. I find Ernesto at a corner table jammed up against the wall. His wife sits next to him on a bench. There are two flimsy plastic chairs on the opposite side of the table, but only one of them is empty. The other one is taken by a brunette. She has her back to me but turns as I approach. She's pretty with big, dark eyes and a figure curvy in all the right ways. On any other night, I might be up for flirting with her but I have zero interest in that right now. The last thing I want is to be set up.

I scowl at Ernesto and he shrugs as if he's innocent in all of this.

"Tanner, I want you to meet my friend Gloria," Jenny says with a bright smile.

"Nice to meet you," I say, forcing a smile.

"You, too," Gloria replies, her cheeks going red. She seems almost as uncomfortable with this as I am, and that helps take the edge off.

I sit and help myself to a margarita from the pitcher in the middle of the table. "You guys been here long?" I ask, taking in the extra empty pitcher and remnants of entree plates crowding the table.

"Might have gotten an early start on happy hour," Ernesto tells me. "See, we got rained out of work *and* the boss never came back after he went for coffee in the morning."

"Told you, I got caught up in errands."

He nods sagely and I can see he's not buying what I'm selling. Still, he's caught because his wife clearly has plans to set me up with her friend, so he can't dig for dirt.

As if on cue, Jenny says, "Gloria, tell Tanner what you do for a living."

"Oh, it's really not that interesting," she demurs.

I turn to her and give her my focus. "Tell me," I say. I might not be interested in dating her, but it costs me nothing to be decent.

She shrugs. "I do payroll for a landscaping company."

Now, that does interest me. Because I'm going to need an experienced payroll person for my own company. This changes the vibe of the night, and I end up talking with Gloria for the next forty-five minutes about her job and even letting her know my plan to start my own business. That is, until Jenny steps in.

"Okay, Tanner, I think the job interview is over now, right?"

"What?" I ask with a laugh.

"I just thought you two would get along on a different level, is all."

"Oh, yeah, the thing is I'm sort of all about work right now. I mean, I don't really have time for much else."

"It's okay, really," Gloria says. She leans into me, the margaritas giving her liquid courage. "I hate setups, too."

Jenny stands. "Come with me to the ladies' room, Glo?"

I watch the women disappear into the crowd before finding Ernesto staring at me dead-eyed.

"What?" I ask again.

"I couldn't tell Jenny this, obviously, but I saw you and your redhead going into her building this morning."

Fuck. He really doesn't miss a thing.

He laughs. "That's a hell of an errand, is all I'm saying."

There's nothing to do but join him in laughing.

"So, is she wanting something more than your fine ass?" he asks.

"What I said before is true. I don't have time for anything but work and helping out Tatum. So, the thing this morning was it."

He studies me, one eye squinting with the effort. "Something else to all this, right?"

"It's complicated."

"Ain't that the bitch of it all?"

"What?"

"Feelings getting in the way of fucking."

The leap he's made out of me saying so little should be easy to dismiss. But this is his talent, his ability to dissect things and discover the root causes of problems. Still, I'm not ready to admit to all the contradictory things I'm feeling about Kayla.

"Anyway, you could have warned me about this setup."

He lets me change the subject, saying, "I was more interested in the potential work setup out of this. She could be a good fit, boss."

Of course, Ernesto knows all about my contractor business plan. He's going to be a key player in it. I should have known he'd have my back with this.

Raising my margarita glass, I say, "Cheers to that."

## 24

### KAYLA

I never had a chance to fill Nicole in on everything yesterday, so my Saturday morning starts early with a phone call to her. While Emerson is still sleeping, I take the opportunity to share every graphic detail of the most amazing sex I've had in forever, followed by the Rad complication, and finally how Tanner inserted himself into things last night only to remind me *again* that he has no interest in dating.

"That boy's mixed messages are annoying," Nicole fumes on my behalf.

"I get it, though. I mean, I still don't know that I have the time to date either. With work and Emmy, I've got so much going on."

"Not to mention Rad appearing out of nowhere and being a presumptuous ass."

I laugh. "Yeah, then there's that. Can you believe how he's dragging Emmy into this?" I glance down the hall but don't see any movement from my daughter's room yet.

"He's always been totally self-involved. You know that."

Sighing, I nod. "I do. But, does he have a point?"

"About what? Don't you dare tell me you're falling for his crap?"

"No, not exactly. But, I do have to consider what's best for Emerson, right? What if what's best for her is for me to do what I can to give her more time with her father?"

"And move to another country to accommodate *him*?"

When I'm silent, she huffs with impatience. "Kay, why do you lose sight of reason when it comes to him? I mean, it's always been that way. When he's not around, you know your mind. You know exactly what you want and how to get it. But whenever he comes into the picture, you doubt yourself. Why?"

She's right. The problem is, I don't understand why. I think there's always that one person who has the ability to get at something deep in your core that for better or worse leads you to make choices you wouldn't normally. Rad's had that effect on me from the start, from that first night in the club when I basically became his groupie. It embarrasses me that I lost myself in him, but at the same time, I can give myself credit for getting over him. Eventually. It was made easier by the fact that he left me to go on my pregnancy and motherhood "journey" without him.

"Thank you for reminding me of that," I tell Nicole. "It's more important than ever that I resist falling back into that old pattern."

"That's right. Look at how far you've come. You have a kick-ass life and that's all no thanks to him."

"Well, I don't know if I'd say it's *kick-ass*."

"You are raising your daughter on your own and you have a solid career. What does he have? Scraping together gigs in

Europe for years while neglecting his kid? And now he doesn't even have a bass player?"

"What?"

"Didn't he tell you? It's on the band's social media. Their bass player quit."

"Ugh," I moan.

"What?"

"That's why he's here. Not to see Emmy. Or at least, not as his only priority. He's here to try to recruit his cousin Cody into the band. That's why he went to Telluride."

"That sneaky bastard."

Taking a deep breath, I release it and feel a little lighter. The pressure has lessened with the knowledge that Rad may not be as invested in us moving as he seems. It was just a convenient thing to pursue in the moment since he was in town anyway. It's much more likely that getting Cody on board has been his primary goal this whole time.

"I guess I'll see what happens when he comes back here and if he's even still interested in his big idea to get us to move," I say, now without any angst about it all.

"And what would you say if he's still forcing the issue?"

When I hesitate too long, she continues, "You say, 'thanks but no thanks.' In fact, you tell him, he needs to rearrange *his* life to accommodate you and Emerson for once instead!"

I bite my lip. I know she's right. But it's still hard for me to envision demanding that of him. Partly because I lose a little bit of myself when I'm with him and partly because I don't want my drawing that line in the sand to be the reason he disappears again.

"It's not your responsibility to make him a responsible father, you know?" Nicole says gently.

She must have sensed the cause of my silent struggle because her words are exactly what I need to hear.

"Thanks, Nic."

"Anytime. Listen, when do you think you and my precious goddaughter can get out for another visit? You remember how quickly infants grow, right? Lucas better not be walking and talking by the time you see him again."

Laughing, I tell her I'll check my calendar at work on Monday and make solid plans.

"Good. In the meantime, pinky-promise me that if you get a chance to have another hot roll in the hay with your Buns-of-Steel guy, you go for it!"

"Yeah, not going to happen. But it was fun while it lasted," I say, even though we both know that I've gotten my ego bruised a little by his multiple rejections of me. And even though Nicole doesn't acknowledge that, I know she gets it. That's exactly the kind of support I need.

## 25

### KAYLA

Emerson and I are just wrapping up lunch when my cell rings. It's Sunday and I've been expecting a call from Rad to hear when he'll be back in town, so I grab my phone with the expectation that it's finally him.

Nope. It's Tanner.

I let it ring, torn over whether to answer. I just don't see the point after he's made it clear—repeatedly—that he's not interested in a relationship. Unless ... he's looking for a booty call? Just the thing Nicole had encouraged me to seek out. The thought of a repeat performance from our morning together is enough to make me reconsider blowing him off, and I take the call.

"Uh, hi, Kayla," he says.

"Hi." I wait for him to take the lead. I'm done getting burned over assuming his intentions.

"So, I'm here at Pioneer Park with Tatum and the boys. And I know it's really last minute, but I wanted to check to see if you and Emerson would be free to join us."

A kids playdate. That's not exactly what I'd been hoping he

was after. "Oh, um, that's nice of you to think of us." I look over at Emerson at the kitchen table, where she's carefully eating around the crust of her last bit of grilled cheese.

"I told Tatum it was a long shot. That you were probably busy, so don't worry about it."

He's so dismissive of the idea that I'm once again at a loss. His mixed messages even extend to a kids playdate, apparently.

"Okay, I won't," I say. "Hope you have fun, though."

"It's just that—"

He cuts off and I hear some background argument for a moment. I'm about to disconnect when Tatum comes on the line.

"Kayla, we can't wait to see you and Emerson. I told the boys we'd wait for you to get something from the ice cream truck, but I don't know how long it'll be there, so maybe you can come soon?"

"Oh, I don't know if we can make it," I say. I have no intention of going, not with the lackluster invitation Tanner just offered. How awkward would it be to see him after that? No thank you. I have better ways to spend my Sunday afternoon.

"The boys will be so disappointed if you don't come," Tatum says. "They've really taken to your Emerson. And to be honest, it's sort of like training for them to hone their big brother skills. Please? You wouldn't have to stay long."

I didn't expect a guilt trip like this. Nor for it to work so well. Emerson has mentioned Matt and Max several times since meeting them at Tatum's house. Other than the sporadic birthday party for a daycare friend, Emerson doesn't have a lot of weekend opportunities to bond with other kids. I'm about to relent and agree to meet them when I remember that Tanner will be a part of this get-together.

"So, Tatum," I said, "I don't know if Tanner told you, but we're sort of ..." I struggle for what to say next.

"Going slow?" she offers. "Yes, he said that. But this is really just about the kids, so it's okay. Right?"

Ah, so he had said something about the relative lack of an "us." Okay, I guess that settles that. He's made it clear to his sister that we're not really dating. So, if I show up, he'll be just as uncomfortable as I will be.

Good.

"We'll be there in about fifteen minutes," I say.

"Great!"

I don't wait to see if Tanner gets back on the line. Instead, I disconnect and tell Emerson, "Guess what? We've got a play-date with Matt and Max!"

Her eyes go as wide as her smile. "Yay!"

THE BOYS SPOT us before Tanner and Tatum do and take off running our way. Emerson squeals and gallops toward them. The reunion between these little friends is sweet enough to take my mind off of the regrets I have for coming. I suppose Tanner's not the only one with mixed emotions, but at least mine are just with myself.

Whatever doubts I'm having, it's too late now. Tanner was lounging on a picnic blanket next to Tatum, who sat in a camping chair, but now he's getting to his feet and looking my way. I groan inwardly as my heart betrays me by beating faster. Yes, he's still just as hot as he's always been, but that's not what this is about. I force a smile and then focus on

Tatum to find she's struggling to get out of the sunken seat of her chair.

"Don't get up," I call and quicken my pace.

Tatum spends another second trying to get up before Tanner offers her his hand, pulling her easily to her feet just as I reach them.

"You didn't have to get up," I say.

"Oh, but I do," Tatum says. "I promised ice cream and I always keep my promise. Okay if I take Emerson with me and the boys to pick something out?"

"Can I?" Emerson asks.

"I can go with you, Tatum."

"No, let me give you five minutes of grown-up talk," she says with a nod to her brother. Her intention is obvious. She thinks she's helping and I don't have the heart to correct her.

"Okay, thank you."

"Let's go, kids," she says. "But not too fast. This pregnant mama likes to stroll, not run!"

The kids, of course, don't listen to her and go running off. But the ice cream truck is parked in the lot not far off, pulled up to the field for operations, so it's safe enough.

"I think I owe you an apology," Tanner says.

I glance at him but then train my eyes back on Emerson. She and the boys are giggling and pointing at the colorful menu on the side of the truck.

"It's okay," I say. "Emerson was really happy to see Max and Matt again."

"No, I didn't mean about today. Or, I guess, yes about today, but about everything really."

Confused, I look at him. "I don't know what you mean."

"I've been giving you mixed signals, and I know that kind of sucks."

I raise my eyebrows. "Yeah, kind of does."

"Thing is, I really like you. I do. You're a really fantastic woman. But you absolutely deserve more than I can give right now."

"You told me this already, Tanner. I don't think I need to hear it again."

He grimaces. "It's just ... I'm so drawn to you. I think about you—a lot. But our timing of meeting now when I can't—"

"Please stop," I interrupt. "You've made yourself clear several times now. I understand that you've got a lot going on. I do, too. And it's not just Rad and his big ideas. I'm in the middle of a big project at work that could make or break me. I've got pressures and responsibilities, too. I mean, I don't know that I'd even want a relationship with you, either, okay?" I threw that last bit in just to give him a taste of his own medicine and almost start to walk it back, but he stops me by laughing.

*Laughing* as if I'd said something hilarious.

"What?" I ask.

Shaking his head, he says, "I guess it's just funny to realize we're in the same place after all."

"Yeah, it is ... funny. I guess life is like that."

Looking back toward the ice cream truck, I see that Tatum has managed to get each kid a treat and that they've all settled on a bench by the pond to watch the ducks while they eat. She's really doing her best to give us time for "grown-up talk," but I'm not sure what else there is to say.

I drop my bag and sit cross-legged on the blanket. Tanner joins me, stretching out on his side. It's a warm day and the sun feels good on my skin, like every part of me is slowly coming alive. Closing my eyes, I inhale the fresh air deeply.

"How is it going with Rad?"

Something about this question irritates me and I lose that fleeting sense of calm I just had. I focus on the back of the kids' heads in the distance. "No news from him yet."

"Have you decided what you'll do?"

"About what?" I say, my voice coming out harsher than I intended.

"Sorry, not my business."

It's not. It's not his business at all because he's told me—so many times—that he doesn't want us to know each other like that. Still, I feel bad for snapping.

"No, I'm sorry. He just puts me on edge. He's always had that talent."

"Yeah, some people have a special gift," he agrees. We're silent for a minute before he continues. "The fuckers."

I'm so surprised by this that it takes me a second to react, but then I do, laughing in appreciation for his choice of words and timing. I meet his eyes and find him watching me with a look of appreciation, like he's enjoying the very smile on my face.

But just like before, he seems to make a conscious choice to move in a different direction, saying, "Thanks for bringing Emerson out. They really do get along well."

With his eyes turned toward the kids, I take a second to follow the swell of his bicep as he leans on his hand. The scruff on his face tells me he hasn't shaved in a few days, and he wears it well. It's sexy rather than messy. A tingle goes through me as I remember the way I'd felt a minor beard rash from him in all kinds of places—behind my knee, in between my breasts, at the small of my back—for hours after I'd left him and gone to work. I'd replayed in my head moments of our time together at the most inappropriate times, like when meeting with my boss. But the way I'd flash on how his hands gripped my hips or how he slid a finger inside me was practically out of my control.

My prolonged silence has him shifting his eyes back to me and my dirty thoughts must be obvious because the corner of his mouth goes up. His eyes drop to my mouth and then further, to the deep scoop neck of the simple white T-shirt I've paired with shorts. I don't dare follow his gaze, but I'm pretty sure he's taking in the fact that my nipples are visibly hard.

He still wants me.

I feel it.

I still want him.

He knows it.

What do I do about it? Should I own up to the fact that I am a woman with needs, so why not make an arrangement with this gorgeous, entirely unavailable guy simply for the sake of hookups? I already know he's damn good in bed. We could just find time to do what we did the other morning when it works for us and leave it at that.

No strings attached.

He reaches out and presses his hand to my knee, his thumb stroking my skin. The heat of his touch makes my decision for me.

"I want to be Angie," I say softly with a laugh.

"What?"

"Never mind. Just kiss me."

He hesitates even as I lean toward him.

"Let's just be hookup buddies. I'm good with that if you are. Neither one of us has a lot of time, so let's just ... have fun."

"You're sure?"

"Absolutely." I say it with such confidence that he reaches up and pulls me to him, kissing me hard. Kissing me with such pent-up desire that if we weren't in a park in the middle of the day, this would undoubtedly end up being a quick and intense release for both of us.

I forcibly pull away from him and we're both gasping with the sudden rush of air between us.

"Fuck, Kayla," he moans, adjusting himself.

"As soon as we can find the time," I tell him with a laugh.

"Tonight? I can come by late, like ten o'clock or so?"

"Tonight?"

"*Yes.*"

I make a show of thinking about it. "If it's tonight, then maybe I won't have to take care of myself when I get home, then? Because I want to so bad."

He looks pained and I laugh again. "Promise me you'll wait." He pulls me closer to him again but doesn't kiss me. Instead, he whispers in my ear, "I want you writhing with need for me by the time I get there."

That just made it a whole lot harder to hold off. Still, I agree. "Same goes for you, though. Not one stroke until I get you."

Smiling, he says, "This is going to be *good*."

I arch a brow and look away.

"No time for being shy, honey." He kisses me deeply one last time before we have to part and remember that we're on a kids playdate.

## 26

TANNER

Those lips. I could kiss those lips all day.
Only that can't happen right now. Not with Tatum and the kids making their way back to our spot here on the grass.

And so, it is with deep regret that I pull away from Kayla and will my dick back into submission.

I watch with distraction as she and Tatum chat easily, my thoughts lingering on the turn of events. Though I have no idea why Kayla has come around to the idea of just hooking up, I'm definitely down for it. I wasn't ready to end our ... whatever our thing is.

This could work, right? She and I can have more fantastic, intensely satisfying sex and leave it at that. No strings attached.

In the back of my mind, I hear all the reasons why this *can't* work. But then I think again of the promise Kayla made me about getting together later tonight. And how she doesn't want me to give myself one stroke before then.

Yep, that's enough to make me ignore all the reasons why I know this whole thing could end badly.

The sun catches in her hair as she gets to her feet, and I watch as she uses her palms to pat her butt free of any stray grass. If I could, I'd get to my knees and help her. Caress that ass, squeeze it hard, give it a slap, and a nibble.

But that's for later, not now. Instead, I watch as she offers to watch over the kids at the jungle gym and then follows after them as they race off.

"So, Tan," Tatum says as she eases herself into the camping chair. "What was that about being 'casual'? Because from what I can tell, you two have gone well past that and straight into being like cats in heat."

The image makes me laugh. "I don't know about that."

"Come on, 'fess up. What's the story with her?"

I pull my gaze away from Kayla in the distance to focus on my sister. "The story? I don't really know that yet. We're just having fun right now. No need to rush into anything serious."

"So, it's not serious?"

I can see I've disappointed her. She wants so badly for me to settle down. "I, uh, well, not at this point."

"Then, you're open to seeing other people? Like my friend—"

"No, not at all. Kayla and I aren't seeing anyone else. This is it." The lie rolls too smoothly off my tongue. Or, I guess I should say the "charade" is far easier to play than it should be. Because deep down, I know that my response came out so easily because it's how I'd like things to be if the timing was right.

Despite that, Tatum nods slowly, skeptically. "I really like her."

"I do, too."

"I mean it. Like, I could see being friends with her, whether you're in the picture or not."

Laughing, I say, "Thanks a lot."

"My point is that you need to be careful, Tanner. She's a single mom. She's got a lot at stake. Don't hurt her."

"And what makes you think I'd hurt her?" The defensiveness in my voice isn't an act. I'm actually offended that she's making this assumption.

"Well, you're not exactly known for having actual relationships," she says dryly.

"That doesn't mean I'm some kind of heartbreaker. I mean, can't two consenting adults enjoy time together without it having to be some big … thing?"

"No. No, they can't."

I laugh at her blunt reply. "Go on. I know you've got more to say about this."

"Someone always wants more in the end. And someone always gets hurt."

The catch in her voice tells me she's no longer talking about Kayla and me. This is personal. Only, despite how close we are, I don't know who she had this sort of bad experience with.

"Who was it?" I ask. "I'll kick his ass for hurting you."

She shakes her head and smiles wearily.

"Seriously, Tate. Who was it?"

"It would be really awkward if you kicked your brother-in-law's ass."

"Marcus? Your husband? I don't get it."

"That's how we started, as friends with benefits.

"How did I not know that?"

"I don't tell you *everything*," she says with a laugh.

"And, so? What happened?"

"So, when we met, we had instant sparks. But he made it clear pretty much right away that he was a career Marine, that he was away a lot, and didn't have time for a relationship. Oh, and he was adamantly against having kids."

My eyes drop to her rounded belly.

"Yeah, I know all that goes against the present reality. Anyway, I figured he and I could just have fun and keep it casual. But that lasted about two-point-five seconds. Because, honestly, I fell for him before we'd gotten past introducing ourselves. There's just something about him, something about him that told me he was my *person*. Because when you know, you know." She's quiet for a moment, smiling at her memories. Then she shakes her head and sighs. "But we had a deal, so I tried. I tried really hard to play it cool, to detach myself from the way I truly felt. But it wasn't long before he realized I was head over heels and broke up with me."

"You never told me."

"I was so hurt, Tanner, that I just wanted to crawl into a hole. I didn't talk to anyone about it."

I do my best to bury my frustration over this revelation of her enduring a low time. I've seen her at her lowest, after all. I was the one to pick up her pieces, to hold her together when our parents died. She was devastated, and I did everything I could to get her through the deepest hole she'd ever crawled into in her life. I hate hearing that she felt anything like that over Marcus. And that I hadn't been there to help her.

"And then?" I ask.

She takes a deep breath and the sadness that had been in her eyes a moment ago is replaced by shining tears. Happy tears. "It wasn't even two weeks later that he came to me to say he'd made the biggest mistake of his life, that he knew if he let me go he'd always regret it. He said he realized he had to be open to at least trying something real with us. And once he did, everything clicked all at once. He wanted me. He wanted us. He even said he'd be open to kids. Because I was his person, too." She rubs her belly.

My agitation from before takes a moment to subside. But her *happily ever after* ending to her story is comforting. Though I wish she had confided in me so that I could have helped her through her heartache, I'm just glad that she was okay.

"I'm sorry you went through that but really glad it worked out. Marcus is a great guy. An amazing dad, too."

She smiles. "He is. I got lucky."

"*He* got lucky that you ever gave him another chance."

Nodding, she says, "You're right."

I laugh.

"But my point about Kayla still stands. Don't play any games with her, okay?"

Holding up three Boy Scout fingers, I nod solemnly. "I promise."

"You're too cute for your own good, you know that?" she asks with a laugh.

Raising my eyebrows, I say, "So I've been told."

## 27

KAYLA

By the time Emerson and I get home from the park, we both need to clean up. It was a hot afternoon—in more ways than one for me. Now that I've decided that I can go along with a purely sexual relationship with Tanner, I'm giddy with the idea of it. It's like I'm reclaiming an essential piece of myself, the part I lost when I became a mother and had to give up being purely selfish. For the last several years, I saw no other way of being. And I wouldn't have changed that mindset. I needed to cast off my own desires in order to be what Emerson needed.

But we've hit a groove now. I've got us on a good path, and she needs me less. At least, she doesn't need me in that all-consuming way she did when she was a newborn, then an infant, and then in the early stages of being a toddler. I realize that Nicole is right: if I'm happy, i.e. sexually satisfied, then I'll be an even better mother.

To that end, Emerson and I spend the rest of the evening in our usual fashion: setting up an elaborate tea party for her stuffed animals, including designing and coloring mini placemats; two episodes of Peppa Pig; dinner of pesto pasta with peas topped with a ridiculous amount of freshly grated Parmesan cheese to entice Emerson to actually eat it; reading books in bed, followed by singing songs.

Emerson had no trouble falling asleep tonight, having been worn out at the park by her new best friends, Matt and Max. I almost doze off in bed with her before the anticipation of seeing Tanner revives me.

Carefully extricating myself from her bed, I make sure the timer on the sound machine that plays soothing ocean waves backed by classical music will run for another two hours. That background noise is more a part of what she considers her "big girl" bedtime ritual than a necessity. Unlike me, she sleeps soundly and can fall asleep just about anywhere. She once fell asleep on the merry-go-round at a carnival. More mornings than not, it's hard to get her up for daycare.

Once I've changed into a lace-trimmed blush-pink slip dress that could pass for a negligee and step into my highest nude heels, I brush my hair and teeth, apply a fresh coat of mascara and lip balm, and go to the living room to wait.

For my lover.

I laugh out loud at that thought. But I suppose that's what I could call him if I were inclined to use that sort of retro description.

After a few minutes, I feel ridiculous at the deliberate way I'm waiting for him. At the way I've dressed. It feels too needy and not at all empowering, which is what I want to focus on taking away from this.

I quickly change into leggings and a loose Gary Clark Jr. concert tank top, throw my hair up into a ponytail, and go barefoot to the kitchen to pour myself a glass of wine. Taking the glass with me to my Mac, I wake it to find the half-written email I'd abandoned this morning. It's the email I send to my staff every Sunday night. I totally forgot about finishing it.

Sitting down, I quickly review what I have so far, and after a minute's thought, I start typing. I'm concentrating so hard that I don't really register the knock on the door. It takes a sharper knock to pull me from my thoughts, and when I realize that it must be Tanner, I turn so quickly that I brush the wine glass off my desk and onto the floor, breaking it with a splash and a crash.

"Damn it!" I hiss, stepping carefully over the puddle and the shards of glass to get the door.

Tanner looks both handsome and concerned. He's wearing jeans and a plain white T-shirt that's molded to his chest and arms so well that he might as well be a Renaissance sculpture come to life. But he's also wearing a troubled expression.

"It's okay. I just knocked over a glass of wine," I say. "Come in."

Not exactly the start I'd envisioned for this sexy encounter, but I can't let the mess sit on the hardwood floor.

"Just give me a minute to clean this up." I head to the kitchen for a towel, broom and dustpan, but Tanner has followed me and takes it all from my hands. "You don't have to do that."

"I'd like to help," he says simply. "Maybe grab a bag to put the glass in?"

"Oh, sure. Thank you."

He not only takes care of cleaning everything up, but does it so meticulously that I don't worry that Emerson or I might later stumble onto a stray shard of glass.

"So, how did this impressive accident happen?" he asks, still on his knees as he wipes the floor with the wet towel.

I laugh and shake my head. "I was so focused on writing an email for work that when you knocked on the door, it startled me. I turned too quickly and *voilà*."

He looks up at me with a smirk. "*Voilà?*"

Smirking back at him playfully, I say, "Yes, *voilà*. It sounds better than saying I'm clumsy, okay?"

He stands. "At least you're cute and clumsy."

"Cute? Yeah, I guess I deserve that." I look down at my basic outfit and sigh. "Listen, I'm sorry. This isn't exactly how I thought tonight would go."

"It's totally fine."

"No, it's not. I'm a mess. I had on another outfit, but then I felt silly. I just wanted to feel comfortable but now I'm 'cute' to you and that's—"

"Kayla, stop."

"I mean, I want this to be good. For us to have that incredible sexual chemistry again, but maybe I'm not cut out for this. Maybe—"

"Maybe you should stop talking and put those lips to better use." He drops the rag, and when he pulls me to him, my breath leaves me with the force of it.

It's exactly what I needed to snap back into the mindset of why he's here. He came for down and dirty sex. Because that's what I promised him. That's what I want. There's suddenly no more doubt about that as I feel a rush of heat in my core.

I wrap my arms around his neck just as his mouth crashes onto mine, his tongue insistent, his lips commanding. The sweet guy who just helped me clean up broken glass is gone. In his place is a man who is showing me he finds me more than "cute." His hands roam my body hungrily, squeezing my ass, skimming my hips, palming my breasts, rubbing his thumbs over my nipples.

"Did you touch yourself earlier?" he whispers into my ear while pressing his hand between my legs possessively.

I swallow hard. "No."

"I fantasized about you getting yourself off."

I pull away to look at him. "Did you—"

"No. I just tortured myself with the vision of you when I was in the shower. I got so hard thinking of you playing with yourself."

I test him now, running my hand over his swollen cock where it strains against his jeans. He moans before taking my mouth in his again, kissing me urgently, rhythmically to match the tempo he's using with his fingers between my legs. When he gently pinches my clit, even though it's still over my clothes, I whimper into his mouth and my knees tremble. He's already brought me to the edge of coming but I want to make this last. I don't know when we'll have another chance to get together, and I want to take advantage of every second.

With this in mind, I grab his belt and pull him with me as I walk backward into the dark kitchen. Just like the other night, the moon is the only light but it's enough to see the hungry look in his hooded eyes. That desire heightens when I push him against the counter and pull off my tank top. I'm glad I'd left on the sexy black bra that had paired well with the slip dress as it gives me just the right lift and offers a teasing cutout at the tops of my breasts. Next, I wiggle out of my leggings, turning a little so that he can get a view of my matching black thong.

"Fuck, you're so amazing," he murmurs and reaches for me.

I pull away from him. His disappointment changes to sweet anticipation as soon as he sees me go to my knees. He pulls off his T-shirt, braces his hands on the countertop behind him, and widens his stance as I unbuckle his belt and jeans. His cock bobs to attention when I pull his boxer briefs down his thighs, the pre-cum glistening in the dim light. I take his girth into both of my hands and give him that stroke I had told him he couldn't have without me. Looking up, I see him bite his lip, making a conscious, tormented effort to keep quiet. But when I draw my tongue against his tip, tasting him with a satisfied moan, he sucks in a sharp breath, shifts on his feet, and grabs a handful of my hair.

Keeping eye contact, I slowly take him into my mouth, arching my neck so that he fills me. His hand flexes and releases in my hair as I find my rhythm and pressure, working my tongue over him as I go. His restrained moans and hisses spur me on, and I increase my speed.

"Oh, Kayla," he bites out. "Honey, that mouth of yours, it's so fucking good."

Giving him this pleasure is turning me on so much that I drop a hand between my thighs.

This doesn't go unnoticed, as he says, "Yes. Touch yourself like I imagined. Let me see you. Take off your panties."

I let him slide out of my mouth and he fists his cock as he watches me stand so I can pull my thong off. But instead of letting me go back to my knees, he reaches for me, kissing me deeply, his hardness wet and pressing against my belly. He unclasps my bra and deftly removes it, and now I'm completely naked before him when he pulls away from our kiss to survey me. I'm too heated to feel self-conscious. Too needy for him to second guess anything about this moment.

So, even when he grabs me by my waist and lifts me up onto the countertop, I don't hesitate to go with it. He hastily kicks off his shoes and the rest of his clothes before stepping in between my legs.

"Show me," he murmurs. After a slow kiss on my neck, he pulls away with my skin between his teeth so that it sparks a delicious mixture of pleasure and pain. Then he looks at me expectantly and I respond to his request, touching my breasts, pinching my nipples, drawing a hand over my belly and to the now throbbing bud of my clit, needing that touch so much.

His eyes go glassy and almost distant as he watches, his hand moving in a slow, firm motion from the root to the tip of his cock. He's so engorged but he's still got enough patience to focus on me first. But I want him inside me. I want the fullness of his cock deep inside of me as I break into a million pieces.

"Help me?" I say.

"What do you want me to do?" he asks, his voice husky. "Touch you, lick you, or fuck you?"

Heat spreads out over my core at the anticipation of any one of those things. "Your pick. Just make me come."

"How close are you? Were you close to making yourself come?"

I nod because that's all I can manage.

He takes my hand away from where I'd been rubbing my clit and sucks on my middle finger, his eyes locked on mine.

"Tanner," I gasp just as he uses his other hand to slap firmly against my clit. My body goes electric, crackling with desire as he slaps at me once more before he leans down and flicks his firm tongue against me. I hook my legs over his shoulders as he ravages me, his scruffy beard rubbing at the sensitive skin between my thighs, his lips and tongue and teeth all working together to get me closer and closer.

Without warning, he slides two fingers deep into me, curling them up and straight into my g-spot right at the moment that he sucks hard on my clit. It takes everything in me not to let out an earth-shattering scream as my orgasm breaks over me in wave after wave. While I try to catch my breath, he takes his time kissing his way up, his lips lingering on my thighs, hips, belly, breasts, and finally my lips.

Grabbing the back of his head, I hold him to me and whisper, "I'm yours any way you want right now."

He meets my eyes and the upturn at the corner of his mouth tells me he knows exactly how he'll take me. I feel a rush of renewed heat in anticipation.

## 28

TANNER

"Bedroom?" I suggest, and Kayla nods. As I help her off the counter, I realize I'll never think of this kitchen the same way.

Fuck, that was hot. *She's* hot. Our chemistry is incredible, and I'm not done enjoying this night yet.

Grabbing my clothes in one hand, I pull her with me down the hall with the other hand. We creep quietly, sharing giddy smiles as we go. When the door is closed, I drop my things and grab Kayla from behind, one arm around her waist and the other across her tits. She leans back into me, and my dick presses back.

The heat and suction of her mouth with that blowjob earlier had me about to burst. I thought watching her lips slide up and down me was the sexiest thing I ever saw until she couldn't keep from touching herself while she sucked me off. There's nothing like knowing a woman giving you pleasure gives her pleasure too. I could have come in the next second after seeing that, but it was an entirely different kind of satisfaction to watch her touch herself. It was even better than I had fantasized about, seeing her legs spread, her beautiful pussy on display for me as she got herself close. I should have had her finish, but when she asked for help, well, I'm a sucker for a woman who needs me. There was no way I could resist. She was right there on the edge, anyway, just needing a little assist. Her body responded so well to my touch that it was all over in a few seconds, her body jolting with wave after wave as she came so hard against my mouth.

And now, I've got her in my hands again as I nudge myself against her backside, letting my dick nestle between her ass cheeks. She doesn't shy away, and the friction has me rock hard as I kiss the back of her neck and breathe in her floral scent.

I roll her nipple between my fingers and she moans. Jesus, the sounds this woman makes even as she's trying desperately to be quiet. It makes my dick jump. She reaches back and grabs my ass, her nails digging into my skin. It's a move that pulls her tighter to me and I'm losing my patience. I need to be inside of her, and I need it now.

Still holding her, I walk us closer to the bed before pushing her down onto it. She turns her face to the side and I see her eyes closed and a smile on her lips.

"Hang on," I say and give her a light slap on the ass. I have a handful of condoms in my jeans pocket and retrieve one before quickly rolling it on.

When I look back at Kayla, she still has that smile, but she's also wiggling her ass a little. As if I need the extra encouragement.

Positioning myself at her entrance, I lean over to whisper in her ear, "Honey, you've got me so pent-up that I really need to fuck you hard. Is that okay with you?"

"Yes. I want that. I need that."

"Just tell me if you need me to go easy."

She rises to her elbow and looks back at me with a challenge of a smile. "Should we have a safe word?"

I think for a second. "Yeah. Let's go with *voilà*."

She laughs, but only for a second, because I don't waste any time. Grabbing her hips, I pull her ass closer to the end of the bed and plunge straight into her wet pussy, making her gasp. Her walls tighten around me, making each thrust that much more intense. The dimples at the small of her back appear and disappear with each deep push. My balls are tight and I lift her hips a bit so that they slap against her still sensitive clit, making her whimper.

As good as this is, I want better leverage, so I climb onto the bed, pulling her with me so she's on her knees.

"Fuck, yes," I groan as I go deeper and faster.

There's no sign of a code word. In fact, she pushes back against me, and we get into a rough kind of rhythm. I want to be like this, sliding almost all the way out before pounding back in forcefully, all night. But my dick is enjoying it too much, and I'm close to coming harder than I have in a long time. This is even better than our first time the other morning. It's freer. It's absolute sexual gratification. And when I reach around and place my fingers on her clit, I know her body well enough now that I can time our orgasms to happen together.

"Are you ready to come for me?" I ask, my breath hot against the shell of her ear.

"Yes. Yes. Yes," she pants with each of my thrusts.

And then we're both letting go, both trying to do so quietly. But it's not easy, and she yelps. I pull back and bring her with me so she's leaning against my chest so that I can put my hand over her mouth. Her cry of pleasure turns into gentle laughter. Then she's kissing my palm tenderly, and it's so at odds with how animalistically I'd just fucked her, that it takes me a second to switch gears. But when I do, I wrap my arms around her and kiss her shoulder and neck over and over, wanting to be tender with her right back.

After a few minutes, we separate and she falls face-first onto a pillow. Leaning over, I kiss her ass, squeeze it, and bite it just hard enough to make her squirm.

"You're obsessed, too," she says with a laugh.

"Damn right," I reply and spank her gently before getting up.

I do a quick cleanup in the bathroom, and when I come out, Kayla is under the sheets and has her eyes closed. I want to get in with her, pull her close to me and hold her through the night. Maybe even wake her at some point to have a slow, sleepy love-making session to counteract the physicality of what we just did.

But that isn't what we agreed to. We're fuck buddies. And fuck buddies don't cuddle.

Still, I don't want to leave without a goodbye. Fuck buddies doesn't mean being an asshole. Pulling on my boxer briefs and jeans, I then sit on the side of the bed, jostling her enough so that she opens her eyes.

I stroke her cheek and we stare at each other for a long moment.

"I'll see you around," she finally says with a small smile.

Something about that makes my chest burn. Maybe it's that she's the one drawing the line now. She had clearly wanted us to be more the last couple of times we saw each other. But she's given up on that because of the way I denied that possibility. She's putting up walls and preemptively pushing me away. I don't blame her. But that doesn't lessen the sting.

Still, I lean down and kiss her gently on the lips. "See you around."

Standing, I quickly pull on my T-shirt, socks, and shoes. When I look back, her eyes are closed again. I let myself out of her bedroom, closing the door with a careful click, and then I do the same on the way out of her apartment.

## 29

### KAYLA

"Had yourself a late one?" Henry asks as he takes a seat at the conference room table. It's our usual Monday morning meeting to kick off the week. I've taken a page out of Tanner's book and brought pastries for the group and am setting out small paper plates and napkins to go with it when Henry's comment makes me shoot him a glare.

"What is that supposed to mean?" I snap. It's true that I didn't get a lot of sleep last night. Tanner hadn't come over until almost eleven, but there's no way Henry could be insinuating that I was up late with a man in my bed. Right?

"Just that your email came through at almost one in the morning," Henry says. "You usually send it by nine o'clock."

"Oh." I glance around at my staff who are all trying to keep their eyes elsewhere during this awkward exchange. "I realized I had it in my drafts, and so you're right, it wasn't sent until later."

There's a tense moment of silence before Tracy breaks

things up by cooing, "Ooh, is this a bacon cheddar scone? I love savory scones!"

"Uh, yes. There's a mix of savory and sweet—plenty for everyone. Go ahead and help yourselves, and then we'll get started. Maybe the sugar rush will get us all off on the right foot," I say with a laugh.

"Yes, I'm sure pastries will really set the tone for the meeting," Henry says with an eye roll.

Thankfully they ignore Henry in favor of pouncing on the pastries, and I use the distraction to collect my thoughts. The problem is that my thoughts don't center on work, but rather on Tanner. Flashes of last night run through my mind: the lusty way his eyes bore down on me when I was on my knees, the way he was practically drooling when he had me touch myself for his viewing pleasure, the forceful way he drove himself so deep inside me that I can still feel the sweet ache. And then there was the look in his eyes when I dismissed him. It was ... disappointment? Hurt? I'm not exactly sure, but whatever it was, it very much seemed like he wasn't eager to leave. What would it have been like to lie with him in bed, to fall asleep against his broad chest? I imagine it would have felt like a perfect fit.

These thoughts don't fit with the reality of our situation, however, and that's why I was the first to give him the "see you around" line. But it's also why I got up extra early and took Emerson to daycare a bit before her normal time so that I could get my coffee—and the pastries—without running into him. I just need a little space to convince myself that I can put up a wall. That I can enjoy him and our intimate time together without losing my heart to him in the process. I'm determined to use my head, to be conscious of making rational decisions and staying centered on the practicalities of my life, unlike I did where Rad was concerned.

Taking a deep breath, I note that everyone has settled into their chairs. It's time to get to work.

## 30
### TANNER

"Must have been crazy busy at the coffee shop, right boss?" Ernesto says.

I hear him, but I'm still lost in my thoughts and am slow to drag my eyes from Kayla's fourth-floor window across the street.

"I mean, because you were gone for almost an hour?"

He's not exaggerating. I hung around Mean Beanz hoping to see Kayla for far longer than I should have. She never showed and it left me wondering if she's avoiding me or if she's unwell and couldn't come in. I started to text her a bunch of times but held off, knowing that if I were to check up on her it would be weird. Weird because we're playing this whole thing casual.

Or so I thought. When she was the first one to put an end to things last night, I was definitely disappointed. I'm craving more. More amazing sex, for sure. But more of *her*.

The thing is, that craving doesn't change the fact that I don't have room in my life to give her more than what we've already got—random, but intensely satisfying, hookups. So,

I've found myself in the unusual position of having to put up my guard, to force myself not to fall for her. The fact that I just spent way too long away from the site in hope of seeing her at the coffee shop proves that I've already started to lose focus because of her.

"Tanner, what are you looking at?" Ernesto whispers in my ear, finally snapping me out of it.

I turn to him quickly and laugh. "Sorry, man. I, uh, it's nothing. Where are we with getting that replacement backhoe?"

"Nah, nah," he says, shaking his head. "You don't get off that easy. Tell me what's up with you and your redhead? You two hook up at the coffee shop or something? That why you were gone so long and came back all spacey?"

"No, nothing like that. I'm just a little distracted today, but I'm shaking it off."

"You still doing that 'complicated' thing with her?"

I consider blowing him off, using my authority as the boss to direct his attention back to work. But I value his opinion and decide to come clean—to a point, that is.

"Her name is Kayla. And she's pretty fucking awesome."

"But?"

"But she and I both have a lot going on in our lives. So, we've agreed that we'll just keep things casual."

What I don't say is this: She's got a busy career, an adorable four-year-old daughter, and an ex who is still in the picture. And I definitely don't say that I can't stop thinking about her and wish I could somehow be what she deserves.

But it doesn't really matter what I don't say because Ernesto has already picked up on it all.

"Nothing casual about the way you've been staring at her

window, buddy. But if that's the game you two wanna play, go for it."

"It's not a game. It's reality. The timing just doesn't work for anything more than what we're doing."

He nods and eyes me for a moment. "Yeah, sure. Casual is probably all you can handle right now."

I don't miss the challenge in his dig at me. But I also don't take the bait. It's time to get to work.

# 31

## KAYLA

I stick to my normal routine the next day, leisurely walking hand-in-hand with Emerson to her daycare at our usual time. Just before we get to the front door, she stops me in my tracks with a question I hadn't anticipated.

"Mama, is Tanner your boyfriend?" As if that wasn't enough to flummox me, she adds, "And is Daddy your boyfriend, too?"

This one requires getting down to her level, so I pull her aside to the retaining wall that lines the building, and we sit.

"Well, those are good questions, Emmy. Do you feel like it's been a little weird to have Tanner around?"

"No, I like him."

I sigh inwardly. Though, there isn't really a need to worry what my daughter thinks of the man who technically isn't part of our lives, I'm still happy that she approves of him.

"Yes, I like him, too," I say carefully. "He's a nice friend. We can all use a nice friend, right?"

She ponders that for a moment before smiling widely. "Like Max and Matt!"

Even as I laugh, I wonder why she's become so attached to those boys. Perhaps because they're a little older than the kids she spends most of her time with here at daycare. To her, they probably seem like they've got it all figured out.

"What about Daddy? Is he your boyfriend?"

"Daddy is not my boyfriend. He's your daddy and always will be, though. And I'll always be your mama. So, the three of us will always be connected. Isn't that neat?"

She nods, but after a moment, her expression darkens. "Is Daddy coming back?"

"Yes," I say quickly, firmly. I want to erase any doubt from her mind, to somehow make her feel she can count on her father even though I don't know if that's a realistic thing to do. As much as I want her to believe her father will be back, is it right to make it feel like a certainty? Because where Rad's concerned, anything could happen. He hasn't even called us once since he left for Telluride.

But my response is all she needs. Either that, or her attention span on the subject has evaporated because she nods and jumps off the wall to her feet, happy and ready to start her day.

I'M STILL DISTRACTED by our conversation when I get to Mean Beanz. I don't even think to look for Tanner since I'm too busy mentally composing a rage text to send to Rad about how he's once again disappointed his daughter with his disappearing act.

The line is moving slowly but it turns out I don't have to wait because my usual—a large black coffee—is suddenly held up before me. I recognize the hand with the offering right away. It's large, strong, and slightly roughed up. And boy, does he know how to use them on me.

"Just in case you're in a hurry," Tanner says.

I look up at him through my lashes, the stress of Rad slipping away. "Thanks so much," I say, taking the to-go cup.

With a nod of his head toward the door, he says, "Walk you back?"

"Yes, that'd be great."

Once we're on the street, the morning sun warms my face, and the contrast of the still cool air has me taking in a deep, restorative breath.

"You doing okay?" Tanner asks.

"Yes. I'm better now."

"Rough morning?"

"It's nothing, really." I pull my hair over one shoulder and glance at him, forcing myself not to linger on the way his muscles look straining against his T-shirt.

He leans toward me in what is now one of his signature moves, whispering in my ear, "Just because we're phenomenal fuck buddies doesn't mean you can't also talk to me about regular things."

Pulling away, I look at him with a smile. "*Phenomenal* fuck buddies?"

"Well, wouldn't you say what we do together is phenomenal? I mean, as I recall, you had a very hard time not screaming my name at the top of your lungs."

I playfully slap him on the forearm while looking up with an arched brow and a smile that tells him he's exactly right.

"Anyway," he continues, "tell me what had you looking so pissed off earlier."

"Did I look pissed off?"

"You're good at many things, Kayla. But hiding your emotions isn't one of them."

I tuck that bit of information away to examine later. "Oh, I see. Well, I guess when you saw me, I was pissed off at Rad."

His face changes and I realize he's not so hard to read either. Or at least, his shifts in emotion are obvious. A second ago, he'd been relaxed and playful. But at the mention of Rad's name, he's gone tense and maybe even annoyed.

"What did he do?"

"It's what he *didn't* do. He hasn't called since he left for Telluride."

"You're upset that he hasn't called you?"

"I'm upset that he hasn't called his daughter," I clarify, wondering in the back of my mind at his apparent jealousy. "And that she asked me this morning if he's going to come back. I hate that he does this disappearing act without a second thought to her. What I hate even more is that my instinct is to tell her that, of course, he'll be coming back. I want to protect her and make everything okay. But me telling her that isn't necessarily honest. I don't know what the hell Rad will do. Is it fair to give her a false sense of security? I mean, I'm basically making her a promise that I don't know he'll keep. Am I just making it worse?"

My rant sits in silence for a moment, and I wish I could reel it all back in. Tanner doesn't need to hear about this stuff. None of that fits with being "phenomenal fuck buddies." But before I can change the subject, he responds far more thoughtfully than I could have imagined he would.

"I'd say it's not your job to lower her expectations," he starts. "Sure, you may have a pretty good feeling based on experience that he'll fuck up, but if you try to prep her to be disappointed, you're teaching her to look at things in a cynical way. She's just a kid. She should hold onto all that childhood innocence as long as possible. There's plenty of time when she's older to get jaded. And just maybe, her father will surprise you and do the right thing."

We're about a half of a block from my apartment but I stop there on the sidewalk, and he does, too. He's got his hands full of his usual catering to-go containers and a large bag of pastries and other essentials. So, there's no way that he can respond when I throw my arms around his neck and hug him.

I don't linger too long. I just want to show him my gratitude for what he's said, for how he's taken me and my concerns seriously. It feels so good to have someone on my side, someone supporting me. I have my parents and Nicole, but only long-distance. Tanner being right here and responding to my mini-crisis with such warmth and genuine care is an unexpected but welcome gift.

Before pulling completely away, I kiss him on the cheek and say softly, "Thank you ... buddy."

"Anytime, honey."

We walk on in comfortable silence until we're at the point of separating. After a second of lingering, he sets down his Mean Beanz purchases.

"Your coffee will go cold," I warn him.

"It'll be okay." With a nod of his head toward the site, he adds, "Those guys aren't picky."

"Hope they appreciate the gesture. I actually did the same thing yesterday—took coffee and pastries to my staff."

"How'd it go over?"

"Sort of mixed. There's some tension in our group. One guy in particular really thinks he should have gotten my job and likes to make digs at me any chance he gets, especially in front of everyone."

He winces. "Shit. That's not a lot of fun."

I shrug. "I just push through. That's all I can really do." I see the sympathy in his eyes, but I don't want to further burden him with my complaints. The bit about Rad was more than enough; now add work issues? No, not appropriate—not even for a *phenomenal* fuck buddy. It's time to go.

"I hope your day gets better," he says as I turn toward the parking garage for my car.

There he goes again with that thoughtful, sweet talk that seems to flow so naturally. He has a way of making me let down my defenses so that I can't help but turn back to him with a big, unguarded smile. But being unguarded with him isn't something I can afford to do, so I reflexively cover my mouth with my hand. With his eyes locked on mine, he steps close and gently pulls my hand away.

"Don't hide that smile," he says. "I like it too much." He brushes his fingers over my cheek, then slowly traces my lower lip with his thumb, tugging at it just so. When he leans down and presses his lips to mine for a long, sensual kiss, I both enjoy the hell out of it and curse the fact that I have to get to work.

"Maybe we can get together again?" I say when he pulls away. "I mean, not now. But... soon."

"Looking forward to it." He bites his bottom lip and does that thing where he takes his time looking me up and down, drinking me in as if he needs to commit the visual to memory for some plan he might have later.

Wanting to tease him the way he teased me with that kiss, I

grab him by the back of his neck and whisper in his ear, "Not one stroke until then."

He tries to wrap his arm around my waist to keep me from slipping away, but I'm too quick. I walk backward a few steps, smiling at him and enjoying the tortured look on his face.

"Then I better be seeing you *very* soon, Kayla."

I nod and turn, putting an extra swish in my hips as I walk away because I know he's still watching me. Might as well have as much fun with this thing of ours as I can.

# 32

KAYLA

It turns out that I hear from Rad that very afternoon, just as I'm packing up my things to leave the office for the day. Or rather, I should say, I hear from him by way of Emerson's daycare, who have called to say a man claiming to be her father has come to pick her up.

"He says his name is *Rad*?" Skylar, the front office girl tells me skeptically.

"Is he annoyingly handsome and presumptuous?" I ask with a sigh.

She stifles a laugh. "That sounds about right."

"Put him on for a second, please."

I hear some muffled banter where Rad is no doubt trying to hit on Skylar.

"Kay Kay, they say I'm not on the approved pick-up list," he says indignantly.

"Well, why would you be? You're never here."

"I'm here now, and I'd like to pick up my daughter and take her to dinner. You, too. We can meet at Blue Pan Pizza."

"*Our* daughter. And ... I might have plans." I think of

Tanner, of our flirting and promises for more *phenomenal* time together. If Rad wants to take Emerson for a few hours, that might give me just enough time for another hookup.

"Nothing more important than family, though?"

It's not lost on me that he has the uncanny ability to guilt me with the very thing he's always evaded: family responsibility.

"Okay, sure. I'll meet you there."

"Great. Now, tell the very beautiful Skylar that I can take my daughter out of here."

Gritting my teeth, I go ahead and give my permission that he can take Emerson. Just before leaving my office, I send a quick text to Tanner so that he's not left thinking we might be able to get together tonight.

**Rad's back in town. Won't be able to get phenomenal tonight, sadly.**

Tanner's reply comes just as I'm parking at the pizza place.

**Glad for Emerson's sake he's back.**

The lack of any innuendo or flirtiness disappoints me. But his response is also a reminder of what a good guy he is. He seems to always think of others, even Emerson. It's the polar opposite of Rad, who only ever thinks of himself.

Inside, I find Emerson and Rad at one of the tables just past the bar. They're sitting on the leather banquette side. She's coloring and he's staring at his phone.

"Hey, Emmy girl," I say and when she looks up at me with the biggest smile, I melt.

"Mama!" She gets to her feet on the padded bench and leans over the table to give me a hug. "You said Daddy would come, and he did!"

Still squeezing her to me, I raise my eyebrows at Rad. I never did rage text him. After talking with Tanner this morning, I realized I needed to calm down and approach Rad when I wasn't so angry. And then work got the better of me. Now, he's here.

"I ordered you a beer and we got the Rocky Mountain," Rad says as I sit across from him.

I ignore the fact that he's ordered me beer, even though I don't tend to drink it, but take issue with his pizza choice.

"You know Emerson won't eat that, right? That's the one with sausage and peppers and olives?"

He shrugs with the nonchalance of someone who has never had to get a picky child to eat. "She can take it off."

Just then, our waiter sets down two glasses of beer and a Coke. I ask for a small cheese pizza and water for Emerson and myself while deftly handing the soda back to the waiter with an apologetic smile. He glances at Rad and seems to understand all too well that the "fun, part-time dad" has miscalculated on ordering.

"Not a problem," he says. "I'll get that order in right away."

"Was it really necessary to take it away?" Rad asks.

"She's four, Rad. She doesn't need to drink that much sugar."

"Like one Coke is going to ruin her forever?"

"You're not the one dealing with bedtime routines or dentist appointments."

He sits back with a sigh. "You know, you're going to have to let me be a parent, right?"

"What does that mean?"

"It means that she's my daughter, and I should be allowed to be her dad just as I am. I'm not going to be you. I'm not going to bend over backward to make everything perfectly easy or one hundred percent healthy. But that doesn't mean it's wrong, okay? It's just different."

I'm struck dumb for a moment by the maturity of this. As much as I might want to push back to tell him he doesn't know the first thing about being a parent because a parent has to actually *be there*, I know he's not wrong about what he just said. If he is really going to be around more, I need to try to let him be himself, whether I would agree with exactly how he does things or not. He's not actually incompetent, he just has an approach that isn't necessarily like mine. And I have to learn to be okay with that.

"Okay," I say. "I'll try not to take over."

Now he's the one who seems to be struck dumb. He must have been gearing up for some pushback from me. It takes a second before he nods.

"So, how was Telluride?" I force myself to take a sip of beer.

"It was great. Looks like Cody's going to join the band," he says, getting animated. "Yeah, we spent some time jamming and writing. In fact, I got the beginnings of a song about you and Emmy that I want to play for you."

"He's going to move to Europe?"

His face falls, likely because I didn't acknowledge his song. I can't let myself be distracted by romantic ideas of songs being written for us. I need to stick to the practicalities of our lives, like where he plans on living.

"Yeah, that's where it's at for me, Kay Kay. There's nothing I can do about that. I wish I could make a living here, you know? I wish American audiences got me like they do there. But they don't, so it is what it is."

I know this continues to be a huge disappointment for him. He's confessed that it's one of his biggest heartbreaks, in fact, that he can't seem to break through here. And I actually feel a little sympathy for him. It's all he knows how to do. It's his passion. But the other part of me feels the same sort of pain for having had to give up my dreams of doing creative work and making a living at it. I did that for Emerson because there's nothing more important to me. I'd do anything for her. But it has never even occurred to Rad to alter his life and dreams for her sake.

So, in the end, he's right: He's not going to be like me.

That means he'll always get the easy path of coming and going as he pleases while I hold things steady, and there's nothing I can do about it. I just have to let him be him. And I'll keep doing what I believe is the right thing for Emerson.

"When do you head home?" I ask.

Before Rad can answer, our waiter returns with a tray, unloading our pizzas and water. I thank him and dish out a slice of cheese pizza from the square pan onto a plate for Emerson, warning her to blow on it.

"Sunday," he says.

Nodding, I do my best to mentally prepare for Emerson missing him again.

"Daddy lives in a hotel," Emerson says. "They bring food to his room."

I laugh. "You mean he's staying in a hotel? And they bring room service food to him when he orders it?"

She shrugs. "I guess so. I want to go there. Daddy said we could order hot choc-late and stay up late watching movies."

When I meet Rad's eyes, he raises his brow as a question.

"When would this be? Tonight?"

"Uh, how about on Friday night? I have a few things I need to do for the band in the next couple of days, but then if I take Emmy on Friday, we'll get some good hang time."

My mind races with all the things that could go wrong in letting Emerson stay with Rad overnight. He could neglect her. He could let her slip in the bathtub. He could let her watch something inappropriate for a four-year-old.

My doubts must be written all over my face because Rad says, "You can trust me for one night. And hey, it'll give you a break. Guess you don't get many of those."

If I didn't know what a good manipulator he is, I might appreciate this rare insight from him into the fact that I am a single parent.

"Please, Mama?" Emerson begs.

She's the reason why I finally say a slow "okay." I need to give her all the chances she can get to be with her father.

They both say, "Yay!" in response and high five each other, making me wonder if he had conspired with her about this before I arrived.

"Really, it'll be fine, Kay Kay," he says. "I'll pick her up from daycare on Friday and then have her back to you before dinner the next day."

Yep, it appears he has plotted this out. At least he wants to spend time with his daughter. I have to take comfort in that.

"I'll leave a bag with her at daycare," I say.

"Cool. Listen, I wasn't kidding about wanting you and Emmy to move to Stockholm."

"It's a funny name," Emerson says.

"What is?" Rad asks. "Stockholm?"

She giggles and pulls a string of cheese from her slice. "Yeah."

"Yeah, I guess so. But I think you'd like it a lot there."

"Why?" She's genuinely curious.

"Well, for one, I'd be there. Wouldn't it be great to see me every day?"

"And Mama, too?"

He looks at me and raises his eyebrows hopefully. "Yes, with Mama, too."

Forcing a smile for Emerson's sake, I say, "Maybe we'll visit. Since we've now got an invitation."

"You were always welcome, Kay Kay. You know that."

The idea that we were "welcome" is laughable, but I hold my tongue. I don't want to argue with him, both for Emerson's sake and because I know it would go nowhere. Rad would never admit that he abandoned and disregarded us. He has a habit of conveniently dismissing the reason we're not together as some sort of serendipity where we each just decided to follow our own journey. His journey was, of course, to pursue music. And, in his mind, my journey was pursuing motherhood.

"And when you visit, you'll see what a great city it is and how amazing it would be for the three of us to be together."

"Just go easy with those big ideas. Eat your pizza."

When he grins and picks up a slice, I realize that he sees my tepid rebuke as a victory. Before I can correct him of this wishful thinking, I hear my phone buzz with a text.

**If tonight doesn't work, maybe early morning? I'm always at the site by 5:30am. I'd love to be your wake-up booty call.**

I laugh out loud and can feel Rad's eyes on me, but I don't acknowledge him. I'm too busy typing my reply.

**I'll leave the door unlocked.**

## 33

### TANNER

It's a little after five-thirty when I let myself into Kayla's apartment and pad down the hall to her bedroom in my socks. I've got my heavy work boots in my hand, having taken them off outside of her place so that I'd make as little noise as possible.

Easing her bedroom door open, I find the soft, soothing amber light of her nightstand reading light. Not that she's reading. She must have fallen asleep after unlocking the door for me because she's turned on her side, her hands pressed together under her cheek and eyes closed. I almost feel bad about waking her. That is until I realize that she's not wearing anything other than the cascade of her red hair falling over her shoulder and breasts. Her smooth, lightly freckled skin is bare down to her waist where the comforter covers her.

Still keeping quiet, I grab the condoms from my jeans pocket before stripping down. Just thinking of being with her gets me hard enough to roll on a condom. When I get into bed, the motion makes her stir and take a deep breath, but she's not quite awake. Her body is so warm, her breasts soft under my hand. I take my time circling her nipples with my fingertips, drawing them rigid until she pushes her ass back against me.

"You're ready to go," she says with a muffled laugh.

Reaching between her legs, I find her deliciously wet. I draw my fingers up the length of her body until they're in her open, waiting mouth. She sucks on them eagerly.

"So are you," I whisper in her ear just as I slide into her from behind.

This time, we're slow with each other, savoring each movement, every sensation. Before long, I switch our position so that I'm on top, wanting to have her legs spread wide under me as I watch the desire in her eyes, the way her tits sway as my dick plunges deep into her over and over again. When I lean down to take her nipple into my mouth, sucking and biting it, one of her hands goes into my hair and the other squeezes my ass. She pushes her hips against me in an insistent rhythm that soon quickens, and I reluctantly leave her beautiful tits to kiss her hard on the mouth, knowing it will help muffle the orgasm she's about to have. It's only a moment later that she falls over the edge, her body shaking as she comes. Once she's regained herself, she smiles sleepily, happily at me. Wrapping her legs around my hips, she urges me on, and I don't hesitate to make love to her until my own orgasm builds to the point that I can't contain it.

Resting on my forearms above her, I feel both of our bodies go slack as we come down from the high that we just enjoyed together.

"Hell of a wake-up booty call," she says with a lazy grin.

I kiss that smile. "It was my pleasure to be of service," I tell her, and she laughs.

. . .

"I'm glad you're not getting up and leaving right away," Kayla says. "I mean, you can. But, this is just... nice."

Stroking her bare shoulder in a wide arc, I kiss her forehead. "I have a little time."

I should have cleaned up and gone right to work, but instead, I cleaned up and got back into bed, telling myself this was worth whatever late start I might get. She fits perfectly in my arms, her head just under my chin, our legs intertwined. I could get used to this.

"So, how are things going with getting your business going?"

That question snaps me back to reality, and I sigh, just thinking of all I still have to do. "I'm getting there, but there are a lot of hoops to jump through. I have to tackle the application, of course, which includes gathering proof of supervisory experience for both me and my buddy Ernesto. Then there's forming an LLC and getting insured. And staffing up, including someone who knows HR and payroll."

She pulls away to look at me. "That does sound like a lot."

"I'll get it done. I have to. Marcus is counting on this when he gets out. He's already got some vet buddies in the area lined up for construction work."

"That's a lot of pressure."

"It's fine. It's what I bargained for."

"What's that mean?"

"I'm the reason Tatum is living here with her boys. I convinced her to move near me, saying I'd help her while Marcus was away when she could have been closer to his parents in New Hampshire."

"Are your parents ..."

She lets the sentence fade, likely because of my expression. I assume my eyes have gone dark at the mention of my parents.

"No, they're not around. They died the day of Tatum's high school graduation. They'd gone to get her flowers and a necklace with a charm they had engraved. They got T-boned by a careless driver. He wasn't even drunk. Just distracted. Tatum wasn't quite eighteen, so I became her guardian. She, uh, she got to a really dark place of depression. You know, blaming herself for what happened, which is ridiculous. It took her a long time to bounce back. I needed to be there for her. And, I guess I never really stopped wanting to swoop in and take care of her. So, when she got pregnant—with twins, no less—and it was clear she'd pretty much be on her own living on base in North Carolina with Marcus back and forth between deployments, I convinced them both to make Denver their home so I could be there for her and the boys. Found them that house and said I'd do all the work on it for free. When it comes down to it, I'm the reason they're here, and I need to make sure that they have roots to stay." I pause and look up at the ceiling. There's a fine crack running from the bathroom toward the middle of the room, suggesting the upstairs unit had a flood at some point. It would be great to see Kayla and Emerson living in a house of their own. I catch myself with those runaway thoughts and try to focus again. "Anyway, I would have tried going out on my own with being a GC eventually, but this just pushed things along."

"You are a really good brother, Tanner. Even more than that. You're a good man."

My instinct is to deny the compliment. Partly because

taking care of my sister is simply the right thing to do. And partly because deep down, a part of me craves that feeling of coming to the rescue. I like to be needed, but I know that's not necessarily a good thing because it all stems from the fact that the only way I got through my parents' death was by taking action. It's a crutch I should have given up a long time ago. But I certainly can't confess all of that.

And so, I don't say anything.

After a moment of silence, she nestles her head into my shoulder again and moves her hand to the back of my neck, massaging the tight knots there. It dawns on me that this is an unspoken show of support. It's the kind of thing a girlfriend would do, which I love. But it also makes me put up my guard. We can't do this kind of... intimacy.

"I don't know why I just unloaded all that on you," I say with a forced laugh. "Sorry about that." Pulling away from her, I sit up on the side of the bed.

"It's okay. Like you said, just because we're phenomenal fuck buddies doesn't mean we can't talk about other things."

I glance back at her, but now she's the one staring at the ceiling. I'd like to think the thing I heard beneath the careful irreverence in her voice just now was the same sort of conflict I'm feeling about all of this. But even if it was, I can't afford to explore that.

Getting up, I dress and leave my work boots off once again. She turns on her side and hugs a pillow, watching me.

"Everything good with Rad?" I ask, mostly to orient myself once again to the fact that she's got this entanglement that just adds to the reasons why we're not meant to be.

"Yeah. He wrote us a song," she says with a weary smile. "Emerson was thrilled. He played it for us over and over last night. She couldn't get enough, stayed up way past her bedtime."

I don't like the idea of her having spent all that time with Rad, but I have to push that knee-jerk jealousy away. "That's great."

"It was nice to see her so happy."

"And you?"

"Me?"

"Did it make you happy?" When she hesitates to respond, I say, "Never mind. That's none of my business."

She opens her mouth to say something but thinks better of whatever it was, remaining silent. I lock eyes with her for a long moment. I don't know what I'm looking for in those pale gray eyes. Maybe … maybe I just want some sign that there might be something real with us. Something worth hanging on to.

But I catch myself before she can give me an indication one way or the other. There's no use in pursuing this. Instead, I lean down and quickly kiss her on the cheek.

"See you around, Kayla."

## 34

### KAYLA

**Me: Everything good with the pickup?**
**Rad: Yes, all good. See you tomorrow!**
**Me: Tell Emmy she can call me whenever she wants.**
**Me: And that I can't wait to see her tomorrow!**
**Rad: Relax, KK. Enjoy your night. It's all good.**

Sighing, I set down my cell and force myself to let go of the worry and ache I feel knowing that Emerson won't be with me tonight and for most of tomorrow. She's never had a sleepover somewhere without me and I imagine her having separation anxiety. In all likelihood, I'll be the one having the separation anxiety. For Emerson, being on this little adventure with her dad will be so new and intoxicating that she'll probably be just fine.

Now that I don't have to rush to pick her up from daycare, I turn back to my computer to get some more work done before leaving for the weekend.

An hour goes by before I shut things down and head out.

By the time I've gotten home, showered, and dressed for maximum comfort, I realize I don't have anything for dinner. It's weird to only have myself to consider for such things. It takes me a minute to decide what I want to eat and when I do, it's more about what I want to drink.

Slipping out of my sweats and into jeans and a V-neck T-shirt, I grab my keys to head out in search of a margarita.

"You came home without Emerson," Mrs. Trujillo observes as I'm locking the door.

"Oh, hi. Yes, I did. She's with her father tonight."

"Yes, I thought I saw him coming around lately. The one with the leather jacket."

I laugh. "Yes, that's him."

"And the other one? The one with the muscles? Is he still your ... friend?"

Shaking my head, I say without malice, "Mrs. Trujillo, you are way too observant about the comings and goings-on around here. Yes, he's still a friend ... on occasion."

"So, you'll be seeing him tonight?"

I'd thought of reaching out to him, of course, when I knew I'd have tonight on my own. But I had to force that idea away. He's made it clear—and I've agreed—that we're not that kind of friends. We certainly don't do Friday night dates.

She nods sagely. "Well, you enjoy your grownup time tonight, sweetie."

"Thank you. I will."

I think about trying to reconnect with one of my art school friends, maybe invite them to join me for a drink so I'm not on my own, but quickly dismiss that idea. I'd let those friendships fall away when I got together with Rad. They may have been salvageable after he left, but then I was pregnant and I just didn't invest the time.

So, I end up sitting at the bar in a place not far from my apartment called Pancho's. It's a bit of a dive, but the margaritas are fantastic and the music is a mix of upbeat pop. The Friday night crowd is loud and in good spirits and I enjoy just soaking up this atmosphere, even if I'm not actively participating in it.

I'm mostly done with my tacos and halfway done with my margarita when another is presented by the bartender.

"Oh, I'm not ready to order another," I say, holding up a hand.

"It was sent by the guy over there," he says.

I follow the nod of his head toward a table tucked into the corner and see Tanner sitting there with several other guys who look a whole lot like they've been here for a while, maybe even since the end of their world day at the construction site. Empty beer and margarita pitchers crowd the tabletop and the guys are all talking over each other.

But Tanner meets my eyes, oblivious to everything around him. I smile and give him a little wave. Without a word to his buddies, he gets up and joins me at the bar. I watch him move through the now standing-room-only main floor, my heart beating double-time as he nears. I'm not the only one watching him, either. He's turned the heads of several women, too.

But it's me who he leans in to kiss on the cheek.

"How is it that you're out on your own tonight?" he asks.

"Emerson is with Rad. Doing a sleepover with him at his hotel, actually."

"Shit, why didn't you call me if you were free?"

"The thought had crossed my mind."

"But?"

"But getting together on a Friday night seemed like too much of a date kind of thing. And we don't do that, do we?"

He looks taken aback by me acknowledging the lines we've drawn. The line he drew first. Repeatedly.

"Anyway," I continue, "I had the craving for a margarita. I've only been here once or twice and did not expect to see you here. So, I hope you don't think I'm stalking you or anything."

His brows come together at that as if to tell me I'm ridiculous for the suggestion. "Yeah, uh, the guys come here sometimes and I got roped into coming along tonight."

I nod. "I can let you get back to them."

He hesitates, examining me as if I'm some sort of puzzle he needs to figure out. At last, he leans toward me so he can whisper in my ear, "I'd rather take you back to my place to have my way with you. All. Night. Long."

That raises images that I find hard to resist. Images of his face between my legs. Images of me riding him reverse cowgirl style. Images of him taking me from behind against a wall in his place. A place I've never been to.

"That kind of sweet talk will get you ... everywhere," I say.

He grins and throws some cash onto the bar to pay for my meal and drink while I down my first margarita and make a dent on the second. I grab the slice of lime from the glass as he pulls me by the hand out of there, sucking on it in sweet anticipation of what I'm about to savor with him.

. . .

WE END up doing everything I imagined and more in a marathon session of sex that leaves me tender and asking if I can use his bathtub at three-thirty in the morning. He draws the bath for me and goes to get some water to quench my thirst.

Stepping into the soaker tub, I feel immediate relief and lean my head back with a sigh. I hadn't had much time to take in his place when we got here. We were too busy tearing each other's clothes off for any sort of tour. But during one interval between fucking, he walked me through the house, both of us naked as we went. With two bedrooms and a study, it's not large, but certainly big enough for him. There's a two-car garage he didn't show me, but it's where he said he has a small home gym for his very early morning workouts. He pointed out all the improvements he's made, and it was clear he took pride in his craftsmanship. And while it is a nice, if minimally decorated, house, it's not a *home*. There aren't many personal touches. It feels like he hasn't really set down any roots.

Or maybe I'm just so out of practice with being in a man's home that I don't know what to expect. I shouldn't judge him for how he's set up his life. We are, after all, in two very different places. He's a single man focused on work, and I'm a single parent focused on my daughter.

That thought makes me check my phone again. Emerson never did call. I didn't get any panicked texts from Rad asking how to handle her. All seems to be well.

Setting the phone back on the edge of the tub, I sink under the water, letting the heat of it soothe me. When I come up for air, Tanner is standing over me, his eyes lingering on my breasts.

"Hi," he says and takes a seat on the floor next to me and hands me a bottle of water.

"Thanks. I know it's super late. I can get an Uber after this."

"I've got a better idea. When you get out of there, we're going to crawl in bed together and pass out."

"I actually don't sleep all that well most nights. I wake up a lot. It's better if I just go home."

"Just stay and see how it goes."

I am exhausted but still don't believe I'll be able to sleep for more than thirty minutes before waking up again. Still, I know he'll pass out and then I can easily leave him be.

"Okay, I'll give it a try."

He nods with finality. "Good. It's too bad you have nothing to sleep in," he says with a grin.

I laugh. "I can't wear my T-shirt? Or borrow one of yours?"

"Nope. House rules. Everyone sleeps naked."

"And you want to actually sleep, right? That's what you said?"

"Well, *try* anyway."

I tsk playfully. "Who would you have taken home to fulfill your insatiable appetite if I hadn't been there tonight?"

He sits up as if I've just slapped him. "No one. I'm not fucking around with other women."

"Uh-huh," I say dubiously. I have no reason to believe he's monogamous with me. Why should he be when he's got this easy no-strings attached arrangement deal?

"It's true. But I guess that means I should ask if you're sleeping with other men? Rad, maybe, Kay Kay?"

Scoffing, I stand and reach for a towel, wrapping it around me as I step out of the tub.

That he thinks I could possibly be sleeping with Rad after all he knows and has seen is so far beyond ridiculous that I can't even answer him.

I just want to get dressed and get out of here. But he puts a stop to that, pulling me into his arms tightly.

I struggle but instead of telling him what I'm really upset about, I say, "I *hate* being called Kay Kay. Don't ever call me that again."

"I'm sorry. I'm tired. I've been up since four-thirty yesterday," he tells me. "Just lie down with me for a little bit."

He lets his embrace slowly loosen without releasing me completely, giving me the choice of what to do next. I could just walk out of here and be done with this weird push-pull thing we're doing with each other. It's what I *should* do since as much as I've been trying to deny it, I don't want to be just phenomenal fuck buddies with him. I want more.

But at this moment, I don't want to do the right thing, the cautious thing. I've been careful for years now, always making decisions that would protect Emerson and the stable life I built for us. But tonight, now, I just want to give in to what will make me feel good, even if I know that it might not be the best decision. I'd rather have the pleasure now and pay for it later.

In a flash, I tighten my arms around him and sink into his strong chest. I must have leaned into him so much that he felt he had to carry me because that's what he does: picks me up and carries me to his bed, where he carefully removes the towel from my body and pulls the bedding up over me. I've been the caretaker for so long without anyone to return the favor that being treated with such tenderness makes me want to cry. My eyes tear up, and I have to close them to hide it.

I feel him get into bed with me, wrap his arm around my middle, and pull me into him. I curl toward him and his arms enveloping me are the last thing I remember before I fall into a deep, uninterrupted sleep.

## 35

KAYLA

The first thing I notice when I wake is the smell of coffee. Cracking an eye, I see a to-go cup from Mean Beanz on the side table next to the bed and I smile. All at once I realize two things: I've slept incredibly well in Tanner's bed, and he's gone out of his way to get me the coffee I'm addicted to.

I can hear him in the study, talking on the phone. It sounds like work stuff, something about overdue deliveries of materials. That he's working like this on a Saturday reminds me of how much he has on his plate.

Moving up so that I'm sitting against the headboard, I take a sip of the coffee and savor it with my eyes closed. After another drink, I pick up my cell and have to blink to make sure that I'm reading the time right. It's eleven forty-five. I've slept longer and harder than I have in ages. Though I feel refreshed, it's also disorienting.

There are a couple texts from Rad, and I scrambled to open them.

The first is a picture of Emerson eating room service pancakes.

Then, there are a few messages:

**Rad: Did you know that Emmy sleeps like the dead? Like seriously, it took me three tries just to get her to wake up for pancakes.**

**Rad: I'm going to take Emmy to a friend's house for a BBQ/jam session. There will be other kids there her age. It'll be cool.**

**Rad: Let me know you're alive, okay? Weird not to hear back from you seconds after I text.**

I RAISE AN EYEBROW AT THAT. Seems he doesn't like the taste of his own medicine. He's never one to text back right away, even when I've been mindful to calculate and align our time zone differences. He only replied as fast as he did to let me know he'd picked up Emerson yesterday because I threatened to call the cops if he didn't.

**Me: I'm alive. Glad you two are having fun. Let me know when you're on your way to drop Emmy off.**

I wait, but there's no quick reply. He'll likely get to it in an hour or two. With that resolved, I go back to enjoying my coffee.

I'm halfway done when Tanner walks into the bedroom. He stops as soon as he sees me, taking a long moment to soak up the sight of me sitting naked in his bed. I don't move to cover up or even look away from him. That lack of self-consciousness I had with him since the day I brought him home to my place has become my default. There's something about him that makes me feel desired but safe—like both a sex object and someone he completely respects. Rad only ever made me feel half of that equation: a desired sex object. It was an incomplete connection. If I didn't know that before, I know that now with complete certainty. All because of the way Tanner treats me, even if we're nothing more than intimate friends.

"Hi," I say and hold up the coffee. "Thank you for this."

"God, you're gorgeous," he replies and joins me, sitting on the edge of the bed.

I smile my thanks. "I can't believe how long I slept. I'll be out of your way in just a couple of minutes, okay?"

"Do you have something you need to do? Is Emerson coming back?"

"Uh, no, she won't be back until about dinnertime."

"Oh. Then there's no rush."

"You're busy. I know you use your weekends for work."

He reaches out and takes the coffee cup from my hand, placing it on the nightstand before leaning close to me and saying, "I can spare a few hours, Kayla."

"Oh, *hours*? What ever do you have in mind?" I ask coyly.

His hand drifts between my breasts, and I drop all pretense of protesting and pull him to me.

We linger in bed, alternating between sex and talking. It's lazy and delicious. It's also a little reminiscent of the way Rad and I would waste away our days. The major difference, I tell myself, is that Tanner and I have real conversations.

We talk about my freelancing days of the past and the side projects I amuse myself with now, including my effort at a new design for Mean Beanz. We talk about his interest in architecture and regret over having never gone to college to study it. We talk about how sensitive I am to Emerson being disappointed by Rad's absence and weak efforts at staying connected, which more often than not involve flowers sent a day late to acknowledge the events in her life that he's missed. We talk about how gratifying it's been for him to take on such a big role in his nephews' lives and how he'll miss being a constant presence once their dad comes home. We talk about passion versus practicality and the sacrifices we've made over the years for various reasons. We confess our ideal visions of the future: his is building his own successful business, which he is making headway toward; mine is having my own graphic design business again. Only this time, I'd really devote myself to it, using all of the good things I've learned from my corporate job while unleashing my creative side.

"You need to go for it," Tanner tells me.

We're lying side by side and he's got my hand in his, rubbing his palm against mine repetitively.

"What I need is health insurance and security," I say, resigned. "That's life as a single mom."

"So, you just put off what fulfills you?"

I think about that for a moment before giving him the simple truth. "Yep."

"Unless, maybe, you got child support? Like a father is supposed to do?"

I turn on my side toward him. "I appreciate your concern, but I'm okay. This is just how things have to be for now. I know what I can and cannot expect from Rad, so I manage on my own. It's not exactly bad, you know? I'm navigating my way through everything just fine."

He squeezes my butt with a mischievous smile. "*So* fine, honey."

Burying my face into his neck, I laugh and grab him right back.

# 36

## KAYLA

The next day, Emerson and I take Rad to the airport for his flight home to Stockholm. It's not something I'd normally do, but he insisted on spending as much time with Emerson until the last minute that he's in the country.

We all get out of the car at the drop-off curb, and I watch as Rad gets down on his knees and pulls Emerson into his arms for the longest hug.

"Daddy, you're squeezing me," Emerson says.

He glances up at me and I see a flash of emotion in his eyes before he blinks it away. He rises, standing at his full height and bringing her up with him.

"Sorry, baby girl. Would it be better if I spun you around?" he asks and starts going around in circles, making her throw back her head with laughter.

Now I'm the one who has to hold back the emotion. It's both unusual and satisfying to see him dote on her. While this connection has come years late, I can't deny that it is real.

"You'll come back soon, right?" Emerson asks when he finally stops spinning her and settles her against his hip.

"As soon as I can. We need to do the video thing more, though, too. We talked about that, remember?"

She nods and plays with the zipper of his leather jacket. I can see a shadow of sadness fall over her face and it pains me.

Rad catches my eye. "She's like a real person now. I ... honestly, I didn't know how to relate when she was smaller. Now she's my best buddy."

I nod but don't say anything. It may be true that he had a hard time relating to his daughter when she was younger and less communicative, but that's something he should have worked on. He took the easy way out. I'm over being angry about it, though, because the bond Emerson and I have is something he'll never really get. Being her mother and being there with her and for her every second since she was born has been my privilege.

"What do we say, Emmy?" he asks.

"Rock on!" she screams, making us both laugh.

I reach out and smooth her curls, enjoying this moment where the three of us can be together on good terms.

"You're not going to move, are you?"

When I look up, Rad has me fixed in his intense gaze. "I was never going to move, Rad," I say with a small smile.

"Because of him?"

"Because of me. Because we have our life here."

He nods. "I really screwed up, didn't I?"

I swallow hard at that. "Yeah, you did."

"I just," he says and pauses. "I just didn't know any better, I guess."

"I guess not."

"I'm going to finish that song about you two. And it's going to be a breakout hit. Watch."

"I hope it is. For your sake. You deserve it."

"Visit me? Promise?"

"We will," I say and open my arms for Emerson.

"Love you, Emmy." He kisses her cheek and then hands her off. "Take care, Kay Kay."

We do a quick one-arm hug, and then he's off.

EMERSON IS sad the rest of that day and the next, but I do my best to distract her and give her plenty of attention. Before long, we get back into our routine and the week flies by.

I don't hear from Tanner. No cute, flirty texts, and no sightings at the coffee shop. Despite what a good time we had at his place, nothing has changed with us. Clearly, one sleepover and a whole lot of pillow talk hasn't changed our casual agreement.

I take his lead on the silence and don't reach out either, even though he was the first person I wanted to call after leaving Rad at the airport. I wanted to tell him how well things have resolved between us, that Rad really seems committed to being a dad now—and that he'd given up on his idea of rekindling something with me. I wanted to let him know that talk of us moving is over. But all of that seems beside the point when Tanner and I don't have anything more than a casual relationship. It's something I have to continually, grudgingly remind myself of. And accept.

By Friday morning, I'm glad it's almost the weekend. But first, of course, I need my coffee. As I wait in line, I smile to myself thinking about Emerson's latest obsession: ostriches.

I've promised to take her to the zoo so she can see them live and in person. And to make up for the fact that Rad never followed through with his promise to take her.

As the line shuffles forward, I try to focus on the day ahead. I have a meeting with my boss this afternoon. I'm presenting the final branding package. Or at least I hope it's the final one. He's had so many tweaks and changes that I feel like I'll never satisfy him. On top of that, I have the sneaking suspicion that Henry has been planting seeds with Gregory that he has an alternative he'd like to present. If he does get that chance, and Gregory likes it better, does that mean I'll be demoted and replaced by Henry? What would that mean for the salary I rely on?

"Hey, Kayla. The usual?"

I've gotten to the front of the line on autopilot and look up to see barista Matt in front of me. "You know it. Thanks."

I move over to the pick-up area, still lost in my thoughts.

"You're still having a rough week, aren't you?"

It's unmistakably Tanner's voice now pulling me out of my thoughts. Looking to my left, I see him leaning against the wall, his own face a mask of worry. I go to him and take his hand instinctively.

"What's wrong?"

He shakes his head in a short, dismissive motion. And before he can clear it, there's something in his eyes that scares me.

"Tanner, talk to me."

"It's, uh, it's all going to be okay. I don't want to get into it."

"Are the boys all right?"

"Yeah, they're fine."

"Tatum?"

A flicker of emotion on his face confirms my guess that something is wrong with his sister. I know enough about him to understand that if something was truly wrong with her, he'd be devastated.

"Please tell me," I say.

"She's okay. It's—"

"The baby?"

He smiles weakly. "The baby's registering as a little underweight. Because of Tatum being anemic. But they're working on a plan to get the baby where she needs to be. You know, so she doesn't end up coming prematurely."

I squeeze his hand. "Okay. It's good that her doctor is working with her, that they're aware of everything now. I'm sure they see this all the time."

"Yeah," he says, and I watch his Adam's apple bob as he swallows. "It'll be fine."

"But it's stressful."

He meets my eyes and something passes between us that feels familiar. It's the same kind of understanding we've shared before, where we *get* each other without needing to say anything more.

"What about you, Kayla? What was on your mind a minute ago?" He rubs his thumb over the inside of my wrist.

"Oh, um, just work stuff," I say.

He's about to push me on this when his name is called for his order. My order is called right after, and we end up walking back toward my apartment together.

"So?" he says. "Tell me."

I glance up at him, surprised that he's come back to this. But he's smiling encouragingly and so I give him a brief rundown of my work woes.

"Yeah, I can see why you'd second-guess your work with your boss nitpicking at everything you present."

I nod. "It's like I'm always *just* missing the mark of his expectations, but I can't seem to figure out what exactly he wants."

We walk on in silence before Tanner asks, "Why do you think you were chosen to lead the team? You know, back when everyone was presenting their ideas to get the spot?"

Thinking back on it, I recall just what Gregory had said in response to my portfolio, and it makes me smile. "Gregory said my work stood out because it was art disguised as corporate marketing. He loved not just the color psychology, but the way I used space and texture. The most important thing, he said, was that he could see *me* in the work, and he liked that because he was tired of what was expected in our industry. He wanted us to move beyond that."

"And do you think you've stuck with what he liked about your style?"

My mind flashes through all the work I've produced on this project. In the beginning, I went with my gut but ended up rejecting it before ever sharing it. It was *too* me. Too free and not corporate enough. Over the following months, I leaned more heavily on a variation of what we already had in place, making adjustments that gave it a fresher, if safe, spin. It was fine. But it wasn't inventive. I can see why Gregory has been rejecting and pushing me all of this time.

"You're right. I've been playing it all wrong," I say. "I just got so caught up in wanting to secure my job that I lost sight of what I could really offer."

"So, time to go back to your style?" he asks just as we get to the spot in front of my apartment where we'll separate.

My heart beats a little faster at the prospect, both out of excitement at being that free and at the possibility that it'll be to my detriment.

"It's worth it," he says, reading me. "Whatever you think you're risking, remember that the odds are in your favor because he already saw what you could do and put you in this position."

My smile slowly grows as I process and accept this idea. It gives me the confidence to overhaul everything. But I don't have much time.

"Go ahead," he says. "Knock 'em dead, honey."

Giving him a quick kiss on the cheek, I turn and practically run to my car. There's so much to do, and I can't wait to get to it.

## 37

### TANNER

I've just picked up groceries and am unloading them into Tatum's refrigerator when a text from Kayla comes through.

I've been hoping she'd reach out to tell me how things went with her boss this afternoon, but her message isn't about that.

**Kayla: How about you and I give Tatum a break and take the boys for the day on Sunday? We could go to the zoo?**

I'm thrown by the offer. It isn't what I was expecting, so it takes me a minute to reply. But before I can do so, she texts again.

**Kayla: But if you're too busy, I'd be happy to take the boys on my own. I can reach out to Tatum directly.**

That motivates me, and I quickly write her back.

**Me: Sounds like a great plan for us all to go. Let's meet at the zoo for lunch?**
**Kayla: Perfect. Looking forward to it.**
**Me: But hang on, what happened with your boss? Is everything okay?**
**Kayla: Yes. Thanks so much for your advice. I owe you.**

Knowing our talk might have somehow helped her makes me smile. And what she texts next widens that grin even more.

**Kayla: I owe you something phenomenal.**
**Me: Looking forward to it.**

"What's put that goofy smile on your face?" Tatum asks with a yawn. She's been more tired than usual, her energy levels way down. She's sitting at the kitchen island, grumpily sipping on the spinach smoothie I made her as soon as I got back from the market.

"Kayla," I tell her honestly, knowing the mention of her name will make her happy.

"Really?" She sits up straighter. "How are things going? You're behaving yourself, right?"

"Everything is fine. In fact, she just came up with a great idea. On Sunday, you're going to chill for the afternoon. I'm going to take the boys to the zoo and meet Kayla and Emerson there."

Tatum's eyes light up and I can't tell if it's at the prospect of some downtime or at the idea that I might be getting closer with Kayla.

But before she can say anything more, I call the boys out

from where they were playing in their room and tell them of our weekend plans.

"Yes!"

"Yay!"

Their quick chorus of excited replies is followed by demands for dinner, effectively keeping Tatum from asking more about Kayla. What can I tell her, anyway? She'd made me promise not to hurt Kayla. I don't have any plans to do that. We're giving what we can to each other, including amazing sex and even some support where we need it. All we have to do is keep being up front with each other about the limits of this thing, and everything will be fine.

At the back of my mind, though, I know that spending the day together without sex being the focal point isn't exactly part of how this whole thing is supposed to work. It's, in fact, very much like having a girlfriend.

I'm just too damn stubborn not to steer clear of getting in deeper with her, telling myself we can still figure this out.

Because if I was really honest with myself, I'd admit it's already too late. I'm in deep.

# 38

### KAYLA

When Emerson takes off running, I assume she's in a hurry to greet Matt and Max. But to my surprise, she bypasses them in favor of Tanner. He's caught off guard, too, as she hugs his leg. He recovers quickly, though, bending down to take her into his arms, giving her a hug and a gentle tap on her nose before setting her down again.

The kids are talking over each other about which animal we should see first when I reach the group.

Tanner looks me up and down in that way of his, the heat of his gaze making me feel like I showed up in a hot-girl outfit. In reality, I'm wearing a simple outfit of form-fitting jeans, a brown leather belt that hugs my hips, and a light oatmeal-colored wide-neck sweater that falls off one shoulder. My wedge sandals give me a little extra height but are still comfortable enough to chase kids all day around the zoo.

"Good to see you," he says, finally leaning in to kiss me on the cheek.

"It would seem so," I reply with a laugh.

He grins. "What's that mean?"

"You have a way of ... checking me out, I guess."

"Huh." He raises an eyebrow. "Not too subtle, then?"

"Not at all."

"Want me to stop?"

"Not at all," I repeat with a smile.

He leans into me again. This time, his lips skip my cheek and find the shell of my ear and I get goosebumps, anticipating what he'll say. But instead of some sexy promise of things to come, he lowers his mouth to bite the soft part of my earlobe before sucking on it briefly. It's such an unexpected move that it sends a wave of longing through my core, and I take in a sharp breath.

When he pulls away, his expression tells me he's entirely pleased with my involuntary reaction.

Shrugging, he says, "Can't become entirely predictable, can I?"

I arch a brow and look away. He's far too sexy for a stroll through the zoo of all places.

"Let's go in," I say, trying to keep the reluctance out of my voice.

WE LET the kids dictate our path, wandering in zigzags as we follow their ever-changing focus. It suits us just fine as we trail behind them a few steps. Tanner seems less stressed about Tatum's condition, though he's still concerned. He tells me about the busy week he has coming up with the combination of planning to pick up the boys from school every day to give Tatum a break, the next stage of the build beginning, and working more on his business, including meeting with a woman named Gloria to try to recruit her for a staff position.

"Sounds like it's coming together," I say as we stop at the flamingos.

"Well, headed in the right direction, anyway."

We watch the kids standing on one leg, pretending to be one of the pink birds.

"Tell me how things went with your presentation," he says once we're walking again.

I smile and tell him how after I left him on Friday morning, I raced to work, canceled all of my meetings, and holed up in my office so that I could revisit and refresh my original designs. I was in the zone for hours leading up to my meeting with Gregory, running on adrenaline and a creative high. Going into the meeting, I must have looked a little wild-eyed, but there was no stopping the thrill I had at sharing my work. I didn't even hesitate to worry whether this would be the entirely wrong move because I had Tanner's words of encouragement still in my head.

"Thank you for that," I tell him.

"You're welcome. But tell me what your boss said," he says with a laugh.

"He ... he *loved* it." My eyes tear up as I recall how Gregory's whole body relaxed inch by inch as he absorbed the whole campaign. "He said that what I was presenting was exactly why I had been chosen to lead the team and that he couldn't be happier."

"That's fantastic. Good for you."

"Even better, he called the whole team into his office to show them my work, telling them they should take it as inspiration and motivation. You should have seen Henry's face.

He's the one who's been challenging me every step of the way."

"Sounds like he better step in line after that."

Smiling, I say, "I can only hope he has a bit more respect for me now, grudging though it may be."

"Yeah, I'd think so."

By this time, we've made it to Monkey Island, and the kids are squealing as long-tailed lemurs put on a show in the trees.

"It's a relief, that's for sure."

"That your job is secure?"

"Yes, that most of all. But also that I can not only find some joy in this work but be rewarded for it. I mean, it's still not exactly what I'd like to be doing in graphic design, but it's not the worst thing in the world."

"Probably makes it a little harder for Rad to convince you to move now, right?"

I look up at him curiously. He brings up Rad *a lot*, but I don't quite get why. Why should he care about him one way or the other? He's made it clear more times than I'd like that he's only open to our *phenomenal* arrangement.

Still, I open my mouth to tell him about the airport, to tell him that Rad knows we won't be moving, but before I can say a word, all three kids are suddenly gathered around us and asking to eat.

"We're so hungry," Max says.

"I want pizza!" Matt says.

"Can I have fries, Mama?" Emerson asks.

I look at Tanner. "I think we'd better get lunch for these kiddos."

Tanner watches me for a beat before turning his attention to the kids. He goes into world's best uncle mode and promises them pizza and fries and ice cream, hyping them up so that they squeal in delight.

It's close to dinner time when we drag the kids toward the exit. At the gift shop, Tanner offers to buy each of them a toy or stuffed animal of their choosing. I watch from a distance as he carries a happily exhausted Emerson in his arms, pointing out different things she might like. She's incredibly indecisive in the best of times, but even more so now that she's so tired from our long afternoon of exploring the zoo. But he's patient with her, and she's so clearly comfortable with him that it breaks my heart a little.

I don't know how long he and I will go on in this way or whether it's fair for me to let her bond with him. Seeing how she greeted him when we first arrived was sweet. She hadn't seen him in over a week, but rather than shy away from him, she embraced him like he was a part of her family. But he's not family and won't ever be. My eyes tear up at that thought.

Just then, Tanner's eyes find mine. His smile dissolves, and he nods in a "what's up?" gesture.

Blinking, I force a smile and shake my head. I focus on Matt and Max, who are playing tug of war with a rubber snake, and I go to them.

"There's more than one," I say, kneeling and pulling another snake out of the bin. "You don't have to share."

"No, this is more fun," Matt says.

"Yeah!" Max agrees and pulls harder.

I laugh. "Okay, but we definitely have to buy that one since you're stretching it all out of shape."

"Okay!" they both say.

When I stand, I find that Tanner and Emerson have joined us. She's holding an ostrich stuffed animal. Thankfully, it's not the obnoxiously large one I'd seen tucked into the back corner of the store. If she had seen that one, I just know she'd be obsessed with it, and I'd eventually cave and get it for her, no matter how expensive or how little room we have for it. The one she's hugging to her chest is about ten inches, the perfect size. It has gangly legs and isn't very cute, but it's fluffy and soft, and I'm sure that's won her over even more.

"What will we name him?" I ask.

"Ollie," she replies. "Ollie os-rich."

"I love it!"

"Do you think Daddy will love it?"

"Um, sure he will."

"Will he be there when we get home?"

"No. Remember, we took him to the airport? But we can call him, okay?"

"Can we take Ollie to Stockhome?"

When I glance at Tanner, I find that his eyes have lost their usual warmth.

"We'll talk about that later, okay?"

She nods, hugs the ostrich tight, and rests her head against Tanner's chest, her eyes fluttering as sleep tugs at her.

"I'll take her," I say and open my arms.

"It's okay," he says. "Just let me pay, and I'll help get her to your car."

"Tanner, I'll take her."

Something in my voice convinces him and he eases her over to me. She flings her arms around my neck and squeezes her legs around my waist. The weight of her, the sweet and salty smell of her, makes me breathe a sigh of relief. She's my everything.

Within a few minutes, we all emerge from the store and head toward the parking lot. We parked in opposite directions, but Tanner insists on following us to our car. I get Emerson into her seat and buckled up without her waking.

"Did you boys have fun?" I ask Matt and Max.

"Yeah, it was cool," Max says. "The lion roared at me!"

"No, he roared at me!" Matt says.

"Because he thought you were me."

"Why would he think that?"

"Because we look exactly alike, dummy," Max replies.

Matt huffs before coming up with a clever retort. "If I'm a dummy, then you're a dummy. Because we're exactly alike."

Tanner and I exchange a look at that, silently enjoying the boys' argument.

"This was a great idea," Tanner says. "Thanks for suggesting it."

"I'm glad it worked out. And I hope Tatum enjoyed her afternoon."

"I'm pretty sure she spent most of it napping on the chaise lounge in the backyard. This thing has really knocked her down, you know? She's exhausted all the time."

The worry has returned in his eyes, and I want to reach out to him, give him some comfort. But I stop myself, thinking I'd better try to keep some boundaries between us before I fall completely for him.

"She'll get through this," I say as confidently as possible.

There's a split second of hesitation before he nods. "Absolutely. There's no other choice, is there?"

The way he says that last bit about no other choice strikes

me as if he's not just talking about Tatum. Or maybe I'm reading into it. I need to stop trying to read subtext into this thing with us. I need to instead remember what he's actually *said*. And what he's said more than once is that there is nothing more possible between us than no-strings fun. I've agreed to that.

So, why does my heart ache at the thought of going on this way?

"Drive safe, okay?" he says.

"You, too."

"Come on, boys. Let's go pick up dinner to bring back to your mom."

"McDonalds!" Max says.

Tanner laughs. "We'll see."

"Bye, boys," I say to all three of them.

Tanner gives me a smile and a nod but doesn't kiss me on the cheek like he usually does. And that ache in my heart spreads throughout my chest.

"See you around," I say as he turns to go.

Looking back at me, his expression is resigned and almost sad. I want to rush to him, throw my arms around him, and kiss him until he smiles again.

But I don't. And he turns his attention to his nephews, putting an arm around each of them as they walk away.

## 39

### KAYLA

I've just finished writing my staff email and sent it for them to read first thing in the morning when a text comes through.

**Tanner: I'm nearby. Can I see you?**

We hadn't talked about getting together tonight, and after the way we left things at the zoo earlier, I wasn't sure either of us would reach out to the other anytime soon. But this is definitely soon. Maybe he wants to talk? Maybe he wants to discuss just what it is that's going on between us? It would be good to get some clarity.

**Me: Sure**
**Tanner: Be right there**

It's a quarter to eleven, and I wonder just what he's doing so close to my apartment. Maybe he was working in his office across the street. That means he was making up for the lost time spent at the zoo with us.

I'm wearing the same top as before, but I've removed my bra and changed into leggings. I don't worry about another outfit, but I do brush my teeth quickly and put my hair into a messy bun. Just as I've swiped on tinted lip gloss, there's a light knock on the door.

My stomach tightens in anticipation of us talking about things openly and honestly. I'm not sure I want to examine everything. I'm not sure I want to admit to all that I'm feeling, especially knowing that it'll just chase him away. There's no choice, though, now that he's here, so I take a deep breath and open the door.

He's leaning a muscled forearm against the doorframe, his head lowered. I open my mouth to speak but stop when his energy hits me. He's radiating need and desperation but also fighting a war of some kind within himself. Despite that practically tangible conflict I sense, when he meets my eyes, all I see is desire.

In the next instant, he leans into me, grabbing me around the waist as his mouth crashes against mine. I wrap my arms around his neck and let out a whimper when he simultaneously picks me up and pushes the door closed with his foot. He carries me down the hall, his lips and tongue commanding my own so that I understand that this won't be about give and take. He's here to take what he wants from me. And I'm ready to let him. He can take the lead and satisfy himself because I know instinctively this is what he needs.

In the bedroom, with the door closed and locked, he lets me slide down his chest so that I'm on my feet again. When he grabs a fistful of my hair and pulls my head back so he can trail rough kisses mixed with nips of my skin, I dig my nails into the skin of his hips.

"You remember our safe word?" he asks gruffly.

I do. It's *voilà*. But I don't really believe he'll hurt me or that this will be too much, so I say, "Yes. But I won't need it."

He looks at me, his eyes hooded by desire, but he doesn't say anything. Instead, he slowly unbuckles his belt and pulls it from his jeans. I watch as it slips through the final belt loop, see the way his hand tightens around it. I don't for a second think he's going to use it to hurt me, and I'm right.

"I want to use this to tie you up. Are you okay with that?"

I nod, never taking my eyes from his.

"Take off your clothes."

I do as he says, stripping off my top and leggings until I'm standing before him in my decidedly unsexy gray bikini underwear. He pulls off his T-shirt and unbuttons his jeans but doesn't take them off. Instead, they just slide lower on his hips.

I stand still when he steps closer to me. He drags the folded belt over my chest, between my breasts, and downward, playing the stiff edge between my legs and watching me for a reaction. I don't say anything, don't gasp, or shiver. I only open my stance a little wider and the corner of his mouth turns up. He pulls me to him, his arm around my waist but still allowing for some room to maneuver the belt against my clit. I want him to kiss me, and I try to take his mouth with mine, but he pulls away, wanting to watch me.

This is so different than any of the times we've been together. This isn't quick and animalistic. This isn't about finding each other's pleasure points. This isn't slow and sexy. This is rough and teasing.

He pulls the belt away from me just as I'm about to come and uses it to spank me. Not so hard that I don't enjoy it, but surely hard enough to leave a mark. And hard enough to make me cry out.

In a contrast of touch, he gently strokes my cheek, examining my eyes to be sure I'm okay. I give him a slight nod and then lift my chin, ready for more. Now, he kisses me, sucking hard on my tongue and pulling away with my bottom lip between his teeth. At the same time, he plunges his hand into my underwear, his fingers finding me slick and ready for him as he thrusts them inside me. He brings me to the edge of coming once again before pulling away, leaving me breathless and ready to beg him not to stop.

"Get on the bed," he says before I can say anything.

As soon as I do, he climbs on top of me and pulls my arms over my head, quickly securing my wrists with the belt to the bed frame. I watch his face as he does this, wondering what's going on in his head, what brought him here in this mindset of wanting this kind of sex. But he's passive, coolly concentrating on his task. Clearly, he wants control, and now he's got it.

He uses that control over the next half hour to repeatedly bring me close to the edge before pulling back. He mixes a little pain with the pleasure, but never so much that I'm tempted to say *voilà*. It's the good kind of pain that only heightens my arousal. I'm so desperate for a release by that point that I'm rubbing my legs together futilely. When he first got here, I'd thought he would simply fuck me hard and not even bother with my needs, but this has been all about me. He hasn't even taken his jeans off, though I can feel his dick hard and insistent against me when he leans close.

Maybe he's torturing us both by not giving into the release and satisfaction we both need so much.

That self-control must have reached its limit, though, because he finally removes his jeans and rolls on a condom. And then he fucks me the way I'd imagined he would—hard, relentlessly, and without any effort to make me come. But I still do because I've been so primed that all it takes is the slightest friction when he moves his hips high against mine, and it's the kind of intense, long-lasting orgasm that racks my body so hard that it brings tears to my eyes. I'm overwhelmed with how good it feels, and I cling to him with my legs around him as he keeps his pace, working up to his own orgasm. His biceps are flexed as he holds himself over me, and I want to grab them, both to feel his strength and to keep myself from slipping beneath him, but my wrists are still restrained.

"Fuck," he hisses, nearly there.

And then he pulls out and twists me so that I'm on my side and he's spreading my legs, plunging deep into me again with a different kind of friction that gets him off within seconds.

His entire body weight settles onto me and though I try to sustain it, I have to wiggle to get him off of me. He moves onto his side, reaches up to easily loosen my wrists, and goes slack. His eyes are closed, and I almost think he's fallen asleep, but his breathing is still hitched from his efforts. When I touch his face, he looks at me, but his expression is hard to read.

Before I can say a word, he gets up and goes to the bathroom, helping himself to a shower. After a minute of deliberation, I join him there, stepping in and wrapping my arms around him from behind. He reflexively holds me in return for a long moment. When he turns to me, we do a silent dance of washing each other, tenderness replacing what we just had in bed.

"Lie down with me for a minute?" I ask when we dry off.

He's about to step into his jeans and looks like he wants to refuse. But then he drops them and lets me pull him into bed, holding me in his arms without another word. He cradles me to him like he never wants to let go. I cling to him the same way, feeling safe and exactly where I want to be.

We fall asleep that way but at some point during the night, I feel his hands moving over my body again. This time, slowly, sensually. He coaxes me into sleepy, sweet lovemaking that is just as satisfying as what we had earlier, but in an entirely different way. Where he had been rough before, he is gentle now. Where he had been wild with need before, he is intent on giving now. It is our bodies joining in an unspoken and easy synchronicity.

Afterward, we fall asleep again and stay in each other's arms until Emerson wakes us up in the morning.

## 40

TANNER

When I wake, I realize two things: I'm not in my bed, and I've slept so well that I haven't moved an inch all night. Kayla is still in my arms, curled into me and breathing steadily. Her rich, red hair has fallen over her face and I gently stroke it back, but she doesn't stir.

I hadn't come over last night with the intention of tying this beautiful woman up. That was very much a spur of the moment thought. What I had wanted in coming over was to satisfy the intense craving I had to possess her body and soul. That need had overcome me when Emerson let it slip that they had plans to go to "Stockhome" as she so cutely calls it. Actually, the urge had begun earlier, when Kayla very obviously avoided answering whether her success at work had made it more likely she would stay here rather than move.

This non-relationship thing we're doing is torture. I want her. I want to give her everything she deserves, including committing all of my free time to her. But I have so little free time. It's not fair to her or Emerson.

Then there's the issue of Rad and the pull he apparently still has on her. Clearly, she's leaving things open with him. I don't know what Emerson's talk of Stockholm means, but it sure sounds like the possibility is there that they will leave to be closer to him. The thought tears me up inside, despite the fact that I have no right to feel that way. It's just, we haven't even really begun anything, but I'm already missing what it could have been.

Instead of talking it out, I turned caveman and claimed Kayla's body last night. And she ... let me. What does that say?

Before I can consider this more, the bedroom door handle jiggles and Kayla's eyes fly open, meeting mine. It takes a second for her to register my presence, but when she does, she puts her fingers over my mouth.

"Mama," Emerson says, sleepily. "I can't find Ollie."

"We'll find him," Kayla says automatically. "Give me one second."

"Okay."

Kayla sits up, blinking herself awake. She'd pulled on my T-shirt at some point, and it looks dangerously sexy on her.

"I'll go with Emerson into her room and maybe you can slip out?" she whispers.

I don't mind her not wanting her daughter to know I spent the night, even if it's not the goodbye I'd hoped for. We'll have to talk some other time.

"Okay. But I need my shirt."

She looks surprised until she remembers what she's wearing. She pulls it off, but before handing it to me, she takes a deep inhale of it and smiles.

The gesture makes me never want to leave this bed, but

that's what I have to do. I get dressed while she pulls on a robe. She kisses me lightly on the lips before going to the door.

"Okay, let's find that Ollie," she says brightly. "Remember, ostriches can't fly, so he can't have gone too far!"

I hear Emerson's giggle and chatter fade a little as they go into her bedroom. Kayla has partially closed the door, so when I head out, it's a smooth exit with no chance of being found out.

It's almost six-thirty, so technically, I'm late for work, but the commute is definitely easy. I head into my office without coming across Ernesto or the other guys who have already started their day. I'd come here last night to bury myself in work, to try to push aside my increasingly desperate need to *consume* Kayla.

Obviously, that didn't quite go as planned.

So, I spent the night fucking her like she was mine. But she's not. It's time to stop playing this half-assed game. We were never meant to be. It's enough now. Because, like Tatum said, someone always wants more. And someone always gets hurt. I don't want that for either of us.

## 41

KAYLA

"Wait, *tied up*? Was it ever too much?" Nicole asks.

It's still early and Emerson is in her room, arranging her stuffed animals so that the recently found Ollie has the perfect place among them. I'm standing at the window in the kitchen, as per usual, watching the construction site across the street, hoping that Tanner is looking back up at me. After having spent the night sleeping so soundly in his arms, it was jarring to wake up and have to get into mom-mode. Thankfully, he understood that I needed him to slip out so that Emerson wouldn't realize he'd been there all night. Tying me up, as it happens.

"Um, no," I say. "It wasn't like that at all. It was sort of thrilling to surrender, actually. You know, I'm always the one in control because I have to be. In my job, with Emmy, making all the decisions. So, this was a sexy change up to all that."

"*Damn*, Angie. You're really taking this thing for all it's worth. I'm proud of you. Maybe even a little jealous."

I laugh. "Well, don't get too envious. This all comes at the cost of knowing no matter how much I like him, no matter how amazing we are in bed together, there's no future. And I feel this ache in my chest every time I have to catch myself from enjoying him too much."

"Aww, Kay." She's quiet for a moment. We both are. Just sitting for a moment with that bittersweet revelation. "Do you think you're going to have to end this before you get your heart broken?"

Biting my lip, I take a deep breath and close my eyes. "It's probably too late for that," I finally say.

"Okay. Well, here's what you need to do. You need to book a trip to come see me already, girl! It'll be good to get away. I want you to email me later today with your flight information so that I can pick you up from the airport. Got it?"

With things more settled at the office now, I feel better about taking a long weekend and agree that I'll get the plans made and shared later today.

I'M IN MY OFFICE, about ready to pack up for the day and head out to get Emerson from daycare, when I check my cell again. I've looked at it a dozen times today, hoping to see something from Tanner, but there's been nothing. When he wasn't at Mean Beanz during my coffee run, I wasn't too surprised because of how busy he said his week was supposed to be. Still, I had hoped we'd have the chance to chat for a minute.

Since that didn't happen and he hasn't reached out, I decide to send him a quick text.

## No Strings Attached

**I'm really sorry I had to rush you out this morning. But I'm glad you came over last night.**

I leave it at that. What I wanted to say is that it's only when I'm in his arms that I sleep well. That I love being with him, whether it's in bed, minding the kids, or talking about things big and small. That I hated to give him back his shirt because I wanted to keep the scent of him close to my skin.

But none of that is what I should say. It's not appropriate. We *aren't* together.

I see the little bubbles pop up beneath my text indicating he's writing back. They bounce for what seems like a long time before disappearing. I wait a little longer, but still no reply.

With a sigh, I grab my things and head out. By the time I get to my car, he's texted.

**Np. And me too.**

Not exactly the sweet or flirtatious response I would have liked, but I suppose it tells me what I need to know. It's a reminder, once again, that he and I truly have no strings attached. There's nothing more to us than the occasional good time. And I need to get back into that mindset. It's what I agreed to, after all.

I DON'T SEE him or hear from him during the rest of the week. By Friday night, Emerson and I are gearing up for our go-to dinner of grilled cheese and soup. I'm just about to get it started when I get a phone call from an unknown number.

I don't usually take calls from numbers I don't know, but something makes me pick up and I answer cautiously.

"Kayla, hi! It's Tatum. Listen, I know this is crazy late notice, but I'm planning on ordering in Chinese, and I wanted to see if you and Emerson could join us."

"Tonight?"

She laughs. "Yes. I'm sorry. I know this is obnoxious to invite you so casually, but I've been meaning to call you for the last several days. I just don't know how it slipped my mind. This pregnancy has really thrown me. Anyway, I've been wanting to thank you for taking the boys to the zoo and thought an easy dinner would at least be a start."

"Oh, you don't have to—"

"I don't have to, I know," she interrupts. "But I really want to. And the boys would love to see Emerson. Come over? I'd love the adult company. Come drink the wine I have that will go bad if someone doesn't have it. I won't even mind watching you drink it!"

That makes me laugh. I look at the can of soup on the counter and think of how happy Emerson would be to see Matt and Max.

"Can we bring anything?"

"Nope! Just yourselves. See you soon?"

"Wait—um, is Tanner going to be there?"

"He has an appointment with a woman for the new business, so I don't think he'll make it."

I'm not sure whether I'm relieved or disappointed by that. Or ... if I should be jealous. Who has a Friday night appointment with a woman about business? Could he be on a date with someone else? I really don't like the idea of that. But I don't have any say in the matter.

In any case, I've already agreed to go for dinner, so I tell Tatum we'll head straight over, and she's thrilled, making me think that she and I could have a friendship without Tanner having anything to do with it.

## 42

KAYLA

Tatum and I are lounging in the backyard with the debris of our dinner abandoned inside while we watch the kids jumping on the trampoline when Tanner joins us.

"Oh, hey," he says, clearly surprised to see me.

He's wearing a button-down shirt with clean jeans and even from a few feet away, I can smell cologne wafting off of him, which seems to answer my earlier suspicion that he was on a date tonight. My stomach sinks, but I force myself to smile.

"Hi," I say. I'm hyperaware of the fact that he doesn't greet me with his usual kiss on the cheek. Instead, he keeps his distance.

"Tan, I didn't think you'd make it tonight," Tatum says. "Are you hungry? There's food leftover."

"No, I already ate."

Of course, he did. On his *date*.

"Maybe we should get going," I say and start to sit up.

"No way," Tatum says. "The kids just started playing. I need you to let Emerson stay and tire out my boys."

The pleading look on her face makes me relent, and I lean back on the chaise lounge. She and I had been enjoying idle chatter for only fifteen minutes before Tanner showed up. I've just started on my second glass of wine, which is a very fine Chardonnay that Tatum insisted on opening for me.

"I'll go say hi to the kids," Tanner tells us and heads toward the trampoline.

"What is the deal with the two of you?" Tatum asks me before he's even out of earshot.

"Shh!" I say.

Tatum laughs. "Well, he sure won't tell me the truth. I'm hoping you will. I mean, I love my brother, but he has not been straight with me about you since the beginning."

I've turned my eyes to Tanner where he's chatting animatedly with the kids, making them laugh. He's such a natural.

"What do you mean?" I ask with distraction.

"Come on, Kayla. I'm not an idiot."

That forces me to look at her. "Meaning?"

"You two aren't really dating, are you?"

When I hesitate, she continues, "I mean, I'd *really* love it if you were because I think you're great together. And I really like you. But it's been obvious to me since that first time he brought you over that there's something else going on here."

"Um, well, I don't know what to tell you."

"I knew it! I knew there was something off about you two," she says triumphantly. But then her face falls. "I just don't know why he felt like he had to deceive me."

"Oh, no," I say quickly, not wanting her to take this

personally. "It's just that ... just that, well." I stop and lean toward her. "We're just using each other for sex," I whisper.

Tatum's brows shoot up and her eyes go wide.

"At least, that's sort of how it started," I continue. "He's made it clear a million times he can't commit to a relationship, and I've got my own busy life. So, we just decided we'd enjoy each other for what we can."

"I see," she says on a sigh. But a second later, her disappointment in her brother fades when what I'd said comes to the forefront of her mind. "What do you mean that's how it started? Do you have feelings for him now?"

I don't know how to answer that, and struggle to say anything. Finally, I shake my head helplessly. "It doesn't matter, Tatum. We're just not meant to be."

"You better believe I'm going to have something to say to him about that!" She starts to heave herself up from her prone position.

I reach out and put a hand on her arm, stopping her before she can rise. "Please don't, Tatum. *Please.*"

She looks at me for a long moment, likely registering the desperation in my face.

"I don't understand, though."

"He's got his reasons. And I have mine. It's okay. This is what we agreed to." I take a breath, exhale, and then a large sip of my wine. "Besides, it sure looks like he was on a date tonight. So, all this is awkward enough."

"But he said—"

"Yes, I know. He said it was a business meeting. But look at him. And did you smell that cologne? Doesn't really say *business*, does it?"

She looks over at her brother, taking him in the way I did

the instant he got here. "Well, I mean, I guess it's possible. But I just don't see why he'd be dating someone else."

"It's fine. Really."

"Really? You're dating other people?"

"Well, not at the moment," I concede.

She shakes her head in frustration.

"Your brother is a good guy. He knows what he can handle and what he can't. I understand if he's not into serious dating. It's fine."

"He needs to get over himself. I warned him. I warned him not to hurt you."

"He hasn't," I assure her. "I went into this with my eyes open. It's not on him, I promise."

She doesn't look convinced, but Tanner's on his way back toward us. I watch him walking in that easy way of his, his legs long and his stride confident. I busy myself with my wine instead of continuing to check him out because it'll only make me wonder how his date went and if he's going to drop in for a late-night quickie with her later.

"Help me up, Tan," Tatum says, her arm outstretched to him.

He easily pulls her upright. "What do you need?"

"Sit your butt there," she says with a nod to the chaise she just vacated. "I'll get you a wine glass since Kayla needs help with that bottle. Then I'm going to get the kids set up with the popcorn and movie I promised them."

"I can help with that," I say.

"No, you stay right there," Tatum says so firmly that I dare not move.

We watch in silence as she goes inside the house.

"She just used her mom voice on you," Tanner says with a laugh.

"I think she did," I agree meekly.

We don't say anything more until Tatum returns with a glass. She hands it to Tanner and leaves him to fill it himself while she goes back inside. Once his glass is full, he holds it up to me.

"Cheers."

I tap my glass to his quickly and take a sip.

"How's your week been?" he asks.

Keeping my eyes on the kids, who still seem full of energy on the trampoline, I reply, "Fine."

He sighs and lets his head fall back against the padded chaise. "Yeah, it's been a hell of a week. Crazy busy."

I nod but don't say anything. I don't know how I'm supposed to act with him anymore. The last time I saw him, we were waking up together after he slept in my bed. It felt so good but too fleeting. And he's made no effort to see me since then, which just about screams that he feels like staying over was a huge mistake. To hammer that home, he's seeing someone else. Like, actually getting dressed up and taking that person out to dinner. That's something he's never once done with me.

I'm relieved when Tatum calls the kids in. Standing, I start to go inside to join them, but Tatum stops me cold.

"No, you both should stay out here. Finish your wine." Again, with the mom voice.

It's silly, but I obey her and sit back down.

"I don't know what's going on with her," Tanner says.

"She's mad at you," I reply with a small, satisfied smile. I can't help it. I like that she's on my side.

"I can see that. Do you know why?"

"I sort of told her about our arrangement."

"You what? Why?"

I sigh. "She knew something wasn't right with us. It was just ... the truth."

"What truth was that?"

His voice has turned cold, but I don't get why. "You know very well what I'm talking about," I say.

Sitting up, he turns to face me. "What I know is that you aren't available and neither am I. So, we've made the most out of what we can get from each other. Does that sound about right to you?"

Now, I sit up and face him. "Why do you sound like you're mad at me?"

He stares at me for a long moment, silent.

"You're the one who was on a date tonight," I continue. "I'm the one who should be mad."

"A date? What are you talking about?"

"I mean, it would have been nice for you to take me out to a nice dinner like this woman tonight. But instead, I get early mornings and late-night booty calls." He looks just as surprised as I feel in saying this. Maybe it's the wine that's loosened my tongue, but I can't stop now. "Which, yes, I know I agreed to, but still. It would have been nice, is all I'm saying."

"Kayla, you and I agreed—"

Closing my eyes, I pinch the bridge of my nose. "I know. I know. We agreed to no strings attached. Ugh, I'm such an idiot. I'm sorry." I throw back the rest of my wine.

"We agreed," he continues, "but it's more than that. It's the fact that you've still got this thing with your ex."

"Thing? What thing?"

He scoffs. "Come on. Talk about dates? What about you having dinner with him? What about your late night after with him fucking *serendading* you?"

I struggle to understand what he's talking about because his version of what happened and my version—the *truth*—are so different. He has some odd idea that Rad had been wooing me with his guitar when in reality there was nothing romantic about it all.

But before I can say anything, he continues.

"You have to admit he's got a pull on you."

I shake my head. "He's Emerson's father. Of course, I'm always going to be connected to him. I can't change that."

"And so you'll do whatever he wants, that's clear enough."

"You don't get it, Tanner." I realize once more that he still doesn't have the whole story. He doesn't know that I told Rad we had no chance of getting back together, that I wasn't going to move to Europe. I'm about to tell him all of that, but he speaks first, revealing just how much he's judged me over how I've handled things with my ex.

"Oh, I get it. I get that you've fallen for his guilt trips so hard that you're willing to turn your life upside down rather than somehow think *you're* the one breaking up your family instead of remembering that he already did that."

"Where is this coming from?"

"It's what I see. I see that you think you're doing the right thing for Emerson. But what you end up doing is tiptoeing around his demands, leaving the door open for him to come right in and step all over you. But you have to know it would be so much better for Emerson to see her mother stand up for what is right instead of being willingly manipulated."

I blink but can't clear my eyes. *This* is what he's thought of me all this time? Whether he has the full story about Rad or not is beside the point. What he's just revealed is how little he thinks of me. The realization *hurts*. He's touched a nerve that I wasn't even aware was there. But it is. And it is far too tender to be poked at like this.

I don't try to stop the tears that fall down my cheeks. Instead, I smile weakly at him and whisper, *"Voilà."*

He looks confused for a split second. And then the understanding that I've used our so-called "safe word" to tell him that he's hurting me and I need him to stop softens his eyes.

Standing, I go to the patio door and put my hand on the wall to try to compose myself. I need to get it together before I collect Emerson to go. Two deep breaths and Tanner's cold, oppressive silence are all I need. I straighten my spine, swipe my cheeks dry, and go inside.

## 43

TANNER

"*F*uck." Though I've muttered under my breath, I still look to see if anyone inside has heard me.

All I can see is the back of Kayla's head as she takes a crying Emerson toward the front door. The kid is upset at being torn away from the popcorn and movie she was promised. I don't blame her. I blame me, actually. I've just fucked up absolutely everything.

*Voilà.*

I hurt Kayla. So much that she had to use our safe word. Jesus, the look in her eyes. It was like I'd reached right into her chest, grabbed her heart, and squeezed it dry.

I've been thinking about her inability to tell Rad in no uncertain terms that she won't move, but I never meant to unleash on her about it like this. It all just came out. And it was so unfair because I have no right to judge her. I know that she's an amazing mother, that she's sacrificed to give her daughter a good life. So, why did I give her shit for being open to what Rad wants? It's not like I even understand the compromises separated parents need to make with each other for the sake of their kid.

But when she tried to act like the only reason we're not together is because of the no-strings attached agreement, disregarding her issues when it comes to Rad, I had to say something. That, on top of her nonsensical accusation of me having been on a date tonight, threw me and I lost it.

"Okay," Tatum says as she comes outside. "The boys are settled again, so 'fess up while we have time."

I watch as she settles herself against the padding of the chaise lounge, at a loss for what to say.

"I mean it, Tanner. What the hell just happened?"

"What did Kayla say?"

"About why she was leaving in a hurry? Not much. Just that she needed to get home sooner than she thought. She kept saying she was sorry. To me, to the boys, to Emerson. But I somehow feel like you're the one who should be apologizing."

"Well, thanks for the vote of confidence."

"Tell me why I should think any differently? Tell me that I'm wrong about what I told you. That someone always wants more and someone always gets hurt."

"Well, she's not the only one hurt in this scenario."

"What's that mean?"

I sigh and shake my head. "I don't know." We sit in silence for several minutes while she waits me out. "I guess the fact that her ex is still in the picture and she's not making it clear to him—"

"Wait a second. You can't have this both ways. You can't set up this casual let's-use-each-other-for-sex-thing with her *and* expect her not to be open to other men. I mean, you certainly didn't hold back."

I squint at her. "What are you talking about?"

"You went out with another woman tonight. Don't you think you're being a hypocrite?"

"Tatum, it was a business meeting."

She rolls her eyes. "Right. On a Friday night. With you all dressed and smelling good, come on!"

"Listen, I don't owe you an explanation, but the truth is that the only time I could meet this woman is after work. She has a full-time job and I'm trying to recruit her away from it. And yeah, I cleaned up because I didn't want to look and smell like a construction worker when I'm hoping to be her boss. That's it."

"Oh." She deflates, her earlier indignation disappearing. "Well, still. Kayla ran out of here with tears in her eyes. What did you say?"

"I, uh, I owe her an apology. I overstepped."

She watches me for a long moment, probably hoping I'll say more. But when I don't, she asks, "What do you want from her?"

What do I want from her? It's a good question. All this week, while I've been avoiding her, not calling and not texting, I've wanted desperately to ditch that self-imposed distancing and go to her. I've wanted to hold her in my arms and linger in bed with her. I've wanted to talk about her day and get her thoughts on mine. I've wanted to see Emerson again. The way she surprised me with that hug at the zoo just about melted my heart. She's as sweet as they come, and to know that she trusts me is a gift.

A gift I no longer deserve now that I've hurt her mother.

"Well?"

I'm pulled from my thoughts at Tatum's urging. Still, I shrug. "Listen, I know you don't want to hear this, but I have my hands full right now. I can't commit to Kayla. I just can't half-ass it with her."

"Isn't that what you're doing now?"

"Tate, I love you, but it's not your business, okay?"

She scoffs and is about to come back at me when Max opens the back door, holding a ringing cell phone out in front of him as if it has cooties.

"It won't stop, Mom. I mean, it stops and then it starts again. And then stops and starts all over again," he complains.

Matt pops his head out of the doorway, too. "Yeah, it's ruining the movie."

Alarm colors Tatum's face. "Give it to me."

Max hands it to her and both boys go inside again.

She answers the call with a shaky hello. I listen as she confirms that she's Mrs. Marcus Dunbar. My stomach drops when she reaches out for my hand and squeezes it tightly.

This is the call every military spouse or family member dreads. Bad news about their loved one. All thoughts of Kayla evaporate as I use my other hand to squeeze Tatum's shoulder.

"You're sure?" she asks, sucking in a frantic breath. She's on the verge of hyperventilating. "You're sure?"

*Shit.* Not Marcus. Not my sister's husband. The father to their two boys and baby girl on the way. We can't have lost him.

"Okay, okay," she says, nodding and swallowing back a lump in her throat. Her eyes are glassy with tears that haven't fallen. "When? Where?"

I cringe to think she's asking when and where he might have been attacked and killed.

But then she gasps and laughs. *Laughs.*

"What's happening?" I whisper urgently.

She looks at me but only shakes her head in wonder. Then she's back to talking to the person on her cell and her tone is completely changed. She's calm. Her eyes clear of tears.

I'm so confused that it's hard to follow the rest of the conversation. When she finally ends the call, I demand to know what the hell is happening.

"It's Marcus," she says with a weary smile.

"Is he okay?"

"He will be. He, um, he had to have a procedure for something called an abdominal aortic aneurysm."

"Holy shit. He's okay, though?"

She nods, and tears finally fall down her cheeks. "That was his commanding officer. He said the procedure went well. They caught it early. But it means he'll be honorably discharged. Tan, he's coming home at the end of next week."

Before I can even process all of this, she falls into my arms, sobbing tears of relief and joy. I squeeze her back and hold her for a long while, my mind racing with all that I need to do now that my brother-in-law is expected home months before we'd planned.

## 44

KAYLA

It's Thursday but already feels like the weekend because I'm only working half a day, then picking up Emerson, and heading to the airport for a very overdue getaway.

But first, coffee. I'm at Mean Beanz for my usual morning addiction. I've pretended these last few weeks that I never met Tanner. It's a way to compartmentalize the hurt of his silence toward me since that night at his sister's house. But it's also easy to do since life has returned to the way it was before I stared at his butt the first morning I ever saw him and started the whole weird thing between us.

I thought he might at least offer an apology for how he characterized my actions regarding Rad, but I've heard nothing from him. I guess my use of *voilà* had the effect of not just telling him to stop in the moment, but to stop forever.

I was hurt by his accusation that I was too weak to handle Rad, that I was being *willingly manipulated* by him. Of course, my initial instinct was to deny that. Because what did he really know about what I'm dealing with, anyway? And how dare he judge me. He knows virtually nothing about my life and the choices I have to make.

But then I realized that was a big part of the problem: I hadn't shared everything with him about Rad. He only knew what he saw first-hand, which was more than one instance of me appearing to be open to Rad's insistence that we move. He also didn't understand that I was only doing that to try to keep the peace, to try to maneuver a way into keeping Rad interested in a relationship with his daughter when it's been so fleeting in the past. The problem is, that wasn't being honest. I never should have tiptoed around Rad in hope that he'd be the kind of father that Emerson needs and deserves. That's always only ever been up to him.

So, if Tanner had reached out to apologize, I would have accepted it. I would have admitted that he was at least partially right in how I was too accommodating to Rad. But I also would have taken the time to explain how incredibly conflicted I've been about how to get what my daughter needs. She absolutely needs her father. I know his absence will affect her not just now but long into the future. Wanting to alleviate the inevitable heartache she'll feel over Rad's weak presence in her life has torn me up. I hate the fact that this is something I can't fix.

I've put Emerson's needs before my own since before she was even born, but I never really considered giving up our life here to move closer to him. Nicole was right when she said Emerson needs to see me happy. Rad is not the key to my happiness.

I never got a chance to tell Tanner all of this, though, and the days passed after that night at his sister's without any word from him. So, I've sucked it up and moved on. No need to dwell upon the relationship that never was, after all. It's been almost three weeks now since I saw him last. He never comes to Mean Beanz anymore, which is just as well. We seem to have run out of things to say to each other.

While I wait for my coffee at the pick-up area, I pull up our flight information on my cell's email.

A moment later, I hear a laugh that is all too familiar. Turning, I see Tanner behind me. He has spied on me just like he did that time I was texting Nicole a photo of his butt.

"So, you gave in, huh?" he asks. "You're going to Stockholm?"

"What?"

He nods at my cell. "Your flight info?"

He's jumped to the conclusion that what he saw was for a trip to see Rad. And for some reason, I don't want to correct him anymore. I don't want him to take comfort in the truth that there is *nothing* there with Rad. Probably because his confrontational tone is so out of line that if he's upset by the idea of me going to see Rad, then let him stew in it.

"Man, I've got shitty timing," he says with a shake of his head.

"I don't understand."

"It's pointless, really."

"What is?" It comes out sharp because I'm annoyed. I'm annoyed that the first time I see him in weeks, he's still not apologizing. I'm annoyed that when I turned around and saw him, my heart skipped a beat because I was so thrilled by his unexpected appearance. I'm annoyed because he's once again acting jealous over Rad, but yet he's never once tried to convince me to be his and no one else's.

And now he laughs at my anger, holding his hands up

defensively. "Easy there, *Kay Kay*. Looks like you're getting everything you want. Right?"

I'd told him once that I hated being called Kay Kay. And I know he's heard Rad calling me that. Now he's using it to further get under my skin.

"What is your problem?" I hiss. "You already made it clear exactly what you think of me. What more do you want?"

He freezes, his smile dying. For a moment, I see something like regret in his eyes. But then my name is called for my order, and I turn away from him.

"Wait, Kayla," he says and grabs my arm.

I jerk it violently from him. "Don't," I warn him. "This is *over*." I just want to escape this moment, this ache in my chest at the way he's turned on me when all I ever had was hope that we could be something.

I grab my coffee and slide through the waiting customers so that I don't have to make eye contact with him as I leave.

Just outside the front door, I suddenly struggle for air and lean against the building to steady myself. Even with Rad, I've never been so hurt that it's squeezed all the air out of my lungs like this. I'm such a fool. I guess I never really did learn my lesson after Rad. I'd lost myself in an obsession with him only to find out that I had basically been in that "relationship" by myself. And with Tanner, I lost my heart to him when he never asked for it. Or wanted it.

Forcing a deep breath, I tell myself, *chin up*. Time to move on.

Because I have no other choice.

## 45

### TANNER

Fuck my life. Like seriously. I am now completely and irretrievably fucked.

All because my ego got the better of me when I saw Kayla looking at flight information on her phone. Of course, the only thing it could mean is she's going to see Rad —either for a visit or to plan out actually moving there. And the raging jealousy that rises in me whenever that guy is involved took over. He's just so fucking unworthy of her that it pisses me off that he is *still* getting her consideration. I don't want to think there's the slightest chance that she might get back with him.

Not that I deserve any say in the matter since I've basically ghosted her without any kind of apology after hurting her.

Everything went to shit that night at my sister's house, though. Yes, Tatum was told that Marcus would be fine with an endovascular stent graft, but he ended up having complications and needed open surgery after that. He responded well to the second procedure, but Tatum's stress level shot through the roof and she needed me more than ever. I spent all of my free time with her and the boys. Two days ago, we welcomed Marcus home and he's taking it easy with his family. Things are looking good for him, thank God.

During all of that, I picked up the phone to call Kayla dozens of times. I wanted to share with her what was happening. I wanted to seek comfort in her words and arms, maybe even see if she would massage the stress out of the back of my neck.

But my head was so messed up that I knew I couldn't adequately apologize for being so completely out of line with her that night at Tatum's. And so, I didn't reach out. I let the silence go on over the days and weeks. Once Marcus was well and settled, I obsessed over how to approach her. All I've wanted is to let her know that I've been missing her so much that I haven't been sleeping. But I couldn't come up with words that would repair the damage I did.

Even without knowing the right words, though, I decided to show up here at "our" coffee shop, hoping that once I saw her in person, I'd know exactly what to say.

Instead, I fucked it all up.

Now, she's on her way to Stockholm, and I have no idea when she'll be back.

## 46

### KAYLA

Nicole's timing is impeccable when she meets us at the arrivals curb at the Louis Lambert Airport.

"Don't get out," I say as I open the rear passenger door for Emerson.

"Girl, you know I wasn't going to," she says with a laugh.

I grin and shake my head. It only takes a few minutes to get the car seat we've brought situated and Emerson buckled in, all the while both she and I coo over Lucas, who is now eight months old and smiling at us and drooling at the same time.

"I can't believe you're really here," Nicole says as we exit the airport.

"I can't either! But I am so happy to see you, Nic. This is so overdue."

"You're telling me."

"Let the weekend begin!" I say with more good cheer than I feel.

"Uh, no, we're not suddenly doing that fake shit with each other," Nicole says.

I glance back at Emerson but she's busy holding up a rattle for Lucas and doesn't seem to be listening.

"What?" I say. "I am excited to be here."

"Yeah, okay. But what else is going on? I can see it in your eyes, Kay. What happened?"

I sigh and then admit, "I saw Tanner this morning at the coffee shop."

"Mama, you saw Tanner?" Emerson says with a big smile. "I like Tanner."

Plastering a smile on my face, I tell her, "I know you do, sweetie. Oh, can you wipe Lucas' chin with that bib?"

With Emerson refocused on the baby, I lower my voice and tell Nicole, "It didn't go well. I'll tell you all about it later."

She nods sagely and keeps driving. That's the thing with Nicole. She might see right through me, but she also sees what I need at any given time, and there are no better traits to have in a friend than those.

WE DON'T GET a chance to get into an uninterrupted conversation until Emerson has fallen asleep and Lucas is quietly nursing. Nicole's husband is away for the weekend at a conference in San Francisco, so that gives us the kind of girl time we haven't had in a very long while.

"Don't think I don't see you enjoying the hell out of my wine," Nicole says with a smirk.

"I thought you were going to pump and dump so we could enjoy the hell out of this together?" I reply, holding up the class of Pinot Noir she's poured for me.

She looks down at Lucas and sighs. "He had other plans. Maybe later."

"You're such a good mama."

"I hope so. But, damn, keeping up with the Lindseys out here isn't easy."

"The 'Lindseys'?"

"For real. I know *four* Lindseys. And they're all *super* moms. Everything is organic, everyone's baby is *way* ahead of schedule for their milestones, and they all do 'Mommy and Me Yoga.' It. Is. Exhausting."

I join her in laughing, but I can see that she's not all that amused by it. It makes me think about this new neighborhood she's been living in since Lucas was born. She and her husband, Jordan, moved to this beautiful, wealthy suburb of St. Louis from the more eclectic Delmar Loop area. The Loop is made up of dozens of minority-owned businesses, including restaurants, retail stores, and beauty salons. Nicole used to tell me that if she never had to leave the Loop, she'd be happy because it was a place where she really fit in. But the house they had there was small and once Jordan got a promotion, he convinced her to move to a more affluent area so they could have more space for Lucas and better security for them both since he travels so much. Their two-story brick house is gorgeous, but it looks a lot like the other houses on this well-tended street, all of which have manicured, large backyards that lead into lush, wooded areas. It's about as different as you can get from the hustle and bustle and variety of the Loop.

"It must be hard being out here on your own," I say.

"No, it's fine. We've got a big, beautiful house with plenty of room for Lucas to run around when he gets older. What more can I ask for?"

I can see she's trying to put on a brave face, so I resort to repeating back to her what she told me earlier. "Uh, no, we're not suddenly doing that fake shit with each other."

Her eyes go a shade darker, but she offers up a weak smile. "It's just how it is. I'm sure I'll fit in with the Lindseys one of these days."

I hate to hear that she's unhappy. And I especially hate to realize that I haven't had a deep conversation about how *she* is doing in far too long. It's been all about me and Emerson and work and Tanner for the last couple of months.

"Oh, god, Nic. I'm sorry for being a shitty friend. I got all wrapped up in my own stuff and neglected you, just like when I was first with Rad, didn't I?"

She shrugs and looks down at Lucas, stroking his chubby cheek gently. "I knew you'd come back around. Eventually."

I suck in a breath and groan for dramatic effect. "I deserve that."

When she meets my eyes again, I can see that all is already forgiven. She's not going to give me a hard time about not being there for her. Part of me is relieved, and part of me wants her to let me have it so that I never again take her for granted.

"It's okay," she says. "We all get involved in our own worlds and lose sight of everyone else sometimes. As long as you come back."

My eyes tear up. "I'll always come back. I promise."

She nods and slips a now sleeping Lucas from her breast. I watch as she covers up and raises the baby to her shoulder so she can burp him, which he does before settling back into her arms to keep sleeping.

"How are things with Jordan?" I ask. "He travels a whole lot, right? Must get lonely."

She scrunches up her nose. "It does. And I may just be hormonal, but there are honestly times where I don't even know if we're a fit anymore."

My eyes go wide at this admission. "Are you serious?"

"At least, that's what I think when we're having two-minute video calls more days than we see each other in a week. I mean, I married Jordan believing I had a partner. I thought we were going to do everything together. But I'm out here in suburbia and he's traveling or doing dinners with clients, and I just feel... left behind."

"Have you talked to him about how you feel?"

"Girl, you know I don't hold back. It's what Jordan said he's always loved about me," she says with a laugh. "Yeah, I've told him. And he says all the right things about how we still are a team, but our roles are just shifting, that things will settle soon, that he loves me more now than ever before."

"Do you believe him?"

She doesn't hesitate. "I do. He even said that if I'm not happy here, we can move back to the Loop."

"That's awesome. Do you think that would help?"

"Maybe? I just don't want to make any rash decisions right now. I'm willing to give all of this more time, let my hormones settle down." She looks down at Lucas again. "And besides, Lucas is showing up one of the Lindseys' kids in their baby music class, and I kind of want to see that through."

We laugh together and the tension I felt just a bit ago of worrying for my friend dissipates. Nicole has always been good at holding her own. I have confidence that she'll both figure out what she needs and make it a reality. Still, I remind her that she can talk to me about her life.

"Even if I'm being super self-involved—"

"Oh, like usual, huh?" she teases.

"Exactly. I mean it, though. Will you pinky-promise me that you'll always talk to me?"

She reaches out and we entwine our pinkies. "You know I will, Kay. And you also know I'm just giving you a hard time, right? That I love you?"

That makes me smile. "I love you, too."

"Now, tell me what happened with Tanner when you saw him this morning."

I take a deep breath and then launch into the story, giving her every detail down from how he made my heart skip a beat to how I had trouble breathing after I walked away from him.

"You have it bad for that boy," she says when I've finished.

I finish the last of the wine from my very large pour and fall back against the sofa. "Why do I do this to myself? Why do I fall hard for the boys who don't want me back?"

"That may have been what happened with Rad, but that doesn't sound like what's going on with Tanner."

"What do you mean?" I say with an incredulous laugh. "He totally shined me for three weeks after telling me that I'm basically a bad example for Emerson because I'm 'willingly manipulated' by Rad. And then when I see him today, he jumps straight to thinking I'm going to see Rad and mocks me for it."

"That's the thing, though. Why is he always so interested in Rad? You've said there were other times when he seemed jealous of Rad even though you two were never supposed to be a thing."

Shaking my head, I shrug. "I don't know. He makes no sense to me. And it doesn't matter. It's definitely, completely over."

"Uh-huh."

"I mean it. There's nowhere for us to go. He really hurt me. I'd be an even bigger fool than I already have been to give him the time of day."

We sit in silence together for a long moment as that settles in. Nicole doesn't try to convince me that Tanner will come through and prove himself worthy of me. She doesn't call him out for being a jerk. She just sits with me and lets me be sad about this. At least for a good few minutes before she tries to inject some levity into it all.

"Hey, at least you got to enjoy dat ass, right?"

I look up at her with a small smile that soon turns into a laugh. She joins me and it feels good to let loose. I've always been able to admit to her my failings, my ambitions, and my fears, and she's always supported me through them in one way or the other. Despite the few times that I've fallen short, I know I've done the same for her. Still, I vow to be a better, more present friend, and I take comfort in the fact that I know our bond will never break.

## 47

TANNER

"You like your meat blackened these days?"

Marcus and I are standing over the grill in the backyard like it's the most natural thing in the world. Thanks to his successful surgery and recovery, it is. But I've been spacing out and let the kebabs go too long.

"Shit. Sorry." I pry one of the ribeye and veggie skewers from the grill so I can inspect the damage.

"That's a ... thorough job," he says with a pat to my back.

"It's jerky. I've turned this meal into dehydrated meat sticks."

He laughs. "Just get them all off the grill. I might have a trick up my sleeve to salvage this."

I give him a dubious stare. "Really?"

"Listen, when you're eating mystery meat in the Core, you get creative with sauces and shit."

"Okay, but if it doesn't work, pizza's on me."

"What's got you all distracted, anyway?"

For a brief moment, I consider telling him everything. "Everything" being that I've fallen for a gorgeous redhead who is still tangled up with her ex. Oh, and that I've very likely hurt her to the point where she'll never talk to me again.

Instead of confessing all of that, I just look at him and shake my head.

"Tatum says you met someone?" Marcus continues, making me wonder if my thoughts are written all over my face.

"It didn't really work out."

"Too bad. You're going to have to settle down one of these days, man."

"Don't you start in on me, too," I say with a laugh. "My sister has been harassing me enough as it is."

"What's that?" Tatum asks, her timing perfect as she joins us with the boys right behind her. She has her hands full with platters, one corn on the cob and the other bacon-wrapped hot dogs.

I move to take the platters from her hands just as Marcus does. It takes me a second, but I back off and let him help her out. It's his role as her husband, after all. She doesn't need me these days like she did when he was away.

"Uncle Tanner, can you set up the Slip n' Slide, already?" Matt asks.

"In a minute, bud," I tell him. "Let me finish with the grill."

"It's okay, I got it covered," Marcus tells me.

And I swear he levels his eyes on me in a way that tells me more than the obvious. He's only been back for less than a week, but it feels like there's been a shift in the dynamics between us all. I don't blame him for wanting to assert himself as the head of the house, especially once he returned and his own boys took a minute to warm back up to him. It wasn't all that prolonged, but the fact that they were clinging to me rather than rushing to him must have felt like a punch to the gut. I probably shouldn't even be here now. I should be giving them more time to reconnect instead of inserting myself into their family. But part of why I jumped on Tatum's invitation for dinner with them is because I'm tired of beating myself up over Kayla. This was an opportunity to distract myself from that, even though I've done a pretty shitty job of it. In fact, all I've really done is change my scenery ... and burned the kebabs.

I hand over the grill tongs to Marcus with a shrug. "At least there are hot dogs?"

"Keep the faith, man. I've got a plan."

"Come on, Tan," Tatum says. "I'll show you where the Slip n' Slide is in the garage."

I follow her in a failed-grill-master-walk-of-shame to the garage, where she points to a beat-up box on an upper shelf. I grab it and turn to go back to the yard, but the expression on her face stops me. It's a look that says she's about to grill me. I just hope I'm not going to get burned like the kebabs.

"What?" I ask.

"What's going on with Kayla?"

She and I haven't talked about Kayla since the night when she got the call about Marcus. Just minutes before that call, she'd been imploring me to make it work with Kayla, but we'd never finished that discussion and, in the meantime, I've let everything slide, taking no action.

"Not much," I admit.

"Have you reached out to her? I remember you said you owed her an apology?"

I wince, thinking of what I gave her at the coffee shop the other day in place of an apology. I was rude to her. Hurtful ...

again. It's been killing me that I treated her that way when the truth is that all I want is for her to know just how sorry I am, to know that I never want to see that wounded look on her face again, that I want to be the one who will care for and protect her. But I haven't reached out to tell her any of that because I'm pretty sure I lost any chance I ever had with her.

"Well?"

I watch Tatum for a long moment, debating what to say. Finally, the truth spills out. "Tate, I really fucked things up and I'm pretty sure she's done with me."

To her credit, Tatum doesn't bitch me out. She doesn't say *I told you someone always gets hurt*. Instead, she gives me a small, sympathetic smile and says, "Tell me everything."

I tell Tatum the whole story, including how I tried to play this whole thing off like I'd never get invested, but that didn't last long. Instead, I craved Kayla like I've done with no other woman before. And yet, in the end, I managed to push her away not once but twice for good measure. And the odds are good that she wants nothing to do with me anymore.

"You know what you have to do now, right?" she asks gently when I've finished.

"I wish that I did, actually," I say with a weak laugh.

"Get over yourself. That's what you need to do."

That's not what I expected to hear, and my eyebrows shoot up. "What?"

"Oh, come on, Tanner. All of this, *I hurt her so bad that there's nothing I can do*, is just a cop-out. You're saying you're not even going to try to fight for her?"

I guess her sympathy has its limits. She's coming at me now in a way that reminds me of how I came at Kayla about not standing up to Rad. And it doesn't feel good to be confronted on my own shit like this.

"Wait a second—"

"Whatever you think you're doing by saying you've lost your chance with her is bull, you know? You're just playing the same games you always have of keeping yourself unavailable because you think you need to be free to save me. But, if you haven't heard me before, hear me now: I don't need to be saved."

I take a minute to absorb the hard truths of what my sister has just told me and realize she's right on all counts. I've avoided serious relationships for a long time out of this sense of obligation I have to be ready to take care of Tatum at any moment. It's not based on logic, I know that. She's an adult, a mother and a wife who knows how to handle herself. Yet, I've never been able to shake that sense of duty I have when it comes to her. It was burned into me when our parents died and she fell apart.

"I did need you," Tatum continues. "When Mom and Dad died, a piece of me wanted to go with them. But you wouldn't let me disappear—into myself or otherwise—and I'm so grateful." She takes a deep breath and blinks back tears. When she speaks again, her voice is steady, confident. "That was a lot of years ago, though. I promise you, I am fine and that it's okay to let go now."

I'll never let go, not of my baby sister. But I get what she means. Her permission to stop putting her ahead of myself is something I didn't realize I needed. It settles upon me with the same feeling of clarity and satisfaction I get when I see the skeleton of a building start to take shape. It's a welcome perspective, and after a moment, I nod with the acceptance of it.

But then she pushes me further, saying, "And Kayla doesn't need saving either."

"Okay," I say slowly, not getting her point.

"She can handle herself. She has all these years on her own with Emerson, hasn't she? Looks like she's pretty damn capable. At least that's my take."

"No, you're right. She's got it together. I'm not trying to save her."

She squints at me. "That's not exactly true, is it?"

"What do you mean?"

"This whole thing with her ex and you getting in the middle of that—what's that about?"

My eyes drop from hers, skimming over the old paint cans lining one wall of the garage. They "inherited" them from the previous owner, and I've been meaning to haul them out of here ever since Marcus and Tatum bought the place at my insistence. It's been on my very long list of things to do, not that it has anything to do with what Tatum's just asked. Still, the distraction of this gives me a second to think about her question. To think about why I've been so fixated on Rad and wanting Kayla to make it clear to him that there's no chance for them.

"I guess what it comes down to," I say slowly, the realization forming as I speak, "is that I need her to make the choice. Between me and Rad. But she's obviously conflicted over whether she should be with her ex for the sake of her daughter. Or maybe she feels like there's still something between them that she can't let go."

"Hang on," Tatum says. "You've never actually told her you want to be with her, right?"

I hesitate. "Well, not in so many words."

"So, she was supposed to read your mind? And just go ahead and cut her ex loose on the off chance that you might want to be more than fuck buddies?"

"Tatum—"

"You dope!" She smacks my arm hard enough to sting.

"Hey!" With my arms still full with holding the Slip n' Slide, I can do nothing but take it.

"You know what would be a good idea? Actually *talking* to her about what she wants."

"What if she wants more than what I can offer? That's always been the bottom line. I'm overcommitted with work. How can I give her what she needs? What she deserves?"

"If you'd only talk to her, I bet she'd tell you she doesn't need you to be her *everything*. She's not helpless like you seem to think all us women are."

"That's not fair."

"I'm only kidding with that last bit. Sort of. Anyway, you need to be honest with her. I'm willing to bet that you can make it work if you do that."

Could it actually be that easy? Could I just be completely truthful with Kayla and tell her how much I want to be with her, but that for the foreseeable future I won't be able to give her as much time as I'd want because of work, and she'd not only understand but be open to that?

"You won't know until you try."

I meet her eyes, startled by how easily she can read me.

She laughs and we share a long, meaningful look. We've

been through a lot together, mostly me trying to ensure that she was managing to get by. But now, when I look at her, I see a happy, fulfilled woman ready to expand her family. The anemia is still an issue, but not as dire as the doctor first suggested. The baby is measuring only slightly underweight at this point, and all signs indicate a healthy rest of the pregnancy.

"I love you, Tan," Tatum says. "And I want the best for you, just as much as you've always wanted for me. If Kayla is your person, don't let anything get in your way from being with her. Believe me, you will regret it for the rest of your life if you let her go."

That sinks in, and I'm suddenly itching to take action. "What am I supposed to do? Fly to Stockholm and track her down?" Now that I'm determined to pursue Kayla, I'm only half-kidding with this suggestion. I don't want to wait another second to see if she could be mine. Because I absolutely want her to be mine and no one else's.

"That would be wildly romantic."

Running my hand through my hair, my mind races with the idea of taking the first flight I can find and figuring out the rest as I go. Because wildly romantic is exactly what Kayla deserves. She deserves a grand gesture. An over-the-top declaration of how sorry I am for how I treated her and how much I hope she'll give me a chance to make it up to her.

"And wildly stupid," Tatum continues, throwing cold water all over my fantasy.

"What?"

"You don't even know if that's where she is, right?"

"Uh, no, not for sure. But she had flight info—"

"On her phone, yes, I know you said that. But she never actually confirmed that it was for Stockholm, right?"

"Well, no, I guess she didn't."

"Because you were a jackass and made assumptions."

"Tatum—"

"The point is, dear brother, that this can all be cleared up really quickly."

I watch as she pulls her cell from the pocket of her pants.

"What are you doing?"

"Just sending a very innocent text. Don't worry."

But I do worry, standing helplessly and watching as she types out a message:

**Tatum: Kayla, haven't seen you in forever. Any chance you and Emerson can come by this afternoon? We're doing a BBQ and have the slip n slide out. I'd love for you to meet Marcus. He's home early!**

"Now what?" I ask dumbly. I know the answer, but she tells me anyway.

"Now, we wait."

## 48

### KAYLA

"Huh."

"What? What's 'huh' mean?" Nicole asks.

It's our last day before heading home, and in a fit of nostalgia, we've been wandering around Nicole's old neighborhood, the Loop. Nicole's got Lucas in his stroller and it's the kind that has a bar where Emerson can stand on it to go along for the ride. We've almost walked all the way from one end of the Loop to the other, stopping for lunch at Salt and Smoke BBQ, dropping into boutiques, art galleries, and a candy store, with plans to take the trolley back to where we started.

Tatum's text came in as we were stopped on the sidewalk, examining the Chuck Berry statue near the Walk of Fame for St. Louis natives who have made a cultural impact.

"Tanner's sister just texted me. Invited me to a barbecue."

"Is that weird? Thought you said you liked her?"

"I do. It's just that she said her husband is home early. He's a Marine and had been in Syria. He wasn't due home for a few more months."

"O-kay," she drawls, still not getting my confusion.

"It makes me wonder if he was injured or something went wrong, is all. And maybe that's why Tanner ghosted me? He was too busy with family stuff?"

"Look at you making up excuses for that boy already." She nudges me with her shoulder to soften the blow of her words.

"No, you're right. There are no excuses for how he acted. I just … I wonder."

"Well, are you going to text her back? Tell her you're out of town and unavailable? Maybe she'll tell Tanner, and he can get jealous, worrying you really are with Rad?"

The idea is tempting, but I ask, "That would be mean, right?"

She laughs. "A little. But I'm certainly not above a little pettiness. What about you?"

I think about it for a minute, wondering if it would go beyond pettiness. If it would end any chance of being with Tanner again. I know I shouldn't want that. I know I should just walk away and be the kind of woman who won't put up with anything less than what I deserve. I know that on an intellectual level. But my heart is telling me not to be so quick.

As a compromise, I text back something I hope isn't too telling one way or the other.

**Me: Thrilled to hear Marcus is home early! Unfortunately, Emerson and I are out of town. We won't be back until just after seven tonight, so too late to make it.**

As if she's been waiting on my reply, I see the bubbles indicating she's working on a reply right away.

**Tatum: Oh darn. Hope jet lag won't be too bad?**

She's fishing for information with that one, and it makes me smile. It has to mean that Tanner has talked to her about his assumption that I was going to Europe to see Rad. My heart flutters a little at the thought that he's right there with her, anxiously awaiting my response. I let down my guard, just in case.

**Me: No, none expected coming from St. Louis - lol.**

This time, there's hesitation before responding. Still, I wait her out.

**Tatum: Safe travels! And let's get together soon!**

"So, he's using his sister to get in touch?" Nicole asks.

She's been following the texts back and forth over my shoulder, reminding me of how Tanner did the same thing more than once.

Clearing my throat, I shrug. "Maybe. I don't know." After a moment, I groan and throw my head back in frustration.

"Are you okay, Mama?" Emerson asks.

Recovering myself, I smile at her and stroke her cheek. It's sticky from the lollipop she devoured earlier. "I'm fine. Let's get that trolley ride!"

"I can't wait!" she replies. "Will they make the bell go ding ding?"

"We'll ask them to do it," I promise. "Let's go!"

I glance at Nicole and can see that she's biding her time to continue our conversation about what the texts mean. The kids take priority, though, so it'll have to wait.

Nicole gets back to grilling me as she drives us to the airport later that day. Emerson has crashed from her sugar high, her head lolling to the side in her car seat. Lucas is awake but happily entertained by the mirror attached to the headrest in front of him.

"Girl, tell me you're at least going to make him work for it," she says.

"What?" I ask with a laugh.

"Don't 'what?' me. It's so obvious you can't wait to see that boy and get right back into it. What happened to 'I'd be a fool to get back with him'?"

"Well, I don't think I said that exactly," I hedge, knowing she sees right through me.

She sighs and shakes her head.

"Come on, Nic, you know I'm no good at drawing the line. If he apologizes, how can I not forgive him? How can I not give him a chance?"

"You can't just fall back on saying you're no good at that. You need to step up and be a grown-ass woman. Don't let him be another Rad who just takes whatever he wants from you without you getting what you deserve."

I think about that for a minute, ignoring the sting that comes with her words because I know she only wants the best for me. And that includes me demanding more, not simply accepting the bare minimum like I've always done with Rad.

"You know, he was wrong about you being a bad example for Emerson," she continues. "At least for the way you deal with Rad. He doesn't know all that goes on with managing a co-parenting situation. He was clearly acting out of jealousy. But on the other hand, think about the example you'd set if you just let him brush off how he hurt you. I mean, the thing my mama always told me was, 'you teach people how to treat you.' Don't teach him it's okay. And don't go teaching Emerson that you being hurt by a boy is so easy to dismiss. You and I both know she picks up on your every emotion. She knows you were done wrong. She knows you were sad. And it's okay for her to know that he made you feel that way—especially if she also knows he's worked for your forgiveness."

I'm struck dumb for a long moment. Finally, I manage a breathy, "Wow."

She laughs. "Thank you for coming to my Ted Talk."

My eyes are shining with tears as I look over at her. I can always count on her to tell me the hard truths, whether I like them or not. She did just that when I was obsessed with Rad but I chose to ignore her words of wisdom. I won't do that now. She's absolutely right. I need to demand more for myself.

"I'd come to your Ted Talk any day of the week," I tell her.

She smiles and pats my hand. "We both have to take care of ourselves, right? Figure out what we need and deserve?"

*What we need and deserve.* That's a phrase she mentioned many times when I was lost in my obsession with Rad, even after he'd left me to go on my own "journey" after I realized I was pregnant. I didn't exactly listen to her then, but I realize she's used the same wording now to emphasize just how far I've come. She doesn't want me to slip back into that old destructive pattern. And neither do I.

I squeeze her hand. "Absolutely." Taking a deep breath, I

nod. At first, it's tentative. But it quickly becomes emphatic. "And *this* is why I chose you as Emerson's godmother. You are the very best role model for her."

She glances back at Emerson, who is still fast asleep. "Oh, believe me, I'll never let her forget you said that."

When she meets my eyes again, we burst out into laughter. It's the healing kind. The kind that is more than cathartic. It's restorative. Enough to make me straighten my figurative crown and set my expectations high, where they should always be.

## 49

TANNER

People are staring at me. I don't blame them. I'd stare at the idiot standing at arrivals with an enormous stuffed ostrich in one arm and an oversized bouquet of wild flowers in the other.

The women passing by give me a dreamy smile, as if they could only wish for such a greeting upon returning home, ridiculous stuffed animal and all. The men give me knowing raised brows as if to say they've had to dig themselves out of the doghouse before too.

After Tatum helped me track down the flight Kayla and Emerson had to be on for their return from St. Louis, I raced over to the zoo gift shop just before they closed. I knew I'd get flowers for Kayla but I didn't want to show up empty-handed for Emerson and the first thing that came to mind was that ostrich she latched onto when we went to the zoo. Since she already had one, I was determined to outdo it. The only thing that fit the bill was the three-foot version they had for display purposes. My most charming powers of persuasion—and a hundred and fifty bucks—bought me the thing from the shy teenage girl at the register.

And, so, here I stand in the airport bag return area, holding onto this flightless bird as if it and the flowers could possibly be the ticket back into Kayla's good graces. Or at least, I'm hoping that they'll be enough of a welcome surprise that I'll get a chance to apologize for being a complete and total ass.

I see Kayla's red hair in the crowd before the rest of her comes into view, and the anticipation is painfully delicious.

When she emerges and I can finally see her in full, our eyes meet, and in that split second, I see what I'd hoped for: an incredible mixture of surprise, delight, and desire.

Just as I let go of any attempt to play it cool and instead smile broadly at her, I see something change in her expression. Her face goes blank, losing that unguarded, happy, reaction to seeing me. And when Emerson calls out my name and breaks free to run toward me, I see Kayla try to pull her back. That gesture, her instinct to keep her daughter from me, lands like a sucker punch to the gut because it means she's not going to fall for this romantic gesture of showing up here. She's not going to let Emerson's affection for me sway her either.

Even as I understand that I've truly fucked up with this whole thing, I can't let Emerson know that. She doesn't deserve to be disappointed by yet another guy. I drop down to one knee just as she reaches me, her little arms flying around my neck.

"Tanner, you brought big os-rich!" she squeals, quickly letting go of me and hugging the stuffed animal tight instead.

"I did, Emerson. I brought it just for you."

"He's bigger than me." Her eyes are as wide as her smile as she gazes at the ostrich. "Look Mama!" she squeals.

"I see," Kayla says, having reached us.

Standing, I debate leaning in for a hug or a kiss on the cheek but can see that she's not open to either. Her posture is stiff, her smile forced.

"Good trip?" I ask.

"Yeah, it was really nice to get away. I needed it."

The implication is clear: she needed to get away from me. And now here I am, all up in her business when she didn't ask for it.

"You went to St. Louis, then?"

"Yes, to see my friend Nicole," she continues. "Not Rad, like you assumed without stopping for a second to ask me a single question."

I grimace and rub the back of my neck. Emerson is still enthralled with the ostrich, fluffing its faux feathers merrily as people stream around us.

"These are for you," I say, offering her the flowers. It's a lame deflection. As if giving her flowers is the sum total of all I have to say. As if they're the only apology she deserves.

She gazes at the flowers but doesn't take them. Instead, her eyes drift away, and I feel like I've lost her. My chest burns with a sudden aching emptiness, like I've been hollowed out. This sense of loss is uncomfortably familiar. But I'm struggling to understand why. The only other time I've felt this kind of internal pain was when my parents passed away. This isn't the same thing. I haven't lost someone I ... love. Right? Is that what I'm feeling? That I love Kayla and the fact that I can't have her has morphed into a physical kind of pain?

"Well, we better get to our baggage carousel," Kayla says, looking over my shoulder.

"I'll help you."

"No need. We got it."

She's put up a wall, and I almost let it keep me out, ready to give up and walk away ... until I see something in her waver. There's a flicker of regret in her eyes. She leans toward me ever so slightly, full of anticipation. Giving me an opening to say something. To do what I came here for. To make my big play and plea of forgiveness.

I'm conjuring the words that I hope will sway her when the moment disappears. My briefest of hesitation confirmed her initial dismissal of me, it seems, because she strokes Emerson's hair and tells her they need to go.

"What about os-rich?" she asks.

"I'll carry him," I say quickly. "And I'll help with your bags. You have your car here?"

"Uh, no. We're going to get an Uber," Kayla says.

Seizing the last chance I may have with her, I say, "I'll give you a ride home."

She tries to decline, but it would be more awkward to claim being happy with a car service rather than take my offer, and we settle on the plan that I'll take them both straight home.

That leaves us standing side by side watching bags go round while Emerson tries out "riding" the giant ostrich.

With nothing left to lose, I slide my hand around Kayla's waist as I lean down and whisper into her ear, "I came here to tell you how sorry I am. I know I fucked up—more than once. I've been trying to think of how I can make it up to you—"

"Flowers isn't the answer," she says and pulls away from my touch.

I cringe, remembering too late how she had told me that sending flowers was how Rad always tried to smooth over his absences. Flowers for when Emerson was born, flowers for Emerson's first birthday, flowers for Emerson's first ballet recital.

"You're right. I didn't mean for it—"

"There's my bag."

She goes to the conveyor belt and grabs a red plaid roller bag. I make a guess that the car seat wrapped in plastic next to it is hers and grab it. Stuffing the flowers into the seat, I then ask Emerson for the ostrich so I can throw it over my shoulder before easing the roller bag from Kayla's hand.

"This way," I say. "I'm not parked too far."

I trudge a step ahead, leading the way to my truck as all the while Emerson talks non-stop about the boy she calls her baby. Her baby is actually Nicole's infant son, and it sounds like Emerson was quick to take on a big sister role. Once we get to the truck, I make a show of buckling in the ostrich right next to Emerson in her car seat and she giggles with delight.

Once on the road, we drive for a while in silence. When I can't stand it anymore, I make another attempt to reach Kayla, to scale that wall she's put up.

"Listen, I was a jacka—jerk," I correct myself with an eye on the rearview mirror. Emerson smiles at me, none the wiser. "I wish I could take it all back, I really do. I've just been thrown by this whole thing. I never expected anything to come from our, um, our time together."

"Nothing more than short-term phenomenal f buddies, right?" she asks with a weak smirk. She's lost her edge, tired, no doubt, by all the disappointment I've unloaded upon her. Maybe it's not fair to push her right now. Maybe I should give her time to unwind from her trip and to absorb the fact that I want to make this all better somehow.

But our drive from the airport won't take that long, and it feels like time is running out.

"That's the thing, Kayla. It has been absolutely *phenomenal*. Every bit of time spent with you has been beyond anything I could have hoped for. Yes, we are great together in be—well, you know what I mean. But I'm also in awe of you as a woman and a mother. And I'm even more in awe of how you make me feel. You make me happy. That may sound simple, but when you really think about it, making someone happy is giving them both joy and contentment. When I think about the time we spent together, I realize that you gave me everything I needed. When I was with you, I didn't want to be anywhere else or with anyone else. And when I wasn't with you, I couldn't wait to be with you again."

I've been glancing at her while talking, wanting to make sure my words reach her, but she's kept her eyes trained on the windshield, her face impassive.

"So, why didn't I just say all that before, you're wondering?" I ask, and her eyes flick toward me for just a moment. "Why did I act like a complete idiot and force you into using our safe word?" Now she looks at me, her eyes shining with tears. "I don't have a good reason, honey. I'm sorry. I ... I just kept thinking you're halfway out the door and back with your ex, and who am I to compete with a rock star anyway?" She raises her eyebrows incredulously. "Yes, he's a douche, but let's face it, he's also a rock star. Not in America, granted, but I figure it's still gotta have its appeal."

"It's never been about him," she says, breaking her silence.

As much as I love hearing that, I have to ask, "Really? Because you were pretty honest with me about the struggle you were going through over how to keep him in Emerson's life."

"That doesn't mean I want to *be* with him," she says with a dismissive scoff. "The very last thing I want is to ever be with him again. Wanting him in Emerson's life is completely separate from him and me being together again. That's so over. And that's what I told him when I dropped him off at the airport. He's absolutely clear on the fact that we are not moving to be with him."

It takes me a second to absorb this revelation. It's everything I wanted to hear, but she's put it all so matter of factly that it almost lessens its impact. Or more accurately, it shows me for the ass that I am since I never asked her point-blank what was going on with him.

"Well, uh, good." I nod, forcing myself to dismiss all that worry over Rad.

"What about you being too busy to 'give me what I need'?"

"I do still worry about that, but I realized—with Tatum's help—that I shouldn't be making that assessment on my own. That I should actually *ask* you what you want and need. And then do my damnedest to deliver. That's what I want to do. I want to give you everything I can. But I have to be honest and tell you that I do have a lot going on with work. That's just where I am in life right now. But I sure as hell don't want to miss out on the chance of being with you all because I didn't come out and talk to you about it."

With that last declaration, I pull to a stop in front of her apartment building and kill the engine. Unbuckling my seatbelt, I turn to her and almost laugh at the way the fading sun is perfectly catching in her hair. She takes my breath away just the way she's done since that first morning I watched her from the site across the street.

"Tell me what you're thinking," I say, taking her hand in mine.

She looks back at Emerson. The kid has managed to pull the ostrich's head toward her to use as a pillow for a nap.

"I'm thinking ... that I'm still really hurt by some of the things you said before."

"I'm so—"

"No, I know you're sorry. And you weren't completely wrong about how I allowed Rad to think I might give in to what he wants. But I was only trying to manage the situation. I was trying to appease him until I could let him down, all so that he didn't disappear on Emerson all over again. Maybe it's not the way you would have handled the situation, but it's how I thought it would work best."

"Totally get that. Especially now that I know you have no desire to be back with him. I let my jealousy get in the way. I should never have judged you like that. I am truly sorry."

She nods, and I breathe easier now that she's accepted my apology.

But then she rips that sense of ease right out of me.

"But I think you were right in the beginning. This isn't good timing for either of us. I appreciate your apology and you coming to the airport, but I think we should end things here."

Before I can digest this rejection, she opens her door and climbs out. I jump out on my side and go to her before she can wake Emerson and take her home.

"Wait a second," I say and then immediately come up empty with anything else to say.

## No Strings Attached

"I need time on my own. Time to truly understand what I need and deserve. It's not just for me, either. I want to be an example for Emmy so she knows she should do that for herself, too."

I get what she's saying and it's definitely something to aspire to. But at the same time, she's also telling me that I don't measure up, that I'm not the guy who can give her what she wants and needs. And after all of this, after me telling her how much she means to me, well, it's just a little too much of a blow to my ego. Or, truthfully, too much of a blow to my heart. I was ready to dive into this thing. I was *this close* to telling her I had fallen in love with her. That I adored her kid, too. That the three of us could be something really special.

Guess I dodged a bullet by not confessing all of that. But, *fuck*. It does still hurt.

She must see as much on my face because she squeezes my forearm sympathetically.

That's not what I need right now. I don't need her pity. I need to get out of here.

Clearing my throat, I say, "Let me help you get your things upstairs. You okay to get Emerson?"

She hesitates but has no choice but to get moving when I start to grab her things. We ride up in the elevator in silence, Emerson slumped against her shoulder.

"Can you grab my keys out of my purse?" she asks when we get to her door.

I do so, unlocking her door for her and placing her bag, the car seat, and the stupid ostrich just inside. I'd left the flowers in the truck.

"Okay, you're all set," I say, ready to go.

"I hope we can still be friendly?"

I look at her expectantly, unsure of her meaning.

"You know, if I see you at the coffee shop? We can still say hi?"

"Sure." I have no plans to ever go to that coffee shop again, and I think we both know it. "Take care, Kayla."

"You, too."

She's still got Emerson in her arms and I give the kid a lingering look. I'll miss her as much as I'll miss Kayla. Funny how quickly and deeply a couple of girls were able to work their way into my life, into my heart, so that I already know their absence will be a void I can't imagine ever filling.

I start to turn, to end this before we ever had a chance. But something stops me. It's a need to finish telling her everything, even if she has no interest. I just want it out there.

"The thing is," I say and she meets my eyes, "I just want you to know that I love you. I mean it. I've fallen in love with you, and I know that you'll now be the woman I compare every other woman to." I smile tightly and swallow. "And they'll never measure up." She takes in a sharp breath, and her eyes go glassy with tears. I shake my head. "I hope you find what you need. What you deserve, Kayla."

I mean it. I want her happiness even if I'm not the one who can give it to her.

But I can't stay a second longer. This time, I do turn to go. I bypass the elevator and go to the stairwell, taking the steps two at a time as I leave my heart behind. Better not to worry about such things anymore. I've got work to focus on.

It'll have to be enough.

## 50

KAYLA

I give up tossing and turning at five-fifteen in the morning and pull myself from bed. I was too stunned last night to process what Tanner was saying. It was the tears rolling down my face that finally startled me into blinking, sucking in a shaky breath, and closing the door.

*He loves me.*

Just as I was taking that in, Emerson woke up, and not in a cute, sleepy way for just a second before falling back into a deep sleep. Nope, she was uncharacteristically wide awake for the next four hours. I had to put my thoughts about Tanner on hold for the rest of the night. And then I had to write my usual Sunday night staff email. By the time I crawled into bed, it was almost one o'clock. My exhausted body fought with my spinning mind and eventually won, if only for fleeting moments of sleep fraught with a classic anxiety dream that I kept waking up from, only to fall right back into. The thrust of the dream was that the building across the street was mostly constructed, and I was looking on helplessly as it started to shake and falter—with Tanner in the middle of it all, somehow unaware of his dire predicament. I tried to warn him, calling out and waving my arms frantically, but I couldn't reach him.

"Yet another one of my super obvious dreams, I know," I tell Nicole over the phone. "I'm obviously worried about losing him. I'm worried that doing so will be a catastrophic mistake."

"Okay, that's a crazy dramatic interpretation," Nicole says with a laugh when I've told her my assessment of the dream.

I could tell she was distracted when I called earlier than usual, but she's used to me telling her about my dreams and lets me go on (and on) while she goes about her morning routine, including brewing coffee for her husband, nursing Lucas, and prepping a yogurt parfait for herself.

"I know," I say, "but after what happened last night, the way he bared his heart to me—"

"Whoa, whoa, whoa. *What?* You *saw* him last night and he *bared* his heart to you?"

That's when I realize that in my sleep-deprived state, I neglected to tell Nicole the *reason* for my dream.

Whoops.

In a near frenzy of words, I tell her everything. I tell her how thrilled I was to see him at the airport, but that I forced myself to be rational, to disconnect from the emotion of it all. That I had her words in my head about demanding what I need and deserve, even when he apologized for how he had treated me, even when he said he wanted to be with me. I tell her how I stood my ground and said our timing was off. Finally, I tell her how he turned back before leaving to confess that he had fallen in love with me and that he couldn't imagine any other woman comparing to me.

"And then?" Nicole demands when I stop there.

"And then ... he left."

"I don't understand, Kay. What did you say to him when he told you he loved you?"

"I, uh, nothing."

"You said nothing? Meaning you stood there and let him walk away? The man who showed up at the airport with a huge bunch of flowers and a ridiculous stuffed animal, the man who made an apology, not excuses, the man who said he'd give you everything he had to give, the man who *when he was walking away* told you he loved you?"

My heart sinks into my stomach. It's that horrible feeling of self-sabotage combined with regret, much like how I felt when I realized I was pregnant and all on my own and that not only would Rad never be what I wanted or needed, but that I should have known that from the start. The regret I felt then was for the way I deluded myself into thinking he was this great love when it was only ever a one-sided infatuation. The regret I feel now cuts deeper because it's hit me that I let the love of my life walk away without telling him how I really feel.

"And you're trying to blame me for it?" Nicole continues, only half-kidding. Her question drags me from my thoughts.

"Well, I mean, I just wanted to do the right thing this time, you know? I didn't want to get lost in my feelings for him like I did with Rad, especially when you told me I had to make sure Emerson saw me demanding what *I* deserved. So, I guess I just ... went with that?"

She groans and I can imagine her shaking her head in frustration. "Girl, you need to do what *you* want. All I was trying to get through to you was for you to be aware of your worth."

"Oh," I say.

"And this *isn't* the same as Rad. You know what your first clue is?"

"What?"

"He freaking told you he *loves* you! When did Rad ever do that?" She answers her own question before I can. "Never. That's when. Kay, I know you were … shattered by Rad. And you ended up feeling like you couldn't trust yourself, but you have to know that you're not the same person now as you were then. You are strong and smart and capable. And fully deserving of the guy with the great ass who says he loves you."

That makes me laugh.

"So, yes, your obvious dream was telling you not to make the mistake of letting him go," she continues.

"Oh god," I say with a sigh. "Do you think he'll even want to see me? You should have seen his face last night. He looked … defeated."

"So, give him a victory."

"Okay. But how?"

"Give him the victory of *you*."

I take that in for a moment. I know she absolutely means what she says. She really believes that I am a prize to be won. "Nic, I love you. Thank you so much for putting up with me."

"Please, girl. Just do me a favor and don't make me wear a hideous maid of honor dress in your wedding."

"Ha ha," I say. But I'm smiling at the vision she's conjured, especially the part about Tanner and me getting married.

That's a hell of a leap, though, considering I have to try to somehow convince him to give me another chance after how hard I let him down last night.

I say goodbye to Nicole and rush to my bedroom, where I throw on the first thing I find. Emerson is sleeping soundly but I can't just leave her. Checking the time, I cross my fingers that Mrs. Trujillo will be returning from her early morning walk.

## 51

### KAYLA

Even at this early hour, I can feel the warmth of the sun on my tank-top bared shoulders as I cross the street. And then I feel the eyes of a couple dozen men on me as I stride onto the construction site, and I'm suddenly aware that my cutoff jean shorts are pretty damn short.

"Hold up, hold up," a Latino man says as I near the trailer I assume is Tanner's office.

"Hi, I'm looking for Tanner." I gesture to the trailer.

He eyes me for a long minute, and I realize that the noise level has gone way down. The crew has quieted their work to take in what I now suspect must be an unusual occurrence: a woman visiting their boss on the site. It crosses my mind that this might not be a welcome surprise for Tanner as it will probably create a whole lot of innuendo among the guys. Too late now.

"You gotta be Kayla, right?"

"What?"

He rubs his chin and takes his time letting his eyes wander from my eyes downward and back again.

"Yeah, you're the hottie who picked up my boy in the coffee shop, right?"

My eyebrows shoot up at that. "Well, I, uh," I stammer, thrown off guard.

"Good for you. I'm all for a woman going after what she wants, you know? My wife, she went after me like that, too. Yeah, I'm all for it."

I smile, still unsure how to take him. "Is he here?"

He bows a little and waves his arm gallantly in the direction of the trailer door.

As I move past him and knock on the door, a couple of wolf whistles and shouts of encouragement come from the other workers. I half-turn and give a wave, generating another, stronger response from the guys, and I laugh.

"Yeah, come in," Tanner shouts back.

My confidence falters and I seriously consider giving up and rushing home. Mrs. Trujillo is in my living room, ready to comfort Emerson if she wakes up early. I could be back there and send her home in a matter of minutes and my daughter would never know I'd been gone. But I'd also have returned without ever trying to pursue my own happiness. And giving up like that is exactly what I *don't* want to teach her.

Pulling open the door, I scan the trailer and find Tanner, examining large-scale plans. He's wearing a blue T-shirt and jeans, and with his palms flat on his desk his biceps and forearms are flexed perfection. And damn, he's sexy.

I have to shake off that rush of desire and focus on why I'm here.

I let the door fall shut behind me, but he doesn't look up.

"So, I made a mistake," I say, and his head snaps up, his eyes meeting mine. He doesn't move otherwise, though. He's frozen in place, waiting for more. I take a step closer to him and gather my courage to keep speaking. "Last night, I mean. I made a mistake." Smiling weakly, I shake my head. "I shouldn't have let you go after what you said. I guess I was in shock or just at a loss for words because no one has ever told me anything like what you did. It was wildly romantic and ... *perfect*, to be honest. I don't know why I reacted so badly, not just with letting you go but before that when you were just asking for a chance. But I do know that it was a mistake. And I'm so sorry I did that." My eyes fill with tears and I shrug, trying in vain to dismiss the emotion. "When I saw you at the airport, I was so happy. I wanted to be the one to run into your arms. But seeing Emerson do that was almost as satisfying. She really adores you, and for good reason. You've only ever been sweet and kind to her."

He straightens, standing tall but still staying put behind the desk. And he's still silent, waiting for me to say more.

Taking another step closer to him, I continue. "And while I appreciate that you are wonderful to my daughter, what I realized is that when I think about what makes *me* happy, it's *you*. You are everything that I want and need in a man. It took me a second to trust myself with that truth, to put my own happiness first."

I don't try to stop the tears from falling down my cheeks. They're a necessary release from the emotional tension I'm feeling. Tanner still hasn't said a word or indicated that he's even open to my apology or declaration of me wanting him. I'm too far gone to stop now, though. Just like he did last night, I'm going to lay my heart bare for him. I only hope he'll have a better reaction than I did.

"The thing is," I say, purposely mirroring what he'd told me, "I want you to know that I love you. I've fallen in love with you, and I know there's no one else who can measure up to you."

As the seconds pass by without a response from him, my chest aches with the realization that it's too late. I've lost my chance. I bite my bottom lip to stop it from trembling. I've been here before. I've survived heartbreak. But this somehow feels a thousand times worse than Rad.

Because this was real. For a brief time, it was *real*. We were in this together, in love with each other. Even if we couldn't get it together enough to make it work.

But now it's over, and I have to accept defeat. Wiping my cheeks, I manage a smile as I nod and look down at my hands.

"Okay, I'll go—"

"What's the opposite of *voilà*?" he asks.

I'm not sure I've heard him correctly. Meeting his eyes, I say, "What?"

"What's the opposite of *voilà*?" he repeats. "See, if the way we were using it was as a safe word to say 'stop' then I need to know the opposite because I don't want to stop. I want to keep going. I want more. I want so much more with you. I want it all, Kayla. Everything, starting now."

I'm so relieved that I laugh and cry at the same time, and I'm sure I'm a mess, but that doesn't stop him from finally coming to me. In just a few strides, his body skims mine as he fixes me in a gaze so full of longing and love and wonder that I couldn't tear myself away from him if I wanted to. He cups my cheeks, his thumbs sweeping away the tears that are now of happiness.

"So, what should it be? Our new word?" he asks.

I'm at a loss. All I want is for him to cement this reunion between us with his lips on mine, so that's what I tell him. "How about you kiss me and don't stop?"

He grins. "'Kiss me and don't stop.' It's a little long. But I can work with that."

I tug at his T-shirt, pulling it up as I urge him toward me. It works to get him to finally do what I'd said. He drops one hand from my face, using it to pull me even closer to him by the small of my back. And then he leans in and takes my mouth with his, kissing me so well that the tears and the ache of just a moment ago are forgotten. In its place is a deep sense of happiness, like this is exactly where I'm meant to be, right here in his arms.

"You know what this means?" he asks, breaking away and lightly pressing his forehead to mine.

"What?" I move to kiss him again, needing to taste him, but he moves his mouth to my ear instead.

"It means you're mine and no one else's," he says softly, but firmly as his lips graze my sensitive skin, making me shiver.

Or maybe I've shivered because of the urgent, possessive way he's just spoken to me.

Either way, I like it.

I meet his eyes. There's no insecurity there. He knows now that Rad could never threaten us. No, what's in his expression is complete confidence. He's claiming me, even though there's not a shred of doubt on my part that I want to be his. I flash to the night when he tied me up, when he asserted himself with me. Then, he couldn't talk to me about what he needed. But now he has, making it clear exactly what he wants. He wants me to be his. Explicitly and with no question. There never was any on my part, but he didn't know that. I'm only too happy to make sure it's crystal clear to him now.

Deciding to put a playful twist on all of this, I grab his butt and reply, "It's been that way since I first saw dat ass."

He raises his eyebrows, amused and fighting off a laugh. And then he kisses me again, and I fully surrender.

To him.

To us.

## 52

### KAYLA

That surrender quickly turns into something heated as we kiss and press our bodies together like we've been starved of each other and this is the only way to satisfy that aching need of deprivation. Our tongues tangle and I let out a whimper when he snakes his hand through my hair, grabbing a handful to hold me even closer.

We haven't touched like this in almost a month and it feels like that first time I brought him home to my place, each of us desperate for the other without any reservations. Then, we never planned on seeing each other again, making us free to find our own pleasure. Now, it's an acknowledgment that we completely and unreservedly *belong* to each other. I am his and he is mine—we've declared as much. And yet, we're still instinctually trying to physically prove it as well.

A loud clanging of metal on metal outside of the trailer door, followed by laughter, has us breaking apart, panting. There's a window near Tanner's desk and another on the door but they're covered by mini blinds, so we're not in danger of having been seen.

"It's just the guys fucking around," Tanner says and kisses me again.

But I've snapped out of our heated moment, my mom-mode overriding everything else. I pull away from his touch.

"No, it's okay," he says, reaching for me. "Don't worry about those guys."

"I need to get back. Mrs. Trujillo is there in case Emmy wakes up but…"

Though I know he'd rather I stay so we could finish what we started, he nods. "Yeah, you're right. You should be there." He pulls himself together and takes a deep breath.

Touching his chest, I look up at him so he can see the agony in my eyes. "I still need you," I tell him. "We just have to postpone this a little bit."

He takes my hand and kisses the back of it slowly, his lips lingering on my skin as if he can't bear to let me go.

"Let me take you to dinner tonight," he says. "You and Emerson. I'll take you anywhere you want to go."

I read this for what it is: a nod toward my moment of jealousy that night I thought he'd been on a date with someone else. It's clear to me now that he'd been telling the truth then, that it had only been a business dinner.

But I don't need to be wined and dined. I never did. I just needed *him*.

"Maybe another time, Tanner." He looks surprised and disappointed by this rejection and I quickly continue. "Tonight, I'd love for you to come over. I make a mean grilled cheese and canned soup. It's Emerson's favorite meal that I make." I waggle my eyebrows suggestively to try to tempt him into this incredibly basic offer.

He laughs. "If it's Emerson's favorite, then it has to be good. I'm in, honey."

"And maybe we can make it a sleepover?"

"That depends," he says, and it's my turn to give him a quizzical look. He pulls me into his strong arms, squeezing me to him. "Do you think Emerson would be okay with that?"

In response, I kiss him, pulling away with his bottom lip between my teeth. "Yes. She loves you. And as long as our bedroom door is locked at bedtime, we're good."

Grinning, he cups my cheek and kisses me deeply once more. "Sounds like a phenomenal time to me."

I quirk a brow at that reference to our attempt at being *phenomenal fuck buddies* back when we pretended we'd be nothing more to each other than a good time.

"Phenomenal," he clarifies, "in a completely committed way with the woman I love, that is. That work for you?"

Nodding, I blink back the fresh rush of tears. "Yeah, that works for me."

"Okay, let me walk you out of here and home."

"It's okay, I know you've got work to do."

"I want to go with you. And I can introduce you to Ernesto on the way. He loves to bust my balls. You'll like him."

"Oh, I sort of already met him," I say. "He's a character."

"What did he do?" He's suddenly on alert, ready to protect me.

"Nothing really. I liked him," I assure him.

It takes a second before he lets his guard down again. "Let's go."

We walk out into the bright sunshine of the day and Tanner keeps his arm wrapped around my shoulders as he introduces me to Ernesto. My lips are tender and still tingling from Tanner's rough kisses and bites, but I don't care how it might look. I'm too deliriously happy to worry about appearances.

It's a simple thing, being held by him like this. But there's such comfort and reassurance in it, making me feel that we are, without a doubt, in this together. And there's no place else I'd rather be than together with this man.

# EPILOGUE
## KAYLA

It took a solid year, but the construction across the street is finally complete, which means I won't be watching Tanner and his crew in the mornings anymore.

It's just as well, since I'm currently packing up my apartment. There are boxes everywhere. Movers will be here soon.

"Honey, you about ready?"

"Yeah. You ready, Mama?"

I turn to see Tanner with Emerson on his back. They're such sweet buddies, like two peas in a pod.

The three of us have been inseparable since the day Tanner and I confessed the depth of our feelings to each other.

We're moving into our own house, and I couldn't be more excited.

"Yeah, I just want to put these boxes of books with the others," I say.

"Don't you dare," Tanner tells me.

"Yeah, don't you dare," Emerson parrots, though she doesn't know what she's warning me against.

"I'll do it," he says.

"I can manage."

"Listen, this is why I have the guys coming to help us. You don't need to be lifting heavy boxes at nearly five months pregnant."

He leans down to kiss me and then leans even farther down so that I can give Emerson a quick kiss, too.

Laughing, I say, "Okay, then I am pretty much ready."

This pregnancy was planned. Tanner and I settled into a relationship so easily that it just felt right to add to our family and give Emerson a sibling. We're planning a small backyard wedding in the new house in just over a month.

The new house is where Tanner's pulled off an amazingly sweet proposal. We purchased a fixer-up, of course, so that Tanner could put his own touches into the remodel and hadn't planned on living in it for a while because of the construction. But we did go there often, wandering through the empty rooms and dreaming out loud what it would be like once it was ready, including having enough space for my office to pursue going freelance again with graphic art design.

With Tanner's encouragement, I approached Mean Beanz with the design I'd fine-tuned and they were receptive to reworking their logo with me. The plan is for me to keep working my corporate job until I've secured several more steady clients. Tanner's construction job ends soon, so he'll be able to put all of his focus into the contractor business and is confident he'll bring in enough income to support us as I pursue my passion. It's just another way that he has proven himself to be all that I ever wanted and needed.

And I support him right back. He's been working so hard at his day job, at getting the business up and running, at getting our house in shape. He was right when he thought he'd be overwhelmed by work and couldn't commit the time he wanted to me. But he was wrong in thinking what he could give me wouldn't be enough. I went into our relationship knowing his free time would be limited but also that it wouldn't always be like that. I was content to make the most of what he could spare, whether that was having "date nights" at ten o'clock in the evening consisting of a cold beer and a hot bath or waking up early to make slow love in the mornings.

No matter what little time we had together, we always made the best of it, including meeting at the new house to go over the work being done and turn it into a chance to all have lunch together in the backyard. That's the only spot in the whole house that has "furniture." If you can call the over-the-top cedar playset Tanner insisted on designing and building for Emerson furniture. It included monkey bars, two swings, a climbing wall, a covered fort, a sandbox, and a picnic table.

While the end result is Emerson's dream playset, I had plenty of fun watching Tanner put it together. More often than not, he'd go shirtless, and I'd watch the sweat roll down his back as he cut the wood to size, hammered and screwed it into the right configuration, and otherwise become my construction guy fantasy all over again.

It was fun to claim a piece of the house as our own in that way, even if the rest of the property was unlivable.

When Tanner suggested we host a little gathering of friends and family in the backyard, I thought it was premature, but he promised he'd take care of everything to make it work, including the food and bringing in tables and chairs. He was so enthusiastic about the idea of sharing our first place with others, that I agreed. He spent the morning there getting everything ready on his own so Emerson and I could just walk in to enjoy it all.

It was only when we arrived to find a party in full swing and the backyard transformed that I realized this was no ordinary day. Especially when I saw Nicole, Jordan, and Lucas there. She'd flown in without telling me and I was so thrilled to see her that I didn't fully register all that was going on. There were Italian bulb string lights crisscrossing the yard, rented in tables and chairs, a steady stream of music from a DJ-quality speaker, and a table full of food from our favorite BBQ restaurant. Tatum and Marcus were there, along with Matt and Max, and their beautiful, healthy little sister, Melody. A few of the graphic design friends I'd reconnected with were there, along with Ernesto and his wife and a handful of the crew guys they were tight with. But it was seeing my parents there that made everything click into place. They don't like to travel. It was usually Emerson and me that went to them. But they were there, smiling the smile of those who can barely keep a secret.

Just as the sunset hit its peak colors, filling the sky with pink and purple, Tanner told everyone to fill their glasses and had the music lowered.

"What's going on?" I asked.

"I just need a minute with my girls," he told the crowd and they all pretended to avert their attention.

He took my hand in one of his and Emerson's in the other, pulling us a few feet away from everyone.

And then he dropped to one knee while simultaneously pulling out a ring.

"Emmy, I need to ask your mom an important question," he said. "But I want you to help her answer, okay? You need to both agree to whatever your answer is, otherwise, it won't work."

She nodded solemnly, suddenly seeming much older than her four and a half years.

Looking back, I can't believe how calm I was. But then again, being with him has always felt so right, so easy.

"Kayla, this all started with you staring at my—you know what," he began, and I laughed.

"What did you stare at, Mama?" Emerson asked.

"Nothing," I said, fighting another laugh. "Just listen."

"It was the best thing that ever happened to me," he continued. "Because it meant we could go from two strangers watching each other to realizing we've got a far deeper connection. Honey, I love what an amazing mother you are. I love how you've jumped back into freelancing and know you'll make a success out of your passion. I love how you love me with your whole heart. And most of all, I'd love for you to be my wife. Will you marry me?"

I'd had tears in my eyes as I watched him say those words. He had been supportive of me in everything from day one. He was there to help with Emerson. He was there to cheer me on when I had difficulties at my corporate job. He was there to make sure that at the end of the day, after Emmy was in bed, that I felt like a woman whose needs could take priority. And did he ever take pleasure in getting those needs met.

"Remember," Tanner said, "I need you both to agree on your answer."

Emerson looked up at me. "I think we should marry him, Mama," she said with a nod.

I smiled at her and smoothed her hair before looking at him. "I think so, too."

"Yes?" he asked.

"Yes. Yes, I'll marry you, babe."

He slipped a gorgeous classic round-cut diamond on a gold band onto my finger and then rose to his feet, pulling me into his arms and dipping me backward dramatically as he kissed me. The spectacle drew wolf whistles, cheers, and applause from our closest friends and family. Besides the day I had Emerson, it was the most special moment in my life.

We spent the night celebrating. Everyone stayed late, but in the end, it was just the three of us, still hanging out in the backyard. I had my head on Tanner's shoulder as we sat leaning against the wall of the house with Emerson spread across our laps, sleeping that deep sleep of hers.

"We should get married here," I said idly.

"Here?"

"If we can recreate half the same wonderful, good time we had today, I'd be in heaven. I don't need anything fancy. All I need is you," I said and looked up at him.

"You're sure about that?"

"Well, you and our kids."

We'd started calling Emerson "his" kid or "our" kid months ago. It wasn't anything to take away from Rad, who we had all visited in Stockholm a while back without issue. It was more to acknowledge how much of a presence he was in her life. He took to being a father figure easily, but he was always conscious of making sure to acknowledge who her dad was. He even went out of his way to play The Rad Band around the house and talk about what a great guitarist Rad was. I once found them watching YouTube videos of performances by the band in far-flung European clubs. So, with him being so careful to make it clear that he was both 100% there for her but also respectful of who her real father was, it seemed a harmless shorthand to call her his kid.

But the fact that I just used the plural—*kids*—took a moment for him to register. As soon as that distinction sunk in, he pulled away so he could see my eyes in the soft glow of the hanging lights.

"What did you say?" he asked.

"All I need when we get married is ... the four of us," I said, my eyes going glassy with tears.

We'd only really started to try to get pregnant a couple of months before, proving once more that I am, luckily, fertile.

"It's still really early. I haven't seen a doctor yet. Just took a home test," I said. "But it does say you're going to be a daddy. An amazing one, I'm sure of it."

"Oh, honey," he said softly. "Did I really just get a fiancée and a baby all in one day?"

I raised my eyebrows. "Looks that way."

"What an amazing day."

Holding up my water bottle, I offered a toast. "To many more."

He tapped his beer bottle against my plastic bottle and then leaned in for a long, slow kiss.

It was a day I knew neither of us would soon forget. I often find myself thinking of it, lingering in the sweet perfection of it along with the delicious suspicion that life is only going to get better.

The movers have come and emptied my apartment. Tanner took charge, both directing them and jumping in to help, as Emerson and I made a ritual of saying goodbye to the place that had been our home since she was born.

Now I'm taking a moment to stare out the same window that oddly enough was the catalyst to all of this. If I hadn't made a habit of watching the crew working in the early mornings, Tanner and I probably would have never connected.

Turns out this was *my* journey.

Tanner comes up behind me, wrapping his arm around my shoulders and kissing my temple. I hear Emerson in what is now her old bedroom, saying goodbye to it.

"Are you ready?" he asks.

Squeezing his arm and leaning back into him, I nod. "Absolutely."

## THE END

---

*Thank you so much for reading Kayla and Tanner's story!*

**If you're craving more steamy stand-alone romance, try Hula Girl.**

**HULA GIRL: What happens in Maui, stays in Maui. Unless you run into your vacation fling back home...**

**Or, for something just as engaging but with more angst, try Tangled Up In You, the first book in my rock star romance series...**

"Tangled Up In You is an intense rock star romance that has something for everyone; sexy angst, heart-breaking betrayal, an epic love triangle, hot, complex connections, enduring friendships, laugh out loud moments, and most of all love - BIG, messy, crazy LOVE." - Shatter My Pulse Romance

**Read on for an excerpt of Tangled Up In You. I hope you'll fall for Gavin and Sophie the way you did Kayla and Tanner!**

## EXCERPT FROM TANGLED UP IN YOU
THE FIRST BOOK IN THE ROGUE ROCK STAR ROMANCE SERIES

Gavin exited the hotel elevator, feeling happily buzzed. The band was staying at Chateau Marmont in West Hollywood for a few days and had already taken full advantage of the pool during the day and the hotel bar during the evenings, including this one.

If he hadn't forgotten his cell phone, he would still be at the bar with the others, indulging in drinks despite being underage. They'd all quickly learned that the late 1920s hotel had a reputation for cultivating a celebrity clientele, carefully marketing the prospect of stargazing opportunities for other guests who craved proximity to fame. And now Rogue was staying there as both minor celebrities and tourists themselves. It meant they got to enjoy the perks of the bar, especially after the management saw how much attention he and Conor could generate. They had an ever-growing crowd of new "friends" wanting their company who were all too happy to pay for the bands' overpriced drinks.

But as soon as he rounded the corner toward his room he knew his evening plans had completely changed.

## Excerpt from Tangled Up In You

"Sophie," he said, his smile wide and beyond his control.

It had taken him less than a second to recognize her.

She sat on the floor in front of his door, wearing a light summer dress with a cropped jean jacket and toying with her own cell phone. Startled, she looked up at him and scrambled to her feet at the same time. "I'm sorry to bother you like this," she said quickly. "I just didn't want to meet again in the middle of a crowded room."

"Come here," he said. He reached out to hug her but she shook her head.

"I just wanted you to know I'm not coming tomorrow. In case it mattered."

"In case it mattered? Of course, it matters. Darlin', I meant it when I said I was desperate to see you."

"You mean, just long enough to send me on my way? Like last year at the Palladium. I won't do that again."

"Jesus, Sophie." He'd known he would have to atone for the shitty way he'd treated her, but he hadn't realized how hurt she would still be. It sobered him up in the worst way, as he realized she was only here to tell him off. Dragging his hand through his unruly hair, he let out a sigh and decided his best hope was to remind her of their history. "So, that's it then?"

"I—"

"You want nothing to do with me? After what we had? I mean, we had something real. Something that I know I fucked up last time. But I'm trying now. You can't walk away like this."

"Gavin, don't—"

"You can't give up. You can't—"

"You broke my heart! You broke it."

*Excerpt from Tangled Up In You*

The raw pain in her voice froze him. When her eyes teared up and darkened, his threatened to do the same. It nearly did him in to see her this hurt. To see that he had caused this.

---

To read more, find Tangled Up In You on Amazon!

## ACKNOWLEDGMENTS

Thanks, as always, goes to my insanely patient family. They give me not just time to write, but endless support in all other ways, too.

Big thanks to these readers who so generously gave me their time and vital feedback:

Jennifer Hayes
Samantha Richman
Kathy Aronoff

## ABOUT THE AUTHOR

Lara Ward Cosio is the author of contemporary romances that are raw, realistic, sometimes funny, and always feature swoon-worthy men and strong-willed women.

If you enjoyed this novel, please share your thoughts in a review on Amazon or Goodreads

To learn more about the Lara Ward Cosio's books visit: LaraWardCosio.com

Join us on a Facebook page called Lara's Rogue Readers - join us!

*Lara Ward Cosio*

LOVE STORIES GONE ROGUE

## ALSO BY LARA WARD COSIO

Tangled Up In You (Rogue Series Book 1)
Playing At Love (Rogue Series Book 2)
Hitting That Sweet Spot (Rogue Series Book 3)
Finding Rhythm (Rogue Series Book 4)
Looking For Trouble (Rogue Series Book 5)
Felicity Found (Rogue Series Book 6)
Rogue Christmas Story (Rogue Series Book 7)
Problematic Love (Rogue Series Book 8)
Rock Star on the Verge (Rogue Series Book 9)

Full On Rogue: The Complete Books #1-4
Rogue Extra: The Complete Books #5-8

Hula Girl: A Standalone Romance